SHIFT

MACKENZIE GREY: ORIGINS #1

KARINA ESPINOSA

Cover design by © Christian Bentulan
Edited by Stacy Sanford

ISBN-13: 978-0692368411
ASIN: B00RW8X7MG

To my sister.
Without you, I would have never learned about sarcasm.

1

I couldn't stand that girl. Seriously. She had a head full of luscious, golden-blonde hair with nothing but air underneath. Ugh. Sometimes I would sit and think of all the different ways I could "accidentally" spit my gum into those locks. Yeah, I sounded bitter, like I was hating on her for no reason, but the bitch stole my boyfriend. Well, ex-boyfriend. Whatever. The point is, she was a home-wrecking man-stealer and I hoped she got the squirts tonight. Yeah, definitely the squirts. That would make me feel better. And with that off my chest, maybe I could get some actual work done tonight.

I'd been re-reading the same paragraph in my thesis while shooting laser beams at Diana Stone for the past hour. *That bitch.* It wasn't enough for her to steal James, but she had to follow me all around campus and rub it in. This was probably her first time at a library. That no-good, smut-looking, pretty-faced hooker!

"Are you okay, Kenz?"

I managed to tear my intense glare away from Diana and to

my best friend, for all intents and purposes. She took the seat in front of me, blocking my view of the tramp. I could only manage a grunt as Amy rolled her eyes at me.

"Are you decapitating her, or is this the gum-in-hair scenario?" she said as she loudly popped open a bag of jalapeño Cheetos.

"Laser beams. And are you seriously going to munch on that in here? You know, the place that's supposed to be quiet?" I marveled, staring at her incredulously.

"Oh, please, I'm not *that* loud." She purposely crinkled the bag, making the sound echo around the room. She had no shame. "Well, Cyclops, since you've probably made her bald by now, can we talk about happy things?" Amy asked, perking up.

I groaned at her giddiness. *I'm so not in the mood for this.*

"I hope this isn't about that frat party you got invited to tomorrow."

"Aw, come on, Kenzie! You rarely go out, and you have no excuse this time." She leaned in closer and whispered, "Tonight is the third full moon, so you should have no problem."

I glared at her through stubborn eyes. "No." Point blank and simple. No way.

"Kenz! Stop being a lone wolf—no pun intended—but you can't be a recluse! I won't let you!"

When she slammed her little fists on the table, I couldn't hold back a laugh. She was a feisty little thing. Standing at a mere five-foot-four with flaming red hair cascading down her back in perfect waves, she tucked a stray lock behind her ear, exposing her half-inch gauges. Just one of the many crazy things she'd done to her body. She boasted two full-tatted sleeves and piercings in her eyebrow, nose, and tongue—yet she was too scared to get her belly button done. Go figure.

Even with all her wackiness, she was the only one I'd trusted with my secret: I'm a werewolf. Yeah, that was anti-climactic, but there was nothing cool about it. I didn't know how it happened, and I definitely didn't know *why* it happened. But I deal with it the best I can. I actually met Amy right before my first Change. It was freshman year and Amy and I were assigned to share a dorm room. We hadn't really spoken to each other besides basic pleasantries, which in Amy's case was a groan from under the covers. She wasn't a morning person.

That night, our Resident Advisor was having our first-floor meeting when the pain struck, beginning at my fingertips and quickly spreading all over, each bone breaking, piece by piece, and rearranging to accept the wolf. Amy was entering our dorm room to get me when she saw me naked with my clothes shredded, hunched over, dripping in a cold sweat, while my spine rippled along my back. Once my canines appeared, she locked me in our bathroom and put the dresser in front of the door.

What I would never forget were her accusatory green eyes as they drilled holes into my body the next morning, like this was some vital information I should have provided the Admissions Office before enrolling. How was I supposed to know this would happen to me? To this day, I didn't know if she was scared or pissed that she got stuck with me. Either way, she covered for me and even went to the extent of getting notes from my morning classes when she found me passed out on the bathroom tile floor.

She stood in the middle of the doorframe, with a pierced eyebrow raised towards the ceiling and her arms folded tightly across her chest. "So, you're a werewolf?" she questioned as I tried to raise my weak body off the ground, failing miserably.

"I guess so," was my quick-witted response before I passed out from exhaustion.

I was still recalling the night of my first Change when Diana Stone sashayed up to our table. *Damn it, can't she just disappear already?* She casually leaned against one of the empty chairs and twirled a strand of hair around her pointer finger. *Ugh, what a cliché.*

Her double D's were bursting out of her V-neck shirt, and I wanted to take a needle to those suckers and pop 'em to a size negative A.

"Oh my gosh, Mackenzie. I didn't know you were here." *Lies.* "I would have invited you to study with me." *Even more lies.* "James is at an away game, so I have the apartment all to myself if you want to study together."

Hold up...what? They're living together?

I could feel my claws extending as they scraped against the wood of my chair. A low growl escaped my throat, and that was all the warning Amy needed to intervene. While it might never be a good time to hear that kind of declaration, tonight was definitely not the right time. It was a goddamn full moon.

"Now, why the hell would she want to spend time with *you*, Barbie?"

Diana's smile slipped for a moment and we caught a glimpse behind her façade. *She must be ugly without make-up. At least I hope...*

"And I've told you plenty of times that my name is Diana...not Barbie," she retorted through a tight smile.

"Well, Barbie, Diana, Airhead—they're all the same, in my

book—beat it before she rips into you. You know, PMSing and all," Amy said with a smirk. Diana ignored her and focused on me.

"I just want us to get along, Mackenzie. You're very special to James, and I truly think we can be best friends." Her smile was so fake, it looked painful.

When I growled, "Get the fuck out of my face, *Diana*," she took a tentative step back. Damn right. She better be afraid. I shifted my gaze to the clock by the check-out desk and saw it was past seven o'clock. I couldn't believe I'd been there so long. Pushing my chair back caused its legs to screech across the library floor, the echo drawing attention from everyone within a fifty-foot radius. I headed for the exit, not bothering to grab my things or even look at the people I left behind.

The cool gust of wind smacked me across the face as I walked out of the library and into the parking lot. It was mid-December in New York City, yet the cold weather didn't do a thing to the burning hot temperature of my flesh. But instead of taking the train and dealing with people staring at me for not wearing a jacket, I hailed a cab to take me to my flat in Alphabet City.

I shelled out twenty-five bucks and told the cab driver to step on it. In the almost four years I'd been going through the Change, I'd never cut it this close. As I heard my bones start to crunch, I tried to even out my breathing and calm down. *Not now, not now, not now.* I probably looked like a crack head itching for her next fix. I ground my teeth and clasped my clammy hands together. The pain was excruciating.

We were stuck in traffic and my legs wouldn't stop bouncing. I felt my bones rearranging. *God, this is so damn painful!* Unable to stand the pain any longer, I told the driver to stop, tossed the money onto the passenger seat, and sprinted the rest of the way home.

As I turned the corner to my street, I ran into a hard body that threw me a few feet back and right on my ass, causing a scream to gurgle out of me as more bones crunched from the impact. As my body trembled in a cold sweat in the middle of winter, a rough hand took hold of my forearm.

"I'm so sorry, are you okay?"

Through teary eyes, I looked up into the face of GQ's Sexiest Man of the Year. He had the softest brown eyes that melted into twin pools of milk chocolate, and that one dimple that dipped into his cheek as he bit his lower lip was the cutest thing I'd ever seen. I couldn't look away. Well, at least not until another ripple of pain shot up my spine.

"I think I need to get you some help."

I quivered so much I couldn't speak. Shaking my head erratically, I shuffled away from his reach. *What am I doing? I've killed too much time already.* With renewed strength, I got to my feet with a groan, fairly sure he heard a bone in my hip snap. Sure enough, his eyes widened a fraction as they zeroed in on my pelvis. Gulping as much air as possible, I pushed past him and ran the rest of the way to my building—ignoring his shouted protests for me to wait.

With shaky fingers, I tried inserting the key into the lock of my apartment building. After a few unsuccessful tries, I was finally able to unlock the door, which I flung open with a crash. Taking three steps at a time, I got to the third floor and slammed my shoulder into my apartment door, leaving it hanging off the hinges. By now, my canines and claws were out and the hair on my arms was thickening. Once I passed over the threshold, I started to strip my clothes off as I stumbled towards the back bedroom.

I let out a shriek as my shoulder bones snapped and I involuntarily hunched over while holding on to the door knob. *I'm almost there, c'mon, hang on*, I chanted as I struggled to open the bedroom door and slam it shut behind me. I reached a distorted arm towards the cage and gripped one of the steel bars, flinging myself inside. Now on all fours, I crawled to the lock and clipped it shut.

As if the sound of the bolt was permission enough, a howl ripped through me and the wolf was set free.

2

PRESENT DAY

I awoke with a start, slightly disoriented. My body felt sore and I rubbed my forearms to get some sensation back in them. I'd slept uncomfortably in Detective Michaels' backseat during a stake-out for which I was supposed to be awake last night. Luckily, since I was only an intern at the NYPD, I could get away with these things. Except I had really been looking forward to including this outing in my paper. Hopefully there would be another one in the future—how twisted was that? I crawled out of bed and turned my laptop on, the light of the screen glaring back at me, making me squint. I already had a missed video call on Skype from my brother Oliver. I redialed and he answered while I was mid-yawn.

"Gross, Kenz. Have you brushed your teeth yet?"

"Oh, put a cork in it, Ollie. Why were you calling so early in the morning?"

He rolled the same gray eyes I had and snorted. "Kenz, it's

8

almost noon. Either you had a late night, or you need to get that alarm clock fixed."

I chuckled. "Yeah, well, I was working last night, sue me. Are you coming home for the holidays?" I crossed my fingers under my desk and hoped he'd say yes. I missed my brother.

"Nah, I'm sorry, Sis, I can't. But I promise to make a trip out there soon. I swear!"

I nodded in disappointment, but understood. My brother was a soldier in the U.S. Army, which meant he didn't have the luxury of always coming home for Christmas.

"Well, I have to get going. Just wanted to check in on my favorite sibling," he said.

This time, it was my turn to roll my eyes. "I'm your *only* sibling, Ollie."

He laughed. "Okay, well I love and miss you. Be safe."

"Always."

I ended the video chat and immediately smelled the bacon Amy was cooking. It was all the motivation I needed to run out of my room. The pop and crackle of hot grease made me lick my lips at the same moment my stomach gurgled.

After my first Change, my appetite quadrupled, and now I could eat a whole cow on my own. I never used to be able to eat this much and maintain such an athletic figure. My body had morphed from an average-shaped girl who still had some mild baby fat, to a girl who looked like she lived in the gym. And let's face it, the most I'd lifted in my life was the damn remote control for the TV.

"Morning, sunshine," Amy said as I walked to the kitchen counter. She threw my bathrobe at me, but I didn't need it. My body temperature was the same as Arizona weather in mid-July. Sleeping in pajamas was asking for a heat stroke. But since I'd just spoken to my brother via video chat, pajamas were a necessity. I tossed the robe on the sofa and sat on one of the counter stools.

I let out a deep sigh and smiled—I felt good. After the three nights of a full moon, shifting was like finally being able to go to the bathroom after holding it in for so long. I know—horrible comparison, but it's the best I got. As calm washed over me, I relished the mild high. My muscles were still sore even weeks after the full moon, but it was nothing compared to the void feeling of the wolf that had been pushed to the farthest corner of my subconscious after being let out to play.

"Eat up." Amy placed a mountain-high stack of bacon and pancakes and a mug of steaming coffee in front of me, and my mouth watered. Without hesitation, I dug in, not bothering to use syrup—much less utensils.

All the window blinds were open, and even though it looked like it might snow, the mild warmth of the sun etched itself on my golden, tanned skin. I closed my eyes in contentment and soaked it all in. *Pure bliss.*

"You're like a Snickers commercial during the full moon. Hungry? Eat a Snickers! Or pancakes and bacon—otherwise you get really cranky."

"Yeah, well, you would be too, if you had my luck," I scoffed, chugging half my coffee in one gulp. "By the way, did Barbie say anything after I left?"

She rolled her eyes. "Of course not, jackass. You blew out of there so quick, I'm surprised you still had your shoes on. And with you gone, she had nothing left to bitch about."

"Ha-ha, very funny," I deadpanned. "I'm just glad I made it on time. I was really cutting it close."

"Luckily, we're the only freaks that live in this damn building. Could you imagine if we actually had neighbors? They'd probably think there's some crazy sex parties that go on here with all the howling you do." She smirked and I flicked her off. "The wolf probably needs to get laid, and she's just screaming for a release. Poor wolfey," she chuckled, and stole a piece of my bacon. I swatted her hand away and glared.

"Please don't talk about the beast and sex. It's gross."

"Get over it, babe. She lives through you, and you've been out of commission for like, three months," she said matter-of-factly.

"It's actually been four, but who's counting?" I rolled my eyes at her over-exaggerated jaw drop. "It's not that big a deal! I'll do it when I'm ready, and not with some stranger that will probably give me a disease that'll make me itch!" How she didn't see reason was beyond me.

"Oh my God, Kenz! You're so freakin' dramatic."

"Whatever. Nothing you say can rain on my parade. I'm free for at least another week and a half until the wolf comes out again, and freedom never tasted so sweet." I sighed, nibbling on a piece of bacon. Talking about sex made me uncomfortable, and I knew my change of subject wasn't subtle.

Amy smirked. "Nothing can rain on your parade?" she questioned. I shook my head. "What about James?" I stopped mid-bite, remembering what Diana said two weeks ago. That slut purposefully told me they were living together.

I'd known James almost all my life. We had grown up together in Cold Springs, New York. We had been best friends and were rarely ever seen apart. Our senior year of high school we decided to move to the city for college, but that wasn't my mistake. My mistake was letting a platonic relationship turn romantic. The summer before college, we got pretty drunk during the Fourth of July festival in town and ended up sleeping together. It wasn't our first time, but it was the first time we actually did it because we wanted each other.

Our first time was before our senior year of high school, because we'd made a pact that if we hadn't lost our virginities by the beginning of the school year, we'd lose it to each other. To say it was awkward and only lasted two seconds was putting it mildly. Afterwards, it just felt like we had checked off something on our bucket list, but that Fourth of July before college was different. There was no awkward talk or weird departure, and it definitely lasted more than a few seconds. Most likely because he had gotten experienced during that school year and knew what he was doing.

It was perfect, really. Who wouldn't want to date their best friend? It also didn't hurt that James wasn't bad looking, either. Although he was scrawny and gangly through most of high school, he filled in nicely that first year of college. He started playing hockey and got into shape. Just over six feet tall, with sandy blonde hair and a six pack you could bounce a quarter on. He was no longer the nerdy looking teenager, but a man. What James didn't know was that I'd never done it with anyone else besides him, which made his betrayal burn that much more. The only other person who knew was Amy.

I didn't know if I was *in* love with him, but I knew I loved and cared for him. Maybe I still did. I'd known we wouldn't last forever, not once I went through my first Change a few months after we started dating. I just never thought he would leave me so abruptly, and for someone else. That was four months ago—at the beginning of this semester—so you could imagine my shock to find out he was already cohabitating with the bimbo. He had never wanted to move in together, so I wondered what made him want to do it with her.

Ugh, okay, Amy officially rained on my parade.

"Did I burst your bubble there, sweetheart?"

I glared at her mischievous smile. She knew damn well that the briefest mention of him would bring me down memory lane.

"I'm a freakin' werewolf, for God's sakes! I'm supposed to be a lean, mean, fighting machine—so why does she bother me so damn much?" I knew I sounded whiny, but I couldn't help but feel distraught.

"There, there, my little she-wolf. She'll catch chlamydia or something, and all will be right with the world again," Amy consoled as she hugged me and combed out the knots in the dark brown mess I called my hair.

Being depressed wasn't really my thing, but it still hurt. To this day, James swears up and down that he didn't cheat on me, but it was hard to believe his assertion when less than twenty-four hours after our break up, he was magically with someone else. What hurt the most wasn't that we were together for three years, but that I ended up losing my best friend of sixteen years. At times I wondered, *What did I do wrong?* I might have become more aggressive and bitchy since the wolf entered my life, but I did everything I could to make it work. I couldn't have been that bad.

I pulled away from Amy and hopped off the kitchen stool with renewed determination. Moping around was the last thing I wanted, or needed to be doing. It was over and done with. Four months was long enough to be over our doomed love affair...right?

"Alright, enough of the love fest. I'm off to The Brew." I waved her off and walked towards my room.

"Not so fast, missy." I turned back around with a raised brow. "It's been two weeks now, and you need to replace the apartment door before we get robbed."

I glanced at the hanging piece of wood that I barreled through during the last full moon and cringed at the sight of the yellow caution tape blocking the entrance. A flimsy piece of yellow film wouldn't stop any thief. *Google better tell me how to fix that.* "Yeah, yeah, I'll do it today," I grumbled.

AFTER PAYING MR. GOMEZ—THE owner of the bodega across the street—to install a new door, I grabbed my school work and headed to The Brew. Amy hated when I spent money unnecessarily if we could easily fix it ourselves, but I just didn't have time to figure it out. The first draft of my paper for my internship was due before winter break, and since I'd been running into Diana Stone more frequently on campus, I'd better stay local if I wanted to get it done.

Amy and I had moved to the East Village after freshman year once we realized the dorms weren't a safe place to change in, which sounds like it would be common sense, but hey—we were eighteen and ignorant. After many months of going through the Change in a storage unit, we got lucky and found an old building with few tenants in a secluded area of Alphabet City. It was quiet and private for such a lively and at times, dangerous neighborhood. And it was only a couple blocks away from the best coffee shop in the city.

I walked in to The Brew with my laptop and books in my bag. The robust aroma of coffee took over my sensitive sense of smell and I closed my eyes, inhaling the creamy java. *Heaven.*

Most of the employees were familiar with me and didn't bother to ask what I'd like. I found my customary little nook in the back and within minutes, Stacey brought me a caramel macchiato.

"Hey, I haven't seen you here in like, a week. How's it going?" Stacey and I had attended some of the same classes during my sophomore year at Columbia University. We were both studying Criminal Justice.

"Yeah, I've been at the library mostly, or down at the precinct. How's school coming along?"

"I actually handed in the first draft of my research paper yesterday, so fingers crossed!"

I politely smiled, but couldn't help but be envious. I was so close to being done with mine, but something always seemed to get in the way.

"Well, I gotta get back," Stacey groaned. "We're doing inventory this week. I'll talk to you later!" I waved as she left to go back behind the counter.

Three caramel macchiatos under my belt and a couple hours later, I arrived at the closing statement of my fifty-page paper and felt like crying tears of joy. I'd been busting my ass all semester and it was almost over—well, the first draft, anyway.

I was cranking out the last bit left when someone cleared their throat behind me. Annoyed by the interruption, I looked back with a scowl.

With his hands stuffed in the pockets of his wool coat, James—my ex—stood there with his boy-next-door smile. *I swear, something always gets in the way of me finishing this damn paper.*

"Hey Kenz, can I join you?"

"If you must," I snapped as I turned my attention back to my laptop. It was no use. James slid into the seat across from me and adjusted his oversized beanie to cover his ears.

"So...what are you working on?"

"Stuff," I responded, pretending to be immersed in my school work.

"Oh, that's cool. Uh ... I haven't seen you around much. Everything good?"

"Yup." I click-clacked away on my laptop—typing random letters in a blank Word document. *Please go away!*

"Damn it, Kenzie! Can we please talk?" I looked up from the screen to see his face flushed, and not from the cold weather. His heartbeat picked up, but I wasn't sure if it was because he was nervous or upset.

"I thought that's what we were doing?" I said, dripping with sarcasm, but he'd lost all patience with me. Yeah, he was angry. He slammed my laptop shut and slid it to the side. My nostrils flared as I looked at the cheating bastard across from me. My temper was not something to take mildly.

"Don't you *ever* touch my shit again." I kept my hands curled into fists at my side before I aimed for his jaw. The nerve!

"Sorry," he rolled his eyes, "but we need to talk about winter break."

"What about it?"

"Well, for starters, when are we leaving? My last final is on the last day, so we can't leave early this year," he said matter-of-factly as I sat there stunned, my mouth hanging open stupidly.

I slumped in my chair, thinking how to respond. I was trying to kill time and hoping he'd say he was kidding, but no luck. He raised a brow, prompting me to answer, and I had to squeeze my hands tighter before I broke his nose.

"Are you on fucking crack? You must be high on something if you think we're going back home *together*."

"Stop acting so immature, Mackenzie. We've been friends since kindergarten. This is no big deal."

I choked on my response. "No big deal? Fuck all that noise, Jameson Theodore." I said his full first name, just like he did to me. That rat bastard. "Go carpool with Diana. I'm sure she's *dying* to meet your family."

He shifted uncomfortably in his seat—averting his eyes and adjusting the collar of his coat. *Oh, no...no no no no!* "I haven't told my folks we broke up." *NO!*

Before he could say what I would bet my unborn child he was about to say, I put my hand out to stop him. "So, tell them. It's a simple solution."

"It's not that simple Kenz, and you know it. My whole family thinks you and I are going to get married after graduation. I just need some time to figure out how to tell them we broke up."

"So what? Are you seriously asking me to pretend to be your girlfriend during winter break?" He nodded sheepishly, and I could feel fumes coming out of my ears. "You are one sick son of a bitch if you think I would *ever* agree to this. Go bring your porn star girlfriend; I'm sure Nana will love her," I said with a smirk, knowing damn well she wouldn't. James's family was filled with very strong-minded, outspoken women. They'd send Diana

Stone packing before she even made it to the front door. And it wasn't that Diana was ugly or anything. She was pretty, unfortunately—but she dressed like a cheap escort.

"You know I can't bring her. If Nana doesn't tear into her, my sisters will. Please, Kenzie, I swear I'll make it up to you. It's only two weeks! Please?" he begged and shot me those puppy dog eyes.

I couldn't believe I was even contemplating it, but in reality, I hadn't even told *my* parents. Which was no big deal in the grand scheme of things, since we rarely spoke and they really wouldn't care, but ... *Ugh, fine.*

"Two weeks, James, but that's it. Don't come sniffing around during graduation, or I'll personally introduce them to Diana myself."

I caved. Amy was going to kill me.

3

Once James left and I was finally able to finish my paper, I went back home to bury myself in a book before work. I had never been big on reading fiction, but when I went through my first Change, I couldn't exactly "google" symptoms of lycanthropy. So I delved into paranormal fiction and familiarized myself with some myths. I hadn't met another werewolf yet, but I doubted I was the only one. I better not be, at least, because if I was, it would be one helluva solitary existence.

After a shower, I combed my hair and pulled it into a messy bun. I was too pissed off at the world (mainly at James) to care about my appearance. I put on my usual "work" attire, which consisted of leather leggings, a long sleeve black tunic, and my boots. As a bouncer at a nearby bar on the weekends, it could get pretty rowdy when those losers drank too much. I was fortunate enough to have the strength and a permanent resting-bitch face to scare them into behaving. Once in a while, I got a brave soul who wanted to test the waters with me, but they learned to regret that decision by the end of the night. I hoped for one of those idiots tonight. After my encounter with James, I wanted to punch someone in the face.

While I tried to distract myself this evening, I couldn't help but be miffed at how dumb I was to agree to his plan. Who in their right mind would do this? Going home for the holidays was supposed to be a break from everything in the city, and all I did was add more work for myself. I was too angry to think it through earlier, but now all I could think about was when he held my hand or tried to kiss me—would I be able to handle that?

I was walking the few blocks it took to get to work when I got a text.

Amy: PPPPAAARRRTTTTAAAYYY 2NITE?!

Obnoxious much? Geez ... there was nothing that would convince me to go to a dirty, smelly frat house. Gross.

Me: No.

Amy: JAMES WILL BE THERE!

Me: HELL NO.

If she thought the mere mention of his presence would change my mind, I didn't know what planet she was living on. He was the last person I wanted to see, much less talk to. I hadn't even called to tell her about him and winter break, so that was more than enough reason to avoid partying with Amy. I would have to tell her soon, since she stays with me and my family during the holidays. I couldn't blindside her at the last minute.

After waiting a few seconds without a text back, I figured she'd given up. I wasn't one to change my mind once I made a decision. Some called it stubbornness, but I preferred to look at it as disciplined. *Yeah, that sounds about right.*

Night life in the city can get wild, and Pete's Bar was no differ-ent. On the weekends, we got slammed with college kids and had to be careful with the underage drinkers. From the outside, Pete's looks like a dump, a hole in the wall, but inside was a hipster's dream hang-out. As such, it was constantly packed and over-flowing.

"What up, Big John?" I greeted and high-fived the other bouncer who worked the door with me. He was a big dude who was an ex-Marine, but soft as a teddy bear. I couldn't ask for a better partner. He listened to me ramble about all my personal problems (besides wolf stuff), and always offered sound advice. Now, whether I took his advice was another story.

"Nothing much, Kenz. Another day, another dollar," he said in his heavy New York accent.

"Right on." I bypassed him and waved at the two bartenders as I headed straight to the back office and got my time card (yes, those things still exist) and punched in.

Sasha and Cole were working the bar tonight, which meant things would run leniently. I hopped onto a stool and reached for Cole, who smacked a kiss on my lips. I've quit telling him to aim for my cheeks since he never listens, so now I just played along.

"Hey beautiful, I've missed you." *Why is everyone acting like I've been MIA?*

"I worked last weekend with you," I said as he handed me a bottle of water.

"I know, but I miss seeing your lovely face. The weekends just aren't enough."

He winked at me, and if I would have been any other girl, I might have drenched my panties. Cole's mojo didn't work on me —especially after walking in on him more times than I could count, in the employee bathroom with random girls. Seriously though, the guy needed to slow down before his family jewels fell off.

"Oh please, who have you picked for tonight?" I started scoping out the bar, trying to pin-point his target for the evening.

"You know, Kenz, I wouldn't have to do that if you'd just be mine," he sighed.

I never knew if he was being serious or not, but it was better not to play with fire. "Not in this lifetime, Cole," I said as I slid off the stool. A predatory grin stretched across his face and the challenge was set. I knew better than to keep playing this game with him, but after James, I needed some harmless flirting. Don't judge me.

"So, how are you feeling?" a voice seductively whispered in my ear, sending a shiver down my back.

I whirled around—ready to go off on the creeper—and came face to face with a very sculpted chest covered in a form-fitting sweater. Under heavy lashes, I peered up at the man before me; my breath hitched as I took him all in. Waves of heat buzzed through me as a sly smile exposed the one dimple on his cheek.

"What?"

"I asked, how are you feeling—after the other night, I mean?" He was holding back a laugh as he pressed his lips into a straight line.

What the hell?

My body tensed and I gripped the seat behind me. "I'm sorry, I don't know what you're talking about."

He nodded and smiled like he was in on some joke. "A couple weeks ago I bumped into you. You looked sick, but you ran off like the devil himself was after you."

I quirked an eyebrow and then realization dawned on me. The last night of the full moon. How could I forget that face? Well, of course I could. I was nearly dying.

"So ... are you okay?" he asked for the third time.

"Oh! Yeah, I'm fine. Just had some, uh ... bad seafood." Did I just admit to having diarrhea? *Get it together, Mackenzie!*

He narrowed his eyes like he didn't quite believe me, or maybe I just grossed him out. Most likely the latter. He ran his finger down my arm in a slow, leisurely pace. I held my breath as I watched him run his tongue over his bottom lip. "Since you're feeling better, how about I buy you a drink?" His voice was husky, and I had to clear my throat a couple times to get my bearings together. Butterflies tickled my stomach, but I didn't think dating should be at the top of my list. Besides, I sucked at flirting.

"Sorry, I'm on the clock. Thanks anyway." Taking a deep breath, I got my shit together and side-stepped him.

He grasped my elbow before I could leave, sending shots of electricity through my body. "My name's Jonah—Jonah Cadwell." His brown eyes were gentle as he stared intently into mine.

"Mackenzie Grey," I offered, shocked that I told him my full name. "I have to go. It was nice to meet you." I slowly slipped away from his grasp and backed up into the crowd. Grabbing a stool from the end of the bar, I headed outside.

Big John was out front waiting for me—rubbing his gloved hands together for some warmth.

"What took you so long, Kenz?" he asked as I plopped myself next to him.

I didn't have an answer for him because I really didn't know what happened. The encounter with that Jonah guy was weird. Maybe Amy was right: I needed to get laid.

"Sorry." I shrugged. "How's the crowd looking tonight?" I changed the subject and settled in on my stool for the next few hours.

"I think we'll slow down in an hour or so. How's your internship at the precinct?"

I sighed.

Instead of taking twelve elective credit hours, I decided to do an internship during the week at 1PP—One Precinct Plaza in Manhattan. It was going great, and I loved going there after school. The only thing that sucked was the research paper I had to write at the end of the year about my experience and what I'd learned.

"It's going," I said solemnly. "This paper is just kicking my butt, that's all."

"Have you finished?"

"Yeah, but only the first draft."

"Well, look at it this way, at least you get to go home for the holidays and take a break. When you get back, you'll be refreshed and ready to kick that paper's ass," Big John said, and I laughed. "Is your brother coming home for the holidays?"

"No. Ollie doesn't have enough leave time," I said, and it dropped my mood even lower than it already was. My older brother Oliver was an active duty soldier based in Fort Hood, Texas. This was going to be the first time in many years that he would be stateside during the holidays, and we still wouldn't be able to see him. I might not be real close to my parents—not that anything was wrong with them—but I was attached at the hip with my brother. We were only two years apart and Skyped each other at least once a week. I hated that he was so far away and that I could never truly tell him everything about myself. He'd freak out if I told him what I was.

"Well, at least you'll be with your parents and Amy. You'll be fine, Kenz." Big John lightly punched my arm and I gave him a fake smile. This day wasn't getting any better.

4

The night flowed smoothly, and for some reason we weren't as busy as a normal Friday night. Some no-name band was playing inside, and they sucked. All I could hear was someone shaking a tambourine, and I thought I heard the unmistakable sound of a banjo in the mix.

I popped two Advils and swished them down with water when a group of three guys walked up to the door. The one in the middle was the biggest of the bunch, but they were all extremely muscular. Each one looked like they were stepping out of a Calvin Klein ad. They definitely weren't the kind of people who typically came to Pete's Bar.

One of the guys—the one farthest to my left—came up to Big John with a hundred-dollar bill between his fingers. The single light above the front door illuminated his face, and I tried to keep my eyes from bugging out. He was the most slender out of the three, but had a pretty face. Flawless, actually. His brown eyes were piercing as he zoned in on Big John.

"You don't have to pay to get in. We just need to see your I.D.'s," I inserted when I noticed Big John was standing stock still —not saying a word. There was no way he could be intimidated by these fools; he was bigger than all three of them combined.

"Sorry, cookie, but we're talking to *him*. Why don't you run along inside and drink a Cosmo?" Mr. Douche Bag said, not bothering to even look my way.

What a sexist pig! Drink a Cosmo? Cosmo, my ass. He's about to get my foot in his.

"Excuse me? You—"

"Please excuse my brother. He can be tactless at times," a familiar voice whispered in my right ear and I froze in place. His strong hand fell on my shoulder in a friendly hold.

With a slight tilt of my head, I was face-to-face with a guy who closely resembled the douche bag in front of me—my recent acquaintance, Jonah. I hadn't even seen him walk towards me. Where did he come from? Better question: what the hell was he doing?

"First off, don't touch me. Second, you guys need to back the fuck up. And last, what the hell are you doing here?" I moved to stand next to Big John and away from the guy who I was starting to think was stalking me. I discreetly nudged my partner to snap him out of whatever la-la-land he was in, but it was no use. He didn't move.

Jonah furrowed his eyebrows and cocked his head to the side, his chocolate eyes drilling into me with an unspoken question. His douche bag brother fixed his eyes on Big John and whispered, "Go." Without missing a beat, Big John robotically turned and walked into the bar, leaving me alone outside.

Whoa ... not cool. We may have a problem.

"Now, why are you being so difficult?" Douche Bag asked as he locked his gaze on me. His brown eyes darkened to black orbs and I took a wary step back.

"What the fuck is wrong with your eyes?" I questioned, but admittedly, I thought it was a really cool trick.

The two brothers in front of me halted to a stop and stared at me with mouths agape. Their similarities were uncanny, and I felt stupid for not recognizing it at first. Jonah's brother should have looked familiar to me, even if they weren't exactly identical.

Crossing my arms, I snapped, "Look, I don't have time for this crap, so can you idiots just go already? Whatever you're looking for, it's not here," I folded my arms across my chest and huffed out.

"Enough."

A deep, raspy voice boomed from behind the two brothers and I flinched. After becoming a werewolf, I lost my fear of many things—which made my visceral reaction much more shocking. My gaze dropped to the ground and I watched as the third guy's boots made their way towards me. The two brothers stepped aside.

A pull in the pit of my stomach tugged at me and kept me from looking up. It kept me still until the boots stopped just inches away from me. I wanted to put space between us, look at who he was—hell, I wanted to punch these bastards in the face. No matter how good-looking Jonah might be, that asshole needed to get his ass handed to him. But I couldn't. The pull in my stomach was like strings puppeteering me. I'd lost all control. I felt the trickle of what I feared most—the wolf was making its way out of my subconscious.

"Heel," the man in front of me commanded, his husky voice vibrating like a wicked secret in my ear.

My insides melted at the sound, and my mind had to do a double take. *Say what?* What the hell was wrong with my damn hormones?

My body swayed in place, wanting to obey his command, but my mind was in full-on defiant mode. The tug in my gut was getting stronger, and I felt a weird energy encompass me. I tried to hold on to the logical part of me that was screaming *No*. The concrete sidewalk was spinning as I focused on one spot on the dirty pavement. Clenching my jaw shut, I breathed in and out of my nose as I tried to break this odd layer of energy that was pressed on top of my skin—making me want to obey.

With a final deep exhale, I let out a bloodcurdling scream as I pushed against the hold on me and stumbled backwards. Hands on my knees, I gasped for air. Sweat beads rolled down the sides of my face and the cold air warmed my skin. As I steadied my heart rate, I was finally able to look up at the man with the boots. I opened my mouth to speak but snapped it shut.

Son of a bitch.

He wore fitted, dark wash jeans with a tight black t-shirt that accentuated his muscles—and boy, did he have muscles—the body of a fighter with the face of a fallen angel. All square-jawed and Roman nose. I couldn't tell the color of his hair in the darkness of the night, but his icy, pale blue eyes were unmistakable. And they were pissed.

Finding my voice—and attitude—I straightened my back and narrowed my eyes, looking directly at him with just as much intensity. "I'm not a damn dog," I gritted out through clenched teeth. Nobody moved, and the noise of the city was cancelled out by the thundering in my ears. I no longer heard the hustle and bustle of the Big Apple.

"Your name," Blue Eyes barked as if it was an order I was obliged to obey.

"Fuck off," I snapped as I fought the urge to comply. *What's going on with me?*

His nostrils flared and his hands tightened into fists. Either he was cold and wanted to warm his fingers, or he wasn't used to being defied. Most likely the latter, which meant he was in for one heck of a fight with me. The night was way too quiet, anyway.

"Who's your Alpha?" he clipped out.

I knew I was testing his patience—and I didn't even have to guess what he meant by his question. I had enough paranormal books under my belt to know he was talking about a leader of a wolf pack. Some of the pieces of our strange encounter were starting to make sense, but wolf or not, I didn't take kindly to rudeness.

"Say what?" I scrunched up my face in confusion.

I always wondered what I'd do if I ever met a pack of wolves. While their loyalty and obedience were admirable—it just wasn't my cup of tea. Nonetheless, I didn't know why I was playing stupid. Nerves, I guess.

The men exchanged looks right before a car door slammed by the curb. Perfect timing.

"Hey babe." Amy walked towards us nonchalantly as the taxi drove away. "Who are the hotties?" she exclaimed, waggling her brows.

My eyes widened and I couldn't hide my concern. This was

the *worst* timing. After four years of friendship, Amy had learned the ins and outs of yours truly, which meant that as she got closer, she furrowed her brows and started to eye the three guys in front of me. My facial expressions weren't easy to conceal, and she knew something was up.

"Hey, go inside and wait for me by the bar. Tell Cole to give you a drink on me," I whispered to her, but she didn't move. "Please," I begged, edging her behind me to the door. Whether she went inside or not, I didn't check. I kept my attention focused on the blue-eyed devil who was now staring at me with interest.

His eyes burned every inch of my skin. I wet my lips and my heart raced as waves of desire washed over me. *This can't be happening.* I wanted to look away, but was locked in his slow perusal of my body. As his gaze reached my lips in mid-lick, a small grin appeared at the corners of his mouth as if he knew what I was thinking and feeling. An involuntary shiver ran down my spine and I was seriously wigging out.

He turned to the douche bag brother and nodded. Douche Bag gave me a curious look and walked away, probably following some silent order from the person I supposed was their Alpha.

"Follow me," Blue Eyes barked out, startling me from my inner thoughts.

"No." My response wasn't as loud or assertive as I wanted it to be, but his presence loomed over me like a dark cloud.

"I said, *follow me.* Do not make me repeat myself."

Building up my confidence again, I gave him a defiant smirk and crossed my arms. "Not in this lifetime, buddy. Didn't your mother ever teach you not to talk to strangers?"

I was being a smartass, but my tone was serious, all the same.

There was no way I was going anywhere with this looney. Stranger danger, hello? While he may be appealing to the point where I had to smash my thighs together like I needed a potty break, there was just too much crazy seeping out of his pores. I had enough of that going on with my schoolwork and fake boyfriend. I certainly didn't need anymore.

A black SUV with tinted windows screeched to a stop next to us. Jonah, who'd been quiet in the background, walked towards it and opened the passenger door.

Great, their ride is here. Good riddance.

"You're coming with me, either by choice or by force. *Do not* make me toss you over my shoulder," Blue Eyes warned, a scowl marring his god-like features.

My left leg stepped back and I crouched my body in a defensive position. Before I could respond with a retort, his whole face transformed and a small gasp escaped my lips. *Holy shit.*

Standing in front of me was no longer the man I ogled not too long ago, but a half man, half wolf. He growled at me and I couldn't help but stumble backwards, bumping into another body. *Amy.* Without looking back, I knew it was her. Being the loyal friend she was, there was no way she would leave me out here alone. *Damn it.*

For the first time since the Change, I didn't know what to do. This was a whole other kind of dangerous situation, one I'd never encountered before. I was facing someone like me who was stronger and had more control than I did. I could barely keep my canines and claws from coming out on my own, but to wolf-out like this guy? Yeah, he had me beat. But being the hardheaded person I was, if I was going down, I would go down swinging.

"Amy, run!" I yelled as I rushed towards the man-wolf. I heard

Amy's little feet shuffle and the door to the bar slammed shut behind her.

He swung an open-clawed hand to my face and I leaned back, just missing it, but I wasn't fast enough. Another hand came from the other side and hit my right cheek. The force threw me a couple feet to the left side of the door, and for a moment, I thought I saw stars. My hand checked my face and I could feel the indentions of four claw marks stretching across. I stared at my bloody hands, wide eyed, and froze. He took the opportunity to pick me up with his grip fastened around the scruff of my neck and squeezed. My toes barely grazed the pavement.

"Shift!" he yelled, his face inches from mine, close enough to kiss his deformed mouth. His blue, slitted eyes bore into me as his lower canines dimpled his upper lip. His jaw and muzzle jutted out in an unnatural, animalistic way, sending tight ripples of skin over his forehead and cheeks. He looked like a monster as he yelled in my face.

I couldn't respond, and was starting to choke as his hand cut off my air supply. My hands scrabbled against the wrist that held me and I scratched at him for release. My body temperature rose, and I felt a heat wave consume me. Panicking, I closed my eyes and tried to grasp at anything.

"Shift, damn it!" he yelled again, and this time, a fierce, loud growl cut through the night air.

It took me a moment to realize it came from me. My claws emerged and I reached for his neck. A new course of adrenaline kicked in, and I rammed his head against mine in a head bump that made him release me. I fell a few feet away, landing on all fours. I managed a look at my arms to see I wasn't a wolf, but I wasn't fully human, either. Then I realized it wasn't a full moon.

What's happening to me?

My momentary victory didn't last long. A needle punctured the skin at my neck as I stared, mesmerized, as the blue-eyed, half-wolf shifted back to his human form. My vision grew blurry as he rubbed at his forehead with a scowl. The last thing I remembered was falling into a pair of strong arms.

5

I stirred and awakened in a bed with warm blankets wrapped around my body, and sighed in contentment. *This feels so refreshing.* I smiled and had to remind myself to thank Amy for buying me a new comforter. These sheets felt as if they were ripped from cloud nine, and I didn't want to get up for class.

"They're soft, aren't they?" a masculine voice said beside me.

I tightened my closed eyes, not wanting to look at who the voice belonged to. I didn't remember having a one-night stand. Wait. I didn't even *do* one-nighters—I'm a self-certified prude. That's when last night's events hit me like a bucket of ice water. I shot up from the bed and saw who was in the room with me. His chocolaty eyes were soft, and a cautious smile played on his lips. *Jonah.*

"Where am I?" My voice was scratchy and dry.

"Here, drink this." He handed me a glass of water, but I didn't reach out to take it. "It's just water. You're probably dehydrated." I shook my head, and realizing I wouldn't take it, set it back on the nightstand. "Do you need anything? I'm sorry about last night, but—"

"I need to go home," I interrupted, flinging the thick comforter off my body and moving to get up. His eyes darted to my waistline, and I realized I was only wearing my almost-see-through camisole and panties. I felt the warmth in my face as I yanked the blanket back over me, this time covering myself up to my neck.

"Where the hell are my clothes?" I yelled, feeling my blood pressure rise. *Those bastards!*

He put his hands out defensively. "It's not what you think! One of the Lunas undressed you, don't worry."

"Don't worry? Who is *Luna*? Give me my shit, asshole!" I grabbed one of the pillows and aimed at his head. He ducked away and darted to the door.

"Okay, okay! I'll go find out where your things are. Just calm down; we're not going to hurt you," he pleaded as if reassuring me. Reaching for another pillow, he hustled out the door before I could throw the next one.

I waited a couple minutes to make sure he wasn't coming back, and then jumped out of bed like it was laced with acid. Tip-toeing around the room, I scanned it for anything that would give me a clue as to my whereabouts—or at least a phone so I could call the police. I was in a modest-sized room that contained only a queen-sized, four poster bed and a matching night stand. I couldn't discern my location from the smells, but the off-white walls gave the windowless room a gloomy vibe.

Besides the door that Jonah escaped from, there was another one. I walked to it—holding my breath—and peeked inside, but there was nothing in there but an empty walk-in closet. With no other alternative, I crawled back into bed and curled up under the comforter.

Surely, Amy had called the cops by now...at least I hoped she did. Unless they took her as well. Damn it. I hated not knowing shit. This was not as glamorous as the movie *Teen Wolf* made it out to be.

The door to the room swung open and slammed against the wall. A small yelp escaped me. I hadn't heard footsteps approach. What the hell?

"Get up and follow me." The blue-eyed jerk from last night came in with Jonah right on his tail. In the harsh light of morning, I could see him clearly. The sunlight flashed on his black hair, lending a tint of blue. I realized he looked even sexier than I originally thought.

Stop, Mackenzie. He's the enemy.

"Sebastian, it's obvious she's not used to our customs. She won't listen if you're ordering her around," Jonah interjected.

Bless his soul, because I was going to lose my shit if they kept bossing me around.

"*Obviously*," I said with a drip of sarcasm that earned me narrowed eyes from both of them. Whatever.

Blue Eyes, who I now knew was called Sebastian, cleared his throat and pulled at the collar of his t-shirt like he was hot. Which he *so* was. Okay, I swore that was the last time I would ogle him.

"Fine," he gritted out. "Follow me...*please*."

I scrunched my mouth to the side and gave him an *Are-you-shitting-me* look.

"I'm not going anywhere without my clothes," I argued as I tightened my hold on the bedsheets, concealing my discomfort.

"Clothes?" he asked, honestly perplexed.

"Yeah? Have you ever heard of them before? I mean, you must have, since you're wearing them." That got me an evil glare. One point for Team Kenzie.

"Sarcasm isn't cute on you, Mackenzie. Now, I'm losing patience, so let's not play games. Let's go."

Was it weird that the only part I focused on was the fact that he didn't think I was cute? Which I was taking way out of context, because it wasn't exactly what he said, but still.

"Well, *my* patience ran out yesterday when I was abducted by a bunch of thugs." Sexy thugs, but I wasn't going to stroke anyone's ego. "So unless you want to go to prison for kidnapping, extortion, and attempted murder, someone better give me my damn clothes so I can go home," I demanded as I flexed my *Law & Order* Ph.D.

Jonah snickered in the background, diverting my attention from Sebastian to him. He leaned against the door and folded his arms, showing off his fitted jeans and the flannel button-up that tightened against his biceps.

I glared at him. "Give me your shirt," I insisted, pointing to his very broad chest. Good Lord, I needed to get out of there. There was far too much testosterone floating around.

He cocked an eyebrow and I rolled my eyes. "There's no way in hell I'm going out there with my goodies on display, since you didn't bring me my clothes when I asked. Do you want me to cooperate or not?" I answered his unasked question.

"Give her your shirt, Jonah," Sebastian ordered, irritation lacing his tone.

Jonah walked toward me, biting his lower lip, with his eyes trained on me as he slowly undid each button. "Don't you think we're moving a little fast? I mean, we haven't even gone on our first date yet," he smirked, showcasing that one dimple on his cheek that could melt my panties off. I could feel the warmth on my face as he flashed that dimple, but I didn't waver under his intensity.

"In your dreams, lover boy." I snatched his flannel from him and quickly put it on—trying not to look at his bare, sculpted chest. "Haven't you ever heard of an under shirt?"

"We wolves wear the bare minimum in case we need to shift in a hurry. Would you like my pants as well?" His roguish smirk turned into a full-blown grin.

I scoffed at his suggestion. "No thanks. I don't have a magnifier with me." I climbed off the bed and saw that his shirt reached just above my knees.

"Enough. I'm not here to oversee children. You received clothing, now let's go," Sebastian barked. Jonah fell in line, all joking forgotten.

They walked out of the room and my bare feet pitter-pattered as I tried to keep up with their long strides. My mouth hung open as I scanned my surroundings, realizing I truly was locked up. We were in a goddamn warehouse. As soon as we exited the room, we started walking on a second-floor landing that wrapped around the building. I peered over the balcony to the main floor, seeing it was scattered with cafeteria-style tables. A few people were lounging casually, until they heard the heavy thuds of Sebastian's boots and looked up in our direction. I could see why I found him intimidating; he walked with an air of authority that would make anyone bow down to him. The silence echoed in the open space and I felt all eyes on me.

Awkward ...

I followed Sebastian and Jonah down the steel stairs, doing my best to ignore the stares as we crossed the main floor. The whispers that floated around the room made my hands sweaty. This could go one of two ways—either this was a welcome-to-the-club get together, or I was about to be mauled and tortured. I realized I overexaggerted at times, but this wasn't one of my novels. There might not be a happy ending in my new reality.

Sebastian stopped at an empty table. "Sit," he ordered. Whether I was being polite or just scared to defy him in front of his people, I complied, my bare thighs making contact with the cold bench as Jonah's flannel shirt hitched up my thighs. I hissed as goosebumps made me wrap my arms around my middle.

Sebastian pulled out a small notepad and pen from his back pocket and leaned forward on the table. "What family do you belong to?" The tip of his pen hovered over a blank sheet of paper.

"Huh?" Though embarrassed I couldn't come up with a more eloquent response, I needed them to break this down for me.

"Your family, Mackenzie, who are they?" he clipped out.

I surveyed the faces of everyone seated around me. Their expressions ranged from curiosity to boredom, and even some mild hatred, if I read those glares correctly.

"Uh ... well, my parents are Thomas and Joyce. My mom's an accountant, and my dad is—"

"It's Grey," Jonah inserted right as Sebastian was about to snap his pen in half. His nostrils flared as he tried to control his temper.

He could have just asked for my last name instead of getting all wolfey. Geez.

"Grey? I don't recognize that family. What pack do you belong to?" Sebastian asked as he scribbled on his notepad.

I couldn't begin to imagine what he could be writing. I hadn't really said much.

"Okay, I think this is where things got lost in translation. I don't belong to a pack. I'm the only one in my family that's a ... a wolf." Suddenly, the soft whispers around me erupted into a mild roar. I looked up at the second and third floors and saw people scattered all over, looking down on us.

"Silence!" Sebastian barked, and I jumped in my seat. The warehouse went quiet. "Who bit you?" he growled, and it made me more nervous. He was getting angrier by the minute, and nothing I said was making it better.

"I wasn't bitten. The Change happened four years ago ... out of the blue," I murmured, bracing myself for Sebastian's rage.

"You never came into contact with a wolf?" Jonah asked in a softer tone that helped me relax a little.

"You guys are the first I've ever met." Jonah gave me a small smile as Sebastian stood up and began to bark orders.

"Jackson, get Charles on the line. Caleb, get me a Luna in here stat. Everyone else is dismissed for the day. Speak of this to no one!"

Even though there weren't more than a couple dozen people milling around, I felt claustrophobic. Everyone dispersed in different directions so quickly, I couldn't keep track of where they all went. In moments, the room was empty.

"Is something wrong?" I looked to Jonah, who seemed like the more sensible of the two. All the witty banter between us was gone.

"Nothing's wrong, Mackenzie. We just don't know how you

could be a wolf." He paused. "There's only two ways to become a werewolf: You're either born into the family, or you get bitten. There are no other options."

Damn, I hoped there was another explanation for this.

Four years ago when the first Change happened, I had asked my parents if "hypothetically" I turned into a werewolf, what they would do. They brushed it off like I had a wild imagination, which only made me more frustrated. It got to the point where I was begging Amy to lock me up at a psych ward. I thought I was losing my mind. But after much calming and a crap-ton of Chunky Monkey ice cream later, I accepted my fate. To have all my insecurities rehashed by these strangers was not something I wanted to go through again. I didn't want to wonder why or try to figure it all out. If I dwelled on it, I knew I'd fall into a depression that I may not be able to pick myself up from again.

I was lucky I had Amy. But this was senior year, and I still had one semester to go before graduation. I couldn't deal with this now.

A curvy woman who looked to be in her late twenties walked over to us. She wore tight jeans and a sweater that showed off her ample assets. Though similar in looks, she wasn't like Diana Stone. She looked classy.

"Is this her?" the young woman questioned, raising a perfectly plucked brow. When the boys nodded, she rolled up her sleeves and sat next to me. "And you guys didn't bother to give her some clothes?" she yelled at them as she took in my incomplete attire.

"I asked, but they wouldn't give them to me," I tattled on the two wolves who were now glaring at me.

"What are you two buffoons still doing here? Go into the

laundry room and get her clothes!" she yelled at Sebastian and Jonah, who scurried off before she finished her sentence. She giggled. "I'm sorry about that. They don't know how to act around pretty girls." Her smile seemed sincere, but if there was one thing I was, it was untrusting. I was a glass-half-empty kind of girl. "My name's Blu." She extended her hand to me, and being the semi-polite person I was, I shook it.

"I thought you were Luna," I admitted. "They said she had my things." She chuckled at my comment, though I didn't understand what was funny.

"'Luna' is the name for a female wolf, so technically, they weren't lying." Her warm eyes sparkled as she gave me a radiant smile that left me wanting to smile back. "There aren't many of us, but the few that are, take care of the pups and house duties," she announced proudly, like it was supposed to be the greatest title in the world.

What are these people smokin'?

"So you sit here all day and clean and change diapers?" I didn't try to hold back on the sarcasm. They might as well know I wouldn't be drinking the Kool-Aid.

"Well, yes and no." She paused. "I'm guessing that's not your thing, huh?" She scrunched her mouth to the side.

"Hell, no. If you think I'm just going to throw on an apron and start breeding, you're out of your mind. You might as well give me my shit now and show me the door." I stood up from the bench and started to leave—only God knew where, because I didn't know which door led to the exit—when she grabbed my wrist.

"I'm sorry, Mackenzie. I didn't mean to dump that on you in the first five minutes. Of course you're not expected to do that yet."

Oh, hell no.

"Yet? Try never. I'm not part of this...this *thing* you guys got going on here. I've been fine on my own for almost four years now, and to be quite honest, I don't plan to stick around."

"But you have to stay—"

"The hell I do." I snatched my wrist back. "You can't make me do shhhhiiii—," I slurred as I felt a pinch on my neck.

Where the hell did that *come from?* My head felt heavy and my mouth went dry before I was consumed by darkness and a familiar pair of arms. *Bastard!*

6

The pounding in my head was like open mic night at Pete's —just a bunch of idiots banging on their instruments. Serious eye boogers glued my eyes shut so I couldn't see well, but I worked my stiff jaw open and closed. I must have been grinding my teeth while I slept. As I rubbed my eyes open, I came face-to-face with what was becoming a regular nightmare: Jonah.

"Ugh!" I rolled over and turned my back toward him. I felt a weight push the mattress down and Jonah climbed over me, lying on his side, facing me again. I pulled the covers over my head to hide. "Go away!" I mumbled.

"Oh, come on, Mackenzie. Let me explain," he pleaded, tugging the covers back down. "I didn't mean to knock you out again, but you ... well ... you're not as easy to *manage* as we thought." He diverted his eyes, which made me narrow mine in response.

"What do you mean, *manage*?"

"Nothing. Look, we're sorry, but you have to understand that our community has a strict set of rules that must be followed—even if you're not part of the Pack. It's just the way things are."

His soft brown eyes were so apologetic, I almost forgave him for shooting me up with a sedative—twice—but I wasn't *that* forgiving. I was about to give him a piece of my mind when I realized our close proximity and the fact that we were in bed together.

He'd put on a shirt to replace the one he'd given me, but I could still see the finely cut ridges of his body and the taut muscles of his broad shoulders. He was quite a sight to behold, and I had to shake my head to clear my thoughts. They were going down a road I wasn't ready to travel, and our closeness wasn't helping.

"Can you back up? You're in my bubble," I said snidely.

He smirked. "Your bubble? Am I making you nervous, Mackenzie Grey?" He scooted closer to me and I held my breath. He placed a hand on top of my hip and leaned forward to whisper in my ear, his neck inviting me to nibble on it. "You should know that werewolves have a very keen sense of smell, and you, Mackenzie, are drenched in fear," he said, and I felt his very soft lips brush my all-of-a-sudden, sensitive earlobe.

Someone cleared their throat from the door.

"Am I interrupting?"

I pushed away from Jonah, who climbed off the bed and met our visitor at the door. It was none other than his douche bag of a brother.

"Nah, we were just chatting," Jonah said, winking at me. "Mackenzie, I'd like to formally introduce you to my twin brother, Jackson."

"Twin?" My eyes bugged out as they switched back and forth

between the two men. I mean, they resembled each other, but Jackson seemed a little older. I tilted my head to the side and tried to get a better look.

"Like what you see?"

Ugh, and he had the same (if not bigger) ego as his brother Jonah.

"Actually, no, Douche. What I'd *like* is to GET THE HELL OUT OF HERE!" I screamed the last part so they'd get the picture. While it might be a single girl's dream come true to be stuck in bed surrounded by a ton of hunks, it just wasn't one of my fantasies. "I'm tired of being jerked around and sedated. Can someone please show me the goddamn exit so I can go home? I promise I won't tell your freakin' secret to anyone," I fumed, slamming my hands on the mattress like a child throwing a tantrum.

"It's not about you telling people *our* secret, it's about finding out who the hell *you* are. There are very detailed documents about wolves and our family lines—and you're not part of any of them," Jackson answered with a scowl.

"Do I have to be here for you to find out?" *Seriously, what's the point of keeping me? It's not like I'm doing anything. They might as well let me leave.*

"Let you leave so you can skip town? No way. Your cute little ass is staying right here," Jackson replied. I felt gross by the fact he thought my ass was cute. He wasn't ugly, but he was such a jerk.

"Skip town? First off, this is the city, and secondly, my research paper is due this week, and there's no way I've been slaving away on it just to *not* turn it in," I said with a hmph.

"A paper? Like schoolwork?" Jonah asked and I rolled my eyes. "What are you going to school for?" he asked, like it was a foreign concept.

"Criminal Justice." The bothers exchanged a look of disbelief.

"What?" I crossed my arms over my chest, feeling awkward under their intense scrutiny.

"How far along are you in your field?" Jackson asked.

I scrunched my eyebrows together, wondering where they were going with this. "I'm in my last year. I'm an intern at One Precinct Plaza."

"Shit," Jonah mumbled. "When do you go in?"

Now I was catching on. They were scared about people finding out I was missing. I was sure that if Amy hadn't been captured here with me, she would have already gone down to the precinct and told them by now. The whole squadron would be out looking for me soon. "I go weekdays after class," I answered with a smirk. *Suck on that, losers!*

Jackson straightened and narrowed his eyes. "I don't believe you. You're probably some English major or something wacky like that."

I scoffed. "I don't care if you believe me or not. If you keep me here any longer, you're looking at all of 1PP crawling up your asses!" I was embellishing, but desperate times ...

"Whatever." Jackson waved me off.

I threw off the covers and jumped out of bed, pulling Jonah's flannel down to cover my rump.

"Sebastian!" I yelled as I stomped over to the door. If they weren't going to let me leave, I vowed to make their lives miserable. Time to find my inner chick, and cry and whine about everything.

Jonah grabbed me from behind, his arm wrapped around my waist, and pulled me back against his chest. "Not so fast there, smarty pants. The big guy is busy. I'm sorry if Jackson hurt your feelings," he whispered softly in my ear and I huffed, trying to ignore the tingle in my belly.

Suddenly, a dark, looming figure stood outside the door frame. The room shrank once he stepped in, clouding the entrance. Sebastian stood there with his hands planted on his hips, a very pissed expression on his face. Would he ever look at me differently?

"What's going on here?" he asked—no, demanded.

"Nothing, Boss, we're just chatting," Jackson said, all joking aside.

"No, they were harassing me," I snipped. Jonah's grip tightened around my waist. I forgot he was still holding on to me and I frowned. Sebastian looked at the three of us and then down at Jonah's arm, and his eyes narrowed.

Not wanting to stir the pot, I plucked Jonah's arm off me and stepped aside. I could see how this might look ... suspicious. Jonah snapped his head my way and gave me a stern look that was the complete opposite of the jokester I'd come to see him as. I shrunk under his glare. I was starting to think all these wolves had some air of dominance to them.

"Come with me," Sebastian commanded and jerked his head outside the room. He didn't wait for me to respond or see if I was following. I looked back at the brothers—who were both glaring at me—and hurried to catch up to Sebastian.

I ran out and saw Sebastian heading down the stairs to the main floor. Barefoot and cold, I hustled to catch up and shivered as my feet came in contact with the steel. It was rare that I ever felt anything other than hot. They must have had the AC blasting in there.

"You're cold," he stated tonelessly, peering down at me once I caught up with him.

"Y-yes." My teeth chattered and his face darkened. He was probably upset with me for being so weak, because I doubt he was upset at anyone else for not taking better care of me. If only ...

"Luna!" he barked, and I jumped at his unexpected raised voice. "Get Mackenzie a pair of sweats and some shoes." The woman who had been mopping the main floor nodded at Sebastian, set the mop against the wall, and hurried to do as he commanded. "Damn Jonah can never do what he's told," he mumbled.

"Are they all at your beck and call?" I mumbled.

He jerked to a stop in front of me, almost making me run into him. "Do you always have a snappy retort for everything?" he accused, and those ice-cold, baby blues froze me in place.

"It wasn't a *retort*, I was merely saying that it seems like everyone snaps to your every whim," I defended myself and met his stare, matching his dominance. I refused to cower under his intensity and run away with my tail tucked between my legs, no matter how scary he might be—or how good looking.

Ugh, I have to stop thinking about him that way. Jonah was able to smell my fear, which means they might be able to smell if I'm aroused. Does that even have a smell? That is so trippy, and also kind of gross.

"They do as their Alpha says, like they should," he responded. "Soon, you will as well."

"Not happening. I'm not joining your little club."

"We'll see." He turned around just as the Luna came up to us with the items he requested. He handed me a pair of gray sweatpants that tightened at the ankles and a pair of pink, fluffy slippers.

"Uh ... can you turn around?" I asked, but he crossed his arms over his chest and narrowed his eyes more intently. *Asshole.*

With Jonah's flannel still on, I tried to discreetly pull up the sweats, but I was sure I flashed my undies either way. Once I slid my feet into the slippers, I couldn't help but let out a sigh mixed with a moan. Not one of my finest moments, but the softness was a much needed reprieve from the cold that was making my toes into little popsicles.

"Better?" Sebastian asked huskily. I raised an eyebrow at him, but he continued, "Come on; I was in the middle of a phone call when you cried wolf."

I chuckled. *I guess he does have a sense of humor.*

I followed him down a hallway across the main floor and down another set of stairs that I assumed led to the basement. There was nothing special about it, it just looked like another floor. We made two lefts and a right, and then stopped in front of a door that he opened without knocking. It was an office, and I saw there was already someone waiting for him. In the middle of the room was a large, oak desk with a laptop and papers scattered all over the surface. Two chairs sat in front of it, and bookshelves lined the small space.

A woman with long, silky blonde hair that reached below her butt was sitting on top of the desk. Her bare legs were crossed, with red pumps on her feet. She had cat-like eyes that narrowed once she saw me standing behind the giant that was Sebastian. This entire scenario looked like the setup for a really bad porno. She was wearing a man's white button up shirt that wasn't even buttoned, with no bra on. And yes, this was my inner prude talking. This chick was ready to do the nasty, and I didn't think she was expecting anyone—much less me—to mess up her plans.

"Not now, V," Sebastian said tiredly, sparing her a brief glance before walking around the desk.

This must be his office. I tried to look around, but felt the glare of the woman he called V, who was still perched on his desk.

"Who's this?" she asked, never taking her eyes off me.

"This is Mackenzie Grey," he replied as he sat down in his chair. "She's a lone wolf." He turned the laptop on and started to look for something in the pile of papers he had.

She smirked. "A lone, eh? How lovely," she purred.

I couldn't hold back a grimace. Not that she scared me, but she made me want to barf. Unless I was reading this all wrong, she came here to bone Sebastian—possibly on top of the desk. Yuck. I hadn't even contemplated the idea that he might have a girlfriend.

Of course he would. He's like sex on a stick. Quick mental note, I better not touch that desk, or even the chairs, for that matter. I didn't know how many times they'd "used" this office.

"Don't you have somewhere else to be?" he asked V, irritated.

"Of course, Bash. That's why I'm here ... remember? I penciled you in for this evening; you promised," she whined and turned to him. Her laced rump peeked out of the shirt she wore when she leaned across the desk to him.

Ew, gross. I diverted my eyes to the ceiling because this was getting really awkward. If there was ever a time I missed Jonah—hell, even Jackson—it was now. At this point, I even missed the crappy music at Pete's Bar.

"Uh ... may I be excused?" I interrupted, immediately wanting to slap myself. I sounded like I was asking my parents to leave the dinner table.

"Yes, you may," V answered snidely as she turned her cat eyes to me with satisfaction.

"No, you may not," Sebastian countered. "We have things to discuss. V, this can wait."

She pouted. "You promised, Bash. You're always so busy." She trailed her hand from his chest down under the table.

Oh, good lord. I *so* didn't need to be here for this. He didn't even look fazed by her, or interested, and trust me, she was seriously working the whole Marilyn-Monroe-I-want-to-seduce-JFK thing she had going on.

"Yeah, *Bash*, you promised her," I smarted. "We can always reschedule. I'll pencil you in for later today," I suggested, rushing out of the office that I felt was giving me a heat rash. I slammed the door shut, the noise echoing through the hallway. I didn't realize how upset I was. It was none of my business, really, and I shouldn't be ticked off that he had a girlfriend, but still ... whatever.

I stood in front of his office door for a few moments until I heard V's giggles turn to moans—answered by a grunt coming from Sebastian that made me haul ass out of there. I retraced my path back to the stairs and up to the main floor—their loud moans echoing through the hallway.

I fumed, the desire to punch someone in the face trickling through my veins when I smacked right into Blu. I'd just reached the top of the stairs as she came out of what looked like a laundry room holding my now clean and pressed clothes.

"Oh, Mackenzie, I'm sorry!" she said, taking a quick step back.

I put a hand out to steady her. "No worries ... are those my clothes?" I said nonchalantly, trying to calm my mood. I realized I was all alone for the first time since I arrived, and if I could find the exit, I would be able to leave this hell hole.

"Oh, yes. If you'd like, I can bring them to your room."

I shook my head. No way. I wanted to change so I could stop looking like a homeless person. I didn't even match! "No, that's not necessary. I'll take them now. I was actually wondering ... where is this warehouse located? No one's told me anything."

She seemed uneasy as she looked around to make sure no one was listening. "I don't know if I should be telling you. Not that I'm worried they'll do anything, because I can kick their butts, but ..."

I was starting to like this chick. She was a rule follower, but she also had a smidge of a rebellious streak. If she wasn't neck-deep with the Pack, she might be someone I'd hang out with.

"Well, let me just ask what I'm thinking. Are you planning on escaping?" she asked.

I stared at her for a long moment, realizing I might have underestimated her. She wasn't stupid, but I saw a spark of intrigue in her eyes that made me wonder if she wanted to jump ship.

"Possibly," I answered honestly, and eyed her cautiously. I had to word this correctly. "Would you be willing to help me?"

She gasped, but I could tell my answer didn't shock her too much, because she glanced around again. *Hook, line, and sinker.* Before she responded, I knew she was on Team Kenzie.

"Are you sure you want to do this? The Pack could protect and help you. You wouldn't be alone," she proposed.

For a moment, I thought she truly cared if something happened to me. Not like V. V probably assumed I was some sort of competition. Which I wasn't. Sebastian could not care less about me. In *that* way, in any event.

"Protect me from what? A mugger? I've been living in New York all my life, Blu. I'll be fine." I brushed off her concern with a laugh. It was obviously the wrong thing to say, because she scoffed like I'd just bitch-slapped her or something.

"A mugger? Mackenzie, there are worse things out there than a human with a gun. Don't you know?"

"Yeah, yeah, I know, like cancer, terrorists, and wearing white after Labor Day. But right now, I don't care about any of those things. I just need to go home. I can't stay locked up here. I'm going crazy, and I have a life out there. I can't just throw that away."

She scrunched her mouth to the side and thought about my words for a moment. "If—and this is a huge if—I help you, will you at least think about joining the Pack?"

I searched her face. Did she really think I would willingly come back to this?

"They'll find you, Mackenzie. Don't think if you escape today, that you can simply disappear. When Jonah found you on the third night of the last full moon, they went on a hunt for you ... and obviously they found you. Now that almost the entire pack knows your scent, you'll be even easier to find the second time around."

My scent? This is all too weird. I wonder what I smell like? Okay, stay on track, Kenz.

"I don't care, Blu, I just need to get out of here, even if it's for a little while," I said, even though there was no way I would let myself get caught again. Wednesday was the beginning of winter break, and I was leaving this damn city. Hopefully two weeks would be enough time for their muzzles to forget about me.

"Fine," she answered, handing me my clothing. "We're in Brooklyn—"

"Brooklyn!" I exclaimed. *Oh no, they didn't.*

"Oh, don't worry, we're in Dumbo. The city is right across the East River."

Like *that* made it any better. They took me out of my comfort zone! How the hell was I going to get home? I grimaced. "Where is the nearest train station?"

As Blu continued to tell me how to get home, I quickly stripped and put my clothes on, but deciding to retain some sense of comfort, I didn't bother to change out of the slippers. Blu went into one of the other rooms in the hallway and got my purse.

"How'd you get my bag?" I asked, startled.

"I think one of the guys went back to your job and snatched it."

If I still have a job, I frowned.

I shoved my boots in my purse, grateful for my infatuation with big, sling-on bags. She walked me outside, but not before making me promise to give her my phone number. Scrambling for a pen in my now overflowing purse, I found one and wrote my cell number in the palm of her hand.

Before I left, I paused for a moment. "Out of curiosity, why are you helping me?" Not that I wasn't appreciative for all she was doing for me, but she was going against her Pack; a group of people she was very adamant about wanting me to join not too long ago.

Her eyes narrowed and she scrunched her mouth to the side.

"Let's just say this isn't my first rodeo. If you make it out of this unscathed and we get a chance, I'll tell you all about it."

I nodded and she pulled me into a very tight and unexpected hug, like we were already best friends. "Be careful, Mackenzie. I'll call you in an hour to make sure you're okay."

"Call me Kenz, and I will. Thanks, Blu." With a small smile, I started my trek toward the A train.

7

I thanked my lucky stars once I crossed over the Brooklyn Bridge. After taking the A train, switching to the Six, and getting off on Astor Place, I hailed a cab that took me straight home. I was tired and cranky, and I wanted a bowl of Chunky Monkey ice cream in which to drown my supernatural woes. How had my life turned upside down in just one day? First with James, and now with this werewolf business? *This blows.*

I dug in my bag for my keys and hurried inside, where a spazzed-out Amy was pacing in the apartment living room. I shut the new door with a loud thud and she jerked around; the relief on her face was instantaneous. She ran over to me and her little arms squeezed me like I was going to disappear any second.

"Oh my God, I've missed you! What did they do to you? Are you okay? Did they feed you? I'll go over there and kick their asses if they didn't. Have you showered? Do you need—"

"Amy, stop, please. Catch your breath," I said as I patted her on her back. She was cutting off my air flow, and I wanted to jump in bed and sleep for the rest of the year.

She pulled away and adjusted my shirt. "Sorry," she replied sheepishly. "They called a half hour ago and told me you'd be coming home."

"Who called?" I froze mid-step towards my room.

"This guy named Joe? Jonah? I don't know, but he said you left without saying goodbye and were most likely headed this way. He wanted me to call him when you arrived," she said as she reached for her cell phone.

I grabbed her arm before she could press the center button of her iPhone.

"Ow! Let go, Kenz!" Amy jerked her arm away and rubbed it.

"You can't call them! I ran the hell away. They're a freakin' cult!" I yelled and her eyes widened.

"He said they were helping you with the whole werewolf thing. I thought ..." She trailed off, and I knew she felt guilty.

They probably painted her a rosy story about helping me to make her think everything was okay. The more I thought about it, the more I had a hard time believing she fell for it. Amy wasn't gullible. She thought everyone had a hidden agenda, and she questioned everything. She was the queen of conspiracy theories.

"Amy," I started, "look at me." She turned around and her eyes dilated rapidly—so fast, it didn't look normal. *What the hell ... ?*

Just then, my phone rang. When I pulled it out of my bag and saw a three-four-seven area code on the screen, I hesitated for a minute. It could either be Blu checking that I made it home, or it was Jonah and Sebastian, probably tracking my number for my location or something crazy like that. I let it go to voicemail and waited to see if they'd leave a message. When the chime came through, I listened to Blu's voicemail.

"Hey Mackenzie, I mean Kenz, I was just calling to make sure you made it home okay. They know you're gone, so be careful. I think they're sending out a team to look for you. Call me back within the next five minutes if you can. Bye."

I re-dialed her number and she picked up before the first ring ended. "Kenz!" she exclaimed through the phone.

"Yeah, hey," I answered, watching Amy from the corner of my eye. She was acting funny, like she was on a bad trip or something.

Blu exhaled. "I was so worried. Like, twenty minutes after you left, Sebastian came out of his office looking for you, and when no one could find you, this place went crazy. Jonah and Sebastian are fighting with each other, and they sent out three teams to look for you. They just left for Alphabet City, so if you can go somewhere else, I suggest you go," she whispered into the phone.

I tensed and looked around as if they'd pop out from behind the curtains. "Thanks for the heads up, but I need your help with something else. Something's wrong with my roommate. Her eyes are dilating like crazy, and she's acting really funny. She thinks I was in werewolf rehab, which in a normal situation where I'd been kidnapped, she never would."

"They probably used compulsion on her so she wouldn't call the police. Just splash some water on her and put her somewhere there's loud noises. She'll eventually snap out of it. But seriously, Mackenzie, you need to leave your apartment. They'll be there soon."

"Okay, thanks Blu. I'll call you later."

We said our goodbyes and hung up. I grabbed Amy's phone as

well as mine and ran into my bedroom. I changed into a pair of jeans, a sweater, and my boots. What I really needed was a goddamn shower, but that would have to wait. I pulled a bag from my closet and started stuffing it with some clothes before moving to Amy's room and doing the same. When I went back to the living room, I saw that Amy had started pacing again.

She was making me nervous. *What the hell did they do to her?* I gripped her heavily pierced face to force her to look up and tried to make eye contact, but she was so jittery, it was hard to keep her eyes still and focused on me. Looking back, it was silly, but I figured I'd watched enough TV about supernatural beings to handle this, so compulsion should be easy...right?

"Calm down," I said sternly. She started to shake. *Damn it.* I cleared my throat and held her firmly still. "Calm down," I repeated. She blinked a few times before she settled and nodded. "Good, now let's go." After bundling up in our winter coats, we grabbed our bags and left the apartment. Instead of leaving through the front entrance, we took the service exit in the back, looped around the block, and backtracked around to the bodega across the street. I went inside where Mr. Gomez's wife was working the convenience store.

"Hola, mija," she greeted with a smile.

"Hey, Mrs. Gomez, can I use your phone?"

"Sure," she answered in a thick Spanish accent. I threaded through the small store to the back where they had a small office, and dialed the last person I ever wanted to ask for help.

"Hello?" James answered.

I let out a deep breath. *Suck it up, Kenzie.* "James? Hey ... " I trailed off.

There was a pause. "Kenzie? Are you okay?"

I sighed. I figured he would hang up on me. It was late and he was probably all tucked away in bed with prostitute Barbie. "No, I'm not. I need your help." Instantly alert, he started firing off questions and taking charge, and I realized I never should have doubted him. I told him where I was, and he was already in his car and on his way to pick us up before I hung up the phone.

Twenty minutes later, James was parked in front of the bodega and we were squeezing in to his silver Toyota Prius. Yeah, he's one of those hipsters who want to save the environment and crap. Total tree hugger.

"Thanks for coming to get us. If you can drop us off at the Marriott by campus, we'll be good," I said while he drove. Not even five minutes into the drive, Amy had knocked out and we could hear her small snores coming from the backseat.

"You don't have to stay at a hotel, Kenzie. You know you can stay with me," he offered, his eyes never leaving the road. "What's going on, anyway?"

Oh boy, I didn't think that far ahead. What should I tell him? *Well, James, I'm a werewolf, and now a whole Pack is on the lookout for me because they can't have a stray running around the city.* Yeah, that was something you heard every day.

"No, it's okay, I don't want to inconvenience you and Barb—I mean, you and Diana. We'll be fine at a hotel." I hoped he didn't hear my slip-up.

"Diana? She won't care. She hates coming out to the apartment anyway, so you'll never see her," he said.

"You guys aren't living together?" I asked with a little too much interest.

He scoffed. "Heck, no! What made you think that?" He turned

to look at me once he slowed to a red light and I diverted my gaze out the window.

That conniving slut! I hated that I had believed her, when all she wanted to do was one-up me. *Dang it, she's smarter than I gave her credit for.*

"Oh, I don't know, I just thought..." I trailed off and let the conversation hang. I didn't want to whine about how his girlfriend was an evil mastermind or anything—especially since I had bigger problems.

We got to James' apartment and he had to drive around the block a couple times before finding a parking spot. He helped me get Amy from the back seat. "Kenz, are you going to tell me what's going on?"

I sighed. "Well, I'm a werewolf, and there's a wolf pack out looking for me, so I have to lay low."

There was a long beat before James hunched over, laughing. After he caught his breath, he said, "I swear, Kenz, that imagination of yours. If you don't want to tell me that's fine, but I hope you'll learn to trust me again."

Sometimes the best thing to do was tell the truth. The truth was always—to some extent—ridiculous and slightly unbelievable. The ones who asked for it usually didn't really want to know, they just wanted to live in their bubble of lies. Which was alright with me, because when this hit the fan, I could calmly say, *I told you so.*

8
_____

Amy and I spent the next three days holed up in James' apartment. She eventually came to, after many hours of me splashing water on her face and clapping my hands by her ears. Trust me when I tell you it was no easy feat. It took about five hours before she was normal again, and let's just say that if she ever met Jonah and the Pack, she would have a few choice words for them. Amy was pissed. She said they barged into the bar shortly after they dragged me to the truck, and she barely had any time to tell anyone or call the cops. Somehow, they compelled her to go back to our apartment, and there they came to an 'understanding.' Yeah, understanding, my ass. But so far, we hadn't heard or seen them since Saturday night, and I couldn't be happier.

We only left the apartment to take our finals, and then when I had to go down to the station. After each brief outing, we headed straight back to James' apartment. He was right when he said Diana Stone never came to visit. We didn't see her at all. It was now Wednesday morning, and I couldn't wait to finish up at the precinct and head to James' so we could hit the road back home to Cold Springs and truly disappear for a while.

I still hadn't heard from Blu. I wasn't worried we'd been outed; I just hoped she was okay. I felt like a total jerk for not contacting her and checking in, but I didn't want to risk it. Sitting at the precinct, stewing on my dilemma, I was snapped out of my thoughts when someone slammed their hands on the desk where I was sitting.

"When were you going to tell me about James?" Amy said, startling me. I thought she was at school.

"Jesus, Amy! Wear a bell next time."

"Don't change the subject. Why are we still carpooling with him? It's not like we have a car and he wants to ride shot gun," she snipped.

I realized I hadn't told her I was playing girlfriend during winter break. *Crap.* With all this wolf business, I forgot about all the other, regular problems. I looked around the squad room and luckily, no one was paying attention to us. We were working on a major case at the moment, so everyone was preoccupied and neck-deep in work.

"Well, the thing is ... " I whispered, and she arched an eyebrow. I teetered under her intense glare. With a hip jutted out, she tapped her small right foot, waiting for my answer.

"Today would be nice, Kenz."

I sighed. "Fine. He hasn't told his family about our break up."

"Mackenzie!" she shrieked and that got us a couple looks.

"Shhh!" I pulled her down as we hovered over the desk. "Are you *trying* to get me fired?"

"Sorry," Amy rolled her eyes, "but this is a big deal and total bullshit. You don't owe that loser any favors."

"I know, I know," I mumbled as Detective Michaels walked up.

"This isn't the place to socialize, Grey!" he barked as he pushed my rolling chair to the side and logged on to his computer that I had been using. "We have another reported kidnapping, but this time in Spanish Harlem. Do you want to tag along, or are you done for the day?"

It was only eleven A.M, and James wouldn't be done with his last final until late in the afternoon. My eyes switched between Amy and Detective Michaels, and my decision was easy. I'd tackle the beast later. "I'm tagging along."

"Get your things and let's go," he clipped out. I scrambled to grab my stuff and follow him out.

"Mackenzie!" Amy yelled, but I waved her off.

"We'll talk later at the apartment!" With that, I was out the door and hustling to catch up.

———

DETECTIVE GARRETT MICHAELS had been a cop with the NYPD for twelve years. For the last three, he'd been assigned to the Major Case Squad. At the beginning of the semester, his partner had transferred out and he drew the small stick when it came to babysitting the intern. At first, he really disliked me—like, a lot—but I'd like to think I've grown on him. Hopefully, at least. I needed a passing grade.

I rode in the passenger seat of his unmarked car as we weaved through mid-day traffic.

"So what's the skinny on this kidnapping?" I asked. This was the fourth case in less than a month and we were starting to think they were connected. We just hadn't found a pattern yet.

"Thirty-two-year old, Caucasian male, last seen two nights ago and presumably taken from right outside his home."

I nodded and pulled out a notebook from my messenger bag. I skipped over a few pages until I landed on the page that listed the rest of the victims. Two women and one man—now two men. They were all different ages, races, and came from various economic backgrounds. No obvious pattern.

"I don't get it," I whispered, mainly to myself.

Michaels grunted. "Who you tellin'? Don't beat yourself up, kid. It's just a stall. We'll get a lead sooner or later."

I narrowed my eyes. "You know how much I hate it when you call me *kid*."

He chuckled. "I know. I do it on purpose, kid."

I groaned.

"Relax. You have one more semester with me, and then I don't have to see your ugly face again," he said. I rolled my eyes.

"*My* face? What about yours? Your mug is so ugly, not even Scooby Doo could solve that mystery."

"Ha. Ha. Very funny, Grey," he deadpanned. "Give yourself a point."

"Yes!" I excitedly reached into the glove compartment and pulled out the little black book that Michaels kept his booty-call numbers in, but which also held our "shit-talking" tally. He was currently in the lead with thirty-seven, and I was now only five points away from catching up.

"Don't add an extra point! At the end of every shift, I count to make sure you aren't cheating."

"Get a grip, Michaels. You're still in the lead."

"Hurry up and put it away. We're here," he said as he pulled up to a spot in front of a water hydrant where he wasn't supposed to park.

We stood in front of a dilapidated building that appeared to house at least twenty apartments. As we got out of the car, I discreetly took a good whiff but couldn't smell anything distinctive. I perked up my hearing, but there were too many people inside the building to pinpoint anything threatening. Opening the front door to the lobby, the stench of stale cigarettes and mold smacked me in the face. I tried to hide my discomfort as we walked toward the elevators. A dirty white sheet of paper was taped on the elevator doors with the words, "Out of Order", so we ended up climbing seven flights of stairs to the designated apartment.

Garrett's breathing became labored by the fifth floor, and I laughed. "Keep up, old man."

"Yeah, yeah, just keep going," he huffed behind me.

Once we made it to apartment 7B, I knocked on the door and waited for a response.

The locks on the door began to unclick and a woman with wild, chestnut-colored hair peeped through the crack of the door.

"Can I help you?" she mumbled.

"Hello, I'm Detective Michaels and this is Miss Grey. We're with the NYPD, and we're here regarding the kidnapping of ... John Hancock?" Michaels read the name from his notebook in confusion.

I had to hold in my laughter. John Hancock? That could *not* be someone's real name—we were obviously getting played. I listened to the woman's heartbeat as she spoke and waited.

"Y-yes, c-come in," she said as she pushed the door wider. Her eyes were the size of tennis balls when she saw me for the first time. "Y-you can't come in!" She pointed a dirty finger in my direction.

"Excuse me?" I shot back, feeling insulted.

"Do you two know each other?" Michaels asked.

I shook my head.

With speed that matched my own, she was now only a hairs breath away from me and I could smell the six cups of coffee she'd had today.

"The children of the moon are not welcomed in my home," she muttered.

I held my breath until Michaels grabbed the lady and pulled her away from me. I kept my face neutral, but couldn't stop my racing heart. *Who the hell is this old kook?*

"Grey, why don't you canvas the area and see if you find anything?" He handed me a couple of evidence bags and nodded toward the stairs.

Without saying a word, I headed back down toward the lobby.

"Wait for me by the car!"

"Yeah," I yelled back. "Have fun with that crazy bitch," I mumbled and tried to curb the urge to punch the wall. I couldn't let my anger get the best of me.

I exited the building, putting on my winter gloves and tightening my scarf. Even though I wasn't cold, I still had to keep up appearances. New York winters were not to be taken lightly.

After walking around the block—twice—Michaels still hadn't come down and I was getting antsy. What if that crazy lady did something to him? No. I'd wait fifteen minutes before I barged in. I leaned against the unmarked cop car and crossed my arms over my chest just as something caught my attention. Directly in front of me was the apartment building's unkempt garden area with bare bushes and dead flowers. Scattered around were soda cans and other garbage, but a pinkish piece of paper stood out to me. It was cut out in a weird shape, and I couldn't see anything written on it.

I pushed off the car and walked toward the item in question. Squatting in front of it, I pulled out a pen from my coat pocket and lifted the paper—except it wasn't. I knew I shouldn't have done what I did, but I had to know. I took off my gloves and touched it.

It wasn't paper—it was skin.

Shit.

MICHAELS EMERGED from the building looking exhausted and annoyed, which meant I couldn't joke with him right now.

"Let's go, Grey. This was a waste of time," he said as he went around to the driver's side of the car.

"We can't," I said as I stood on the sidewalk. "Garrett—"

"Mackenzie, I don't have the patience for this right now. Get in the car!"

"Shut up and let me finish a goddamn sentence!" I barked, and felt my face turn beet red in anger. It was no easy feat to keep a werewolf's temper down. "I found something, and you need to call it in." I lifted the plastic bag that held the evidence I'd found.

"What is it?"

"It might be John Hancock. It's skin."

His eyes widened a fraction and he reached for the radio in

his pocket to call for backup.

It took over two hours for the troops to canvas the area and re-interview the crazy bitch upstairs, who I learned was named Jane Hancock. John was her son. She'd given a wacky story to Michaels about how her son was taken by a shape shifter. I was starting to understand why he'd gotten so frustrated—the lady had a couple screws missing—which sounds absurd coming from a shifter myself, but her whole story was nuts. She said her son was part Fae. In other terms, he's a fairy.

"What's going to happen to Ms. Hancock?" I asked Detective Michaels as we waited for CSI to finish cleaning up.

"They're taking her in for a psych evaluation. They didn't find any drugs in her apartment, so it's possible she has a mental disability. We're still not sure if she even *has* a son. It could all be in her head," he said and looked to me. "Good catch today, Grey. I guess there might still be hope for you in the force."

I snorted.

"But the next time you tell me to shut up, I'm dropping you from your internship."

With that, he walked away and left me to flip him off behind his back. The jerk.

"I saw that, Grey. Now go home and enjoy your holidays."

IT WAS late in the afternoon when I made it back to James' apartment, where I found Amy sprawled out on his couch waiting for me. Her flaming red hair was pulled up in a messy bun and all her tattoos were covered up by her winter clothes.

"It's about time your ass came home. You can't avoid me forever, Kenz."

"I'm not trying to avoid you; we had a break in the case today, and *I* found it!" I was so giddy I was about to jump out of my skin —no pun intended.

I took off my coat and pushed Amy's legs aside so I could sit beside her.

"Kenz, I'm happy for you, really," she started, and I steeled myself for what was coming, "but when were you going to tell me James was coming home with us? You don't owe him shit. Don't do the bastard any favors."

"I know, but—"

Just then, James burst into the living room where we had been sleeping for the past couple days. He was out of breath and sweating—which would be fine if it wasn't cold outside.

"What the hell—?"

"Kenz!" he yelled just as Jonah, Jackson, and Sebastian barged into the apartment behind him, filling it with their oppressive frames. I wanted to giggle, but had to swallow it. James looked like the nerd he was in high school standing next to these guys. But right now wasn't the time to be thinking about that.

"I swear, the bad guys always get you just as you're about to make your getaway," I said as I threw my hands up in the air. This was total bullshit. I wasn't even two hours away from leaving this damn city.

"Who the heck are these guys, Kenz?" James squealed as Jackson grabbed him by the collar of his coat.

"We wouldn't have found you if this loser didn't reek of your scent. Is he your boyfriend?" Jackson asked. I didn't answer right away, because I was watching the reaction of the other two were-wolves in the room. Jonah's features turned so dark, it betrayed the smirk on his face. Sebastian's upper lip curled into a growl, but that was nothing new. He seemed to always be brooding—he looked the same, and that sort of ticked me off too. Why should he care? He had V.

"Scent? What are you guys, dogs?" James asked, and my face fell.

Wrong thing to say.

I looked at James, who saw my widened eyes and realized he might have made a boo-boo.

"Dogs?" Jackson exclaimed. Either he was about to throw him across the room or punch him.

I grabbed James before he could make it any worse, and with strength that I'm sure shocked James out of his stupor, I pulled him behind me where Amy was. She was noticeably silent, but I didn't have time to check on her.

"You guys need to get out," I said with as much authority as I could muster.

"You didn't answer the question, Mackenzie. Is he your boyfriend?" It was Jonah who asked, and I noticed his eyes had lost the soft pools of chocolate and were now a bright gold.

Holy shit.

I swallowed whatever spit I had left in my dry mouth, squared my shoulders, and stood up straighter. These fools weren't going to intimidate me! Well, that was what I told myself.

"Yes, he's my boyfriend."

And all hell broke loose.

Amy shrieked like a damn whistle, James grabbed onto my shirt like the pansy he was, and Sebastian and Jackson held on to an out-of-control Jonah. He hadn't wolfed out, but his canines were out and he was snapping them at us—well, mainly at James, my pretend boyfriend.

"Heel!" Sebastian barked, and it was like watching a well-trained dog react. He didn't actually heel like one, but he stopped his thrashing. His chest rose and fell like he was short on oxygen. "Enough with the twenty-one questions. Where the hell do you think you're going, Mackenzie?" Sebastian asked. I looked at him and noticed his eyes were glowing. They weren't the pale blue I'd seen before.

What's up with these guys and their eyes?

"I'm going home. It's winter break, and my family is expecting me for the holidays." I kept it short and simple. They could do their worst, but there was no way I was missing this trip home. I barely talked to my parents as it was; I had to show up for school breaks.

"Where is home?" he asked with a hand still holding Jonah back.

"Cold Springs. Upstate New York."

"You can't go alone," Sebastian said. His words woke my feisty best friend out of whatever daydream had trapped her.

"She won't be alone, you asshole!" She pushed past me and stood up to the big, bad wolves in all her five-foot-four glory. "You can't just come barging in here, filled up with testosterone and shit, and expect her to do what you say. Fuck that noise."

I giggled at how badass Amy was. Not even a trio of beefy werewolves could make her quiver.

"And you are?" Sebastian asked.

She crossed her arms over her chest defiantly. "Amelia Elizabeth Fitzgerald, bitch, and don't you forget it."

I smirked with pride as I watched the range of emotions that crossed through all three of their faces. From shock, to anger, to respect. Jackson's was the funniest, as he was awestruck. Oh, boy.

James' grip on my shirt tightened, reminding me that he was still scared and hiding behind me. I rolled my eyes. "Let go of me, Jameson," I whispered and tried to shrug him off. He whined a little but released me.

"Trust me, we won't, Amelia," Sebastian said, and I thought I saw a smile he was trying to cover up. "Will you be going to Cold Springs with Mackenzie as well?"

I was shocked at how ... *nice* he was being to her. Why didn't he talk to me like that?

"Yes," Amy said with conviction. For the last three years, she'd spent winter break with my family since her parents were usually on some fancy vacation in Europe and didn't pay attention to her when she was there. Amy came from a wealthy family, but her appearance wasn't something they condoned. With all the tattoos and piercings, they wrote her off as a screw-up. Funny enough, Amy was one of the smartest people I'd ever met and was at the top of her class. It was their loss if they didn't recognize her brilliance. She would be running the world pretty soon if she got her way.

When Sebastian's gaze turned from my best friend to me, he no longer looked friendly. "I can't let you go alone, Mackenzie." His face twisted in rage, like I'd done something wrong.

Man, I can never win.

"Oh, come on!" I expelled. "I'm not even part of your Pac—," I caught myself before I said something in front of James that could land us both in hot water. I didn't know what their rules on human knowledge were, but I preferred not to test it. "Packet," I corrected, and felt incredibly stupid. I didn't have enough time to think of something better. "I'm not part of your packet, so you can't dictate what goes in it." *Someone save me, please.*

Amy whirled around and raised a pierced eyebrow at me. I rolled my eyes, exasperated. What did they expect? I couldn't be witty all the time. *Sheesh.*

"Then you'll take another document from the packet with you," Sebastian offered smoothly, playing along with my analogy, although he wasn't happy about it.

"Oh, no! No, no, no, no way!" I said like a child. I swore, I was throwing too many tantrums lately. What was up with me?

"This isn't negotiable, Mackenzie. You don't understand everything yet, but hopefully by the next full—by the next week or so, you will," he said and cleared his throat.

"Kenzie, what the hell is going on?" James whispered behind me.

Jonah lurched forward again, but Jackson had a good hold on him as he continued to stare at an oblivious Amy. I chuckled. He was totally smitten.

"I'm sorry, James, I'll explain everything to you later." I put a hand on his arm, directing him to the bedroom. A growl came from someone behind us—most likely Jonah—but I didn't look to see who it was. I was nervous about leaving Amy in the room alone with them, but I had a funny feeling that Jackson would protect her.

I closed the door behind us and leaned against it. "What the hell is going on?" James exclaimed in a loud whisper.

I flinched. Not because he scared me, but because I would have to come up with a really good lie to cover this up. And no matter what happened between us, James was still someone I didn't want to lie to. "Well?" he prompted.

Come on, Kenz...think. "They're cops," I blurted, almost rolling my eyes at my own stupidity. Cops? Really? It was the best I could do ... geez.

"Cops? What did you do?" he asked with concern.

"Nothing, I just ... I was on patrol with Michaels last week, and was involved in a hostage situation. They're just keeping an eye on me because the guys are still at large."

"Oh my God, Kenz, are you okay?" He pulled me into a tight hug and I let him, sagging into his embrace.

It wasn't because he believed me, but because everything from the past couple days was now catching up to me. I needed some form of comfort, even if it was from the douchebag who cheated on me.

"I'm fine; I just want to get home so I can get away from all of this," I sighed into the crook of his neck. He kissed the top of my head and rubbed circles in the middle of my back. I missed this, the familiarity. But I needed to cut it out. No point in getting comfortable with something that wasn't real, no matter how much I wanted it to be.

I pulled away and he tucked my wild strands of hair behind my ear. "So why did those guys jump me on campus?" he asked.

That was going to be a little harder to cover up. I needed to deflect.

"I don't know, but I need a favor from you."

"Anything, Kenzie," he said, his voice so soft and warm that I wanted to curl up in it. But I knew it wasn't real, it was just something I was used to.

"Can you start packing up your stuff so we can head out soon?" No matter what happened, we were going home. Whether Sebastian wanted to allow me or not, I was going home and getting away from all the crazy here in the city.

"Of course." He gave me a soft kiss on the forehead.

I went back to the living room and quietly shut the bedroom door so James wouldn't hear or see what was going on, in case things got out of control, like they were now. I walked in to an unstable Jonah and a growling Sebastian. Their emotions were directed at me. What the hell did I do this time?

Amy stood behind Jackson, pretending to help him keep control of the two wolves, but all she was doing was talking shit.

"Keep the pissing contest to a minimum, you jerk offs," she said as I cleared my throat behind her. She turned and greeted me with a megawatt smile. She was having too much fun.

"Everything okay?"

"Oh yeah, you know, the usual," she said and winked.

I went to stand beside Jackson and he exhaled a sigh of relief when he saw me. "What took you so long? I don't know what you did to get their panties in a twist, but I can't control an Alpha if he loses it too," he said, and there was real worry in his expression.

"Sorry," I mumbled and snapped my fingers in front of Sebastian's face. "Dude, get over yourself. I'm going home, and there's nothing either of you can do about it. I don't talk to my parents much, and I only see them during summer and winter breaks." That stole their attention.

"Fine. I'm coming with you," Sebastian commanded.

"Bash, you can't," Jackson interjected. "You have to attend the Summit in two days, and you haven't prepared." Sebastian growled at him and I started to get a little worried. How pissed could this Alpha be?

"I'll go," Jonah volunteered, and we all looked at him.

"You think you can control yourself?" Jackson questioned, but Jonah only nodded. "She's going to be there with her *boyfriend*,

Jonah. Be truthful with yourself. We can't afford any slip-ups, with the Council coming in a few days."

"The Council?" I asked, ignoring the rest of his statement.

"Wolves have two main councils, the European and the American," Jackson explained. "When a Summit is called, that means something serious is going down and all the Alphas meet. Luckily, this is just an American Summit, but we still need to be careful."

I nodded and watched Jonah, who was carefully watching me. Sebastian's growl broke our stare off and he snarled, "Fine. Jonah, you'll go with them, but do not interact. Watch from a distance and report directly to me—constantly."

I rolled my eyes. This was awfully dramatic for something that wasn't even a big deal. "I still don't get why I need to be watched like a hawk. I think I at least deserve to know what's going on." Something was off with this whole scenario. Maybe they were trying to recruit me for their Pack, but they shouldn't be acting as if I were in the Witness Protection Plan, either. Something was going on, and if my gut was any use, it had something to do with this Summit.

"We aren't the only monsters that lurk in the night, Mackenzie. If we...accidentally exposed you, then you're not safe to wander around on your own," Jonah said, which was the most he'd said since they arrived.

"Exposed me? What, did you guys put out a memo about me?" I laughed, but I was the only one.

"We didn't recover you in the most discreet of ways," Sebastian admitted, and he seemed ashamed.

You're damn right you didn't, I thought as I watched the three of them divert their eyes. I was surprised no one noticed the scene outside of Pete's on Friday night. I was lucky to still have a job after that whole fiasco. Amy had told Big John I got sick and would be out until after winter break.

"So what? Are other wolves looking for me?" I asked, wondering for the first time what other Packs might be established in New York City.

"No, but lone wolves are fair game to vampires and other creatures of the night."

I choked on saliva as I stared at the three of them, hoping they were joking.

"Vampires? Really?" I scoffed, unconvinced. This couldn't be real. Well, I was a werewolf, so it made sense, but nope, still didn't believe it.

"This isn't a joke, Mackenzie. If you value your life, you'll take this seriously," Jonah said.

Amy came to me then and nearly squealed in my ear. "Oh my gosh, Kenz, this is like Twilight!"

Jesus, effin Christ. God, I hope she doesn't make me watch that movie again.

"Take it down a notch, would ya?" I murmured to Amy, trying to look relaxed, something I was far from being. It was easy to joke about this stuff when you were oblivious to the truths. I'd always speculated about the existence of other creatures, but never thought it was possible (which was outrageous, considering what I am). But when you're ignorant, it's easy to pretend. Now, not so much.

"Sorry," she mouthed to me and I nodded. I knew she didn't mean to get excited—if I was her, I would be too—but unfortunately it wasn't her, it was me.

Maybe Jane Hancock wasn't as crazy as I thought.

9

_____

We packed up James' Prius with the few things we had taken from our flat. Jonah would follow us there in a beat-up 4Runner that he'd come in, while Sebastian and Jackson went back to Brooklyn by train. The ride up was mostly quiet, with no one wanting to ask questions or bring up the three brutes who had paid us a visit. Mainly because James was around and there was no way I was telling him anything, which made the trip packed with sniffles, sighs, and shifting in our seats. *Awkward.*

The drive upstate to Cold Springs, New York was only about an hour and a half from the city, and that was with light traffic. It made it the perfect opportunity to bring up my new acting role to Amy. I still hadn't told her that I was playing James' girlfriend for the next two weeks.

"So, Amy, how are you feeling?" I asked as I turned around to face her. She was sitting in the backseat behind James.

"Uh...fine, why?" She arched an eyebrow at me.

"Oh, no reason, just wondering—"

"Mackenzie Grey, please don't beat around the bush, you suck at it," she cut me off.

I sighed. "Okay, fine. If anyone asks, James and I are still together, got it?" I said, skipping the B.S. routine. I should know better than to sugarcoat things with Amy, or with anyone, for that matter.

"What?" *Or maybe I should have.* "Are you crazy? That piece of scum!"

"Hey! I'm right here, you know," James interjected, but she ignored him.

"That bastard cheated on you with blow-up Barbie, and *now* you're going to do him a solid so he doesn't have to tell Nana?" she exclaimed.

Obviously, there was no need to go into details with her. She figured it out. This would be Amy's fourth Christmas with us, and she'd already met the Carsons. James was the only boy in a family overflowing with women, and they watched over him like a hawk. If he and I hadn't been best friends since we were five, I didn't think they would have accepted me. James rarely had any girlfriends in high school, but when he did, they never lasted long. If the sisters didn't make them cry and run for the hills —Nana did.

"I didn't cheat! And Diana isn't a blow—okay, but I didn't cheat, I swear!"

"Oh, shut it, Carson, your opinion doesn't count for diddly squat. You can sing that tune 'til cows fly and it still won't ring true," Amy snapped as she glared at the back of his head. "But *you*," she pointed to me, "need to call this off. I knew something wasn't right with us carpooling with this fool. It would have been easier if we'd just taken the train."

"Amy, it's only for two weeks, don't worry. It'll be over before you know it, and James promised no funny business, right?" I looked at James, who was staring out at the road ahead.

He shifted uncomfortably. "Well, we have to sell this performance, so some hand-holding and cuddling may be required. Maybe even a kiss or two," he replied sheepishly.

My nostrils flared. "You've got to be fucking kidding me," I said through my teeth. He better be joking, because I was about to lose it. That was *not* part of the deal, and there was no way I would have agreed to it if it were. "You might as well tell them the truth when we arrive, because I never agreed to that."

"You might not have agreed, but you should have known we would have to, Kenz. My family has seen us together, even before we dated. They know how close we were."

He wasn't lying there. James and I had always shared a special friendship. Even before things got romantic, we were inseparable, always holding hands, having sleepovers—in a platonic way, of course. But things changed, and I didn't think I could handle acting that way again. Not after being in a relationship with him.

"No kissing, James. I will agree to hand-holding and *very* little cuddling," I relented, and then retreated into myself for the remainder of the trip while Amy and James bickered.

I wish I'd ridden with Jonah.

As soon as I saw the sign that said 'Welcome to Cold Springs', I smiled at the wave of relief that crashed into me. Twenty-four hours earlier, I wasn't too sure I'd actually make it home. I'd never been very close with my parents. Nothing was wrong with them; I loved them unconditionally, and sometimes missed them more than I normally would. There was just a little disconnect between us, I guess. We talked the bare minimum and saw each other only for summer and winter breaks. I called once a week to check in, though the conversations never lasted more than fifteen minutes. Unlike my brother Ollie, with whom I could talk for hours.

"Home sweet home," I mumbled under my breath and sagged into my seat.

Within five minutes, James was pulling into the tiny driveway and my mom waved at us from the kitchen window.

"Shhh!" I said to Amy and James, who were still at each other's throats. I didn't want to look suspicious.

My parents emerged from the front door of our small brick house. My dad wore his usual long sleeve fishing shirt and jeans, and my mom sported a pair of ratty jeans and a red sweater.

"Honey!" she said, engulfing me in a hug that always felt forced.

Okay, maybe I was over-exaggerating. I never was a touchy-feely kind of person, much less a hugger.

"Hey Ma." My dad came around and patted my back. I guess I got it from him; he wasn't big on hugs, either. "Dad." I nodded at him.

"How was the ride up?"

"Not bad, the traffic was surprisingly light," James said as he shook hands with my father and hugged my mom, lifting her off her feet. I caught Amy rolling her eyes, so I nudged her.

"Well, that's good. And why is Amy so quiet back there?" My dad looked around James for her and she came up to greet my parents as well. Amy may look different in her appearance, but my folks didn't care. If anything, they loved her like she was one of their own.

Once the greetings were done, James kissed my cheek. "Well, I'll see you guys later. I better go say hi to my folks," he said, waving as he walked next door to his house.

The moment we stepped inside the house, it felt so warm and homey. It was nothing fancy and it kind of smelled like old people, but I loved it. It was home.

"I have you both set up in your old room, Kenzie," my mom said.

"What about Ollie's room?" I asked, right about the time someone grabbed me from behind and lifted me off the ground.

My brother twirled me around and I squealed with excitement. Just then, my acute hearing kicked in and I heard heavy thuds running up the driveway.

"Amy, tell my brother to put me down!" I yelled so Jonah could hear me. We'd left the front door open, so I was sure he was watching and thought I was in danger. He didn't come in—I guess he got the message.

Ollie put me down and I turned around quickly, almost knocking him down with the barrel of a hug I gave him. Okay, maybe I was a hugger with *certain* people. If I saw very little of my parents, I saw even less of my brother. It was always a treat when we got to hang out.

"How many times have I asked you not to call me Ollie anymore?" he grinned at me.

"Oh, please, that'll never happen. Oliver is an old man's name; it doesn't suit you." I lightly punched him in the arm. I couldn't actually punch him, or with my super strength he'd fly out to the front lawn, which was saying something because my brother was in the Army. Standing at six feet-five inches tall, he was all muscle and bulk. He stood before me in his ACU uniform, which told me he must have just beaten us home.

"Why didn't you tell me you were coming?" I asked. We'd just spoken last week, and he didn't mention anything.

"I wanted to surprise you, Sis." He ruffled my hair and I tried to duck away. "Oh, snap, I didn't even see you, Red," he teased and picked Amy up in a swallowing hug.

For the next couple hours until dinner was ready, Ollie, Amy, and I hung out in my room and caught up on life, joking and plain-out bull-shitting the time away. It'd been at least a year since I'd seen him. Ollie was two years older than me, so we always got along and had the same circle of friends.

"Are you and Carson still together?" he asked me, and Amy snorted.

"Way to be discreet." I glared and then turned to my brother. "It's complicated." I tried to avoid his eyes, because my brother was protective of me. It didn't seem like it to an outsider looking in because we joked a lot, but unless you wanted to be handled by Ollie, it was better if you did right by me.

"Did he do something to you, Kenz?"

I saw the dark glare he shot at me, scaring me into telling the truth.

"Ollie, relax." I rolled my eyes. "Can we talk about this another time?"

"No, we will talk about it now. Amy, what did he do?" He was on his feet in a flash.

Shit.

"He cheated, and now has her pretending they're still together for Nana."

That little snitch.

"That piece of shit loser!" he exploded. "He thinks just because he's living in the city he can get all the ass he wants?" Oliver said as he ran downstairs.

We hustled out of my room behind him and caught up with him on the sidewalk just as he was heading for the Carson household. I snatched the sleeve of the sweater he had changed into, and with a burst of my wolf strength, pulled him to a stop, standing between him and his destination.

"Ollie, stop! You can't do this. I'm old enough to handle myself. Please, I'm okay," I protested, but I saw the fury in his eyes. After all, I was his baby sister. If a girl broke his heart, I'd want to kick her ass, too.

Jonah was parked in his 4Runner across the street and I heard his car door open and slam shut. *This can't be good.*

My insides floated into a mob of butterflies as he walked toward us, strutting across the road in his brown leather jacket, jeans, and boots. His eyes shone golden, and I didn't know if he heard what we'd been talking about. I hoped not, because I told him James and I were dating and kind of wanted to keep it that way. You know, avoid temptation and all.

"What's going on?" Jonah said as he stepped beside me, staring my brother down. Ollie wasn't the Alpha male type, but he wasn't a punk, either. This could end badly.

Oliver sized him up and scoffed, "None of your business." *Damn, wrong answer.*

"When it comes to Mackenzie, it becomes my business," Jonah countered evenly, his words unfurling like silk.

It made me want to lean into him. Sweet baby Jesus, something was seriously wrong with my hormones.

My brother looked at him more closely, trying to place who he was. "Who the hell are you, and how do you know my sister?"

"I'm a friend from school. What's going on here?"

"A friend from school? All the way out in Cold Springs? I don't think so. Mackenzie?"

Ollie swiveled his head to me and I was stuck. Like a deer caught in headlights, I stood there dumbfounded.

"He's a friend I invited," Amy saved the day. "He didn't have anyone to spend the holidays with, so I told him to tag along."

After marinating on her answer, Ollie stuck his hand out to Jonah. "Oliver Grey."

"Jonah Cadwell." They shook hands, and I felt like I could breathe once more. Jonah was about to ask what was going on again, when I gave my brother 'the look.' He knew what it meant —keep your mouth shut.

"My bad. My lovely sister knows how much I hate her ... *boyfriend*," he said through a tight smile. "I was hoping she'd kicked his ass to the curb by now."

It wasn't far from the truth. Ollie had never cared for James. Said he seemed too flakey, and unfortunately, he was right.

Jonah smirked. "Ah, I see. Yeah, I'm not too fond of him, either. Were you on your way to his house? I wouldn't mind accompanying you."

I wanted to punch him in the throat. He wasn't supposed to rile my brother up even more than he already was!

Ollie thought about it for a moment but then shook his head. "I like you. Where are you staying during the break?" *Oh, no.*

"A little bed & breakfast on Main Street."

"Cancel the reservations. We have a futon down in the basement. You're staying with us," he declared.

With those words, my whole world collapsed. Yeah, I know, dramatic, but Jonah wasn't even supposed to be here to begin with!

"Thank you, that sounds great." Jonah turned on his megawatt smile.

I couldn't wait to corner him when we were alone. He would rue the day he was ever born ... or I'd at least get a good kick to his balls and run.

"I told Gary I'd meet him at Angelina's Pizza before dinner, but don't think this conversation is over," my brother said as he narrowed his eyes at me. I nodded and he started to walk down the street.

I knew he wasn't meeting Gary, his best friend from high school. My mom already told me he couldn't make it for the holidays this year. But my brother needed to blow off steam, so I decided not to argue and just give him the space he needed. I hadn't even been here a day and drama had already begun. *Great, the shit-storm followed me from the city.*

The three of us stood there awkwardly—or at least Amy and I did. Jonah looked like a damn fashion model. The bastard.

"I need to head over to the B&B and get my things. Come with me?" Jonah asked with a heated gaze.

I wasn't ready for that. His eyes devoured me as if they were seeing me in a new light. Or he thought that since my brother didn't approve, James was now inconsequential.

"Yeah, why don't you go with wolfey, and I'll catch up with Ollie," Amy the traitor said. My eyes widened. I willed her to stop walking, but she only winked and turned her back to me.

When she was a distance away, Jonah quirked an eyebrow. "Wolfey?"

"Don't ask," I grumbled and walked over to his car. *Might as well get this crap over with.*

He chuckled. "Fine. I like your brother, by the way. We seem to ... oh, how should I say this ... we seem to have a lot in common." He smiled.

Once we were settled in the SUV, I turned and faced him. "Let's clear the air right now, because I'm not good with insinuations. What's your deal with me?" Amy was right; I hated beating around the bush. I preferred getting straight to the point, not because of my personality, but because I was oblivious to social cues. Someone could be mad at me and I wouldn't know, no matter how many hints they dropped. I normally didn't pay attention, but with Jonah—even Sebastian—I felt like I was out of the loop. I didn't like guessing or playing Nancy Drew.

He watched me, but instead of saying what was on his mind, he turned the key in the ignition and pulled away from the curb. If he thought I was going to drop it, he didn't know how annoying I could be.

"Hello? I asked you a question," I snipped as he turned into town, away from my neighborhood.

"Not now, Mackenzie."

Challenge accepted. I spent the next fifteen minutes of the ride to Kittleman House where he was staying repeating, "How about now?" I could see the vein in his neck pop every time my voice rang. I channeled my inner Diana Stone, and by the look of Jonah's tight face, she had the same effect on him as she did on me. He was annoyed.

Not for the first time, I wondered, *How does James handle it?*

We parked and I followed Jonah inside the bed & breakfast—

still asking the same question—until we went upstairs to his room and he shut the door.

With great force, he gripped my shoulders and slammed me against the wall. If I'd been human, I would have been injured, but it didn't faze me. Before I could stop him, his mouth was on mine, forcing me to open up for him. I slunk against the wall and he held me around the waist. He was forceful but gentle at the same time. His hands slid down to my thighs and behind them, picking me up—wrapping my legs around him—and walked backward toward the bed and laid me down. With one hand supporting me, he ran the other through my hair and pulled as he tugged on my lower lip, making me gasp. He nipped across my chin and down to my neck, and my back arched from the sensation.

I was stuck in a daze as my insides swirled with an unfamiliar feeling that kept me from stopping this much sooner than I should have. I gripped Jonah's hair and pulled him away. His brown eyes flashed gold as he stared down at me with a hunger that James never showed in our years together. With my eyes wide, I tried to catch my breath. This was wrong on so many levels.

"That's *my deal*, Mackenzie. I want you," he purred with an inkling of possession in his tone.

My body vibrated beneath him at his response, but it wasn't from fear, it was excitement. My eyebrows furrowed at his revelation. I'd never been so bold in my life. This couldn't be right. I didn't want this.

But I did. And he could see it.

His mouth came down on mine once more and a growl rippled through his chest. I gasped for breath as I tightened my legs around his waist and rolled him onto his back. I grinded against him and his moans electrified my senses. My hands roamed through his hair and I wanted more. Our kisses intensified, our breathing became heavier, and our hands craved skin. I wanted him so much my insides ached, and no kiss or touch was enough to feed my desire.

My eyes suddenly opened and I sat up, still straddling him. Out of breath, I gazed into his golden eyes. Without seeing mine, I knew my eyes had shifted colors as well. I could feel her.

"Jonah ... " I whispered. "Something's wrong." I rolled my hips and tilted my head back.

He gripped my waist and pushed me down harder so I could feel all of him. "No, babe. Nothing's wrong. It's your Wolf. She wants me, too."

I shook my head, trying to clear out the fog. This shouldn't be happening. I pushed off him and crawled off the mattress like it had bed bugs. Feeling disoriented, I stumbled to the nearest corner. I shook my head, looking down at my stomach as if the wolf was there. I could feel her trying to claw her way out of me. She'd never done this before, and it scared me.

She couldn't have this much control over me, could she? *No, no she can't.* She was nonexistent, aside from the three days of the full moon. And now ... now she was making me into someone I wasn't. I wasn't the kind of girl to, I don't know, do these kinds of things. I'm a prude.

"God ... this can't be happening to me," I prayed to someone and no one at all.

Jonah cautiously walked toward me with his hands held up and stood a good distance away. "I'm sorry. I shouldn't have been so aggressive and taken advantage of you that way," he said, and I quirked an eyebrow.

Okay, he was pushing it now. I scoffed, "You didn't take advantage of me."

He shook his head. "Yes I did. You didn't know it, but I did." He covered his mouth and looked as if he were thinking about what to say next. His lean frame sagged. "Even though it's been almost four years, you're still a pup. You weren't raised by a Pack or even another wolf, so you don't understand the relationship you have—or should have—with the wolf. I knew that, and I still pursued you. It was wrong."

He looked ashamed, and while I understood what he was saying—and yeah, if it was true, then I should be punching him in the face—I didn't want to.

"Jonah," I started, "we can't—"

"I know. *James*," he said, and walked to the other side of the room where his untouched duffle bag was.

I didn't bother correcting him. James wasn't the reason we couldn't be together, but it would do for now. The real reason—and I knew it was stupid—was that I couldn't be intimate with anyone right now, not so soon after James. I might not have showed it much, and I possibly didn't love him the way I should have, but James was still very special to me and was the only guy I'd ever been with. The only one who'd ever seen me naked, for God's sake. I wasn't ready to be like that with anyone else, no matter how much my wolf wanted it.

10

As soon as I bid everyone goodnight and my head hit the pillow, I was out like I'd drunk a bottle of Nyquil. I think a blizzard could have come through and I wouldn't have twitched a muscle.

When I finally woke, I peeked over at the alarm clock on my nightstand and saw it was just after ten in the morning. Amy and I were sharing my bed, and I could tell she was still passed out. She wasn't a morning person, so it was better if I let her sleep. I quietly slipped out of bed, padded across my room, and headed for the bathroom.

After quickly brushing my teeth and washing my face, I ran a comb through my hair and went downstairs. It was the day before Christmas and my parents were already out of the house. They were probably down on Main Street helping with decorations. I meandered past Ollie's open bedroom door and peered inside, but his empty bed told me he had left as well. I just hoped he didn't run into James—or anyone in the Carson family, for that matter. Oliver wasn't shy with his feelings, and he didn't care who he told off.

I went down to the TV room where I found Jonah channel surfing. He was the last person I wanted to deal with after yesterday, especially considering how awkward we were around each other afterwards. I'd be lying if I said I wasn't attracted to him. I'd be blind if I wasn't. Everything about him was warm and fuzzy; I wanted to curl up with him. Don't even get me started about his smiles ... every time that one dimple popped out, I just wanted to lick it. Oh, God ... what the hell was wrong with me?

"Morning," I said as I sat on the other empty lounger across from him.

"Hey," he said, not looking away from the TV.

Okay. Maybe he's not my number one fan.

"How'd you sleep?" The futon in the basement was as old as Moses. I was surprised we still had it.

"Just fine."

"Are you mad at me?" If he was pissed at me, I needed him to tell me outright.

"Nope."

Ugh!

"Jonah, stop being short with me. If you're ticked off, just tell me. You're not going to hurt my feelings, I just don't want to play cat and mouse with you."

"I didn't say I was upset, Mackenzie," he said as he continued to flick through the channels.

"You know what? Whatever, I don't care. Better yet, I'll call Sebastian and tell him to send someone else so you can head back to the city. It's obvious this isn't going to work." I got up and started to head for the stairs to get my phone.

"I'm leaving soon anyway, so there's no need," he said before I left the room.

Huh?

"You're leaving?" I asked, stunned.

"Yeah. Bash sent a team out here yesterday and we'll be alternating. I'll be out of your hair in no time."

What is his problem?

ONCE I WAS SHOWERED and dressed—Amy was still sleeping—I headed out to start my girlfriend duties. The first thing I had to do was go over and greet the Carsons. I knew I was already going to get an earful for not stopping by yesterday, but I wasn't up for it. I was still pissed at Jonah for acting ... well, for acting like his damn brother. He was being a total douchebag. Gosh, I would've understood if I'd told him the *real* reason I didn't want to get involved, but I have a pretend boyfriend! That's a legit excuse!

Oh my gosh, and I fake-cheated on him. *Shit.*

I knocked on James' front door and then let myself in. It was cold as heck outside, but fortunately, people around Cold Springs didn't usually lock their doors. I wasn't waiting. Even with a coat I shivered in my boots, and I had a higher body temperature than most.

"Hello?" I called out and walked to the kitchen where James' mom, Cindy, was with Nana.

"Oh dear, it's about time you came by to visit. What took so long?" Nana said from the dining table, her voice reminiscent of a pack-a-day smoker.

"Hey, Nana, I'm sorry. I wasn't feeling well yesterday, so I didn't want to come over and be a Debbie downer," I yelled so she could hear me. She hated wearing her hearing aid. I went over to Ms. Cindy and kissed her on the cheek. Between the two of them, they raised all five of Ms. Cindy's kids. Her husband died of cancer when James, the youngest, was only ten years old.

"Rubbish! You still should have come by to see this old woman," Nana grumped as I went to sit next to her.

"Is James still in bed?"

"He just woke up; I think he's in the shower," Cindy offered and continued to wash the dishes.

"So, when's the wedding?" Nana asked.

In response, I choked on my own saliva. Cindy brought me a glass of water and gave me a look that said, *Be patient with her.* There was only so much patience I had with her son. If he didn't tell them the truth soon, Nana would have a heart attack from the news.

Oh no, I shouldn't have thrown that out into the universe. Crap, I take it back!

"Nana, they're too young," Ms. Cindy said. I nodded emphatically in agreement.

"Young?" she scoffed. "I was seventeen when I married your father. Now *that's* young."

"And that was during WWII. We're in different times, Nana."

While they continued to bicker about how young James and I were, I zoned out. I didn't want to be a part of this conversation. I felt like a fraud. James needed to hurry up and save me from this drama he created. Last year, I would have been all for this. Maybe not the marriage part (I had too much I wanted to accomplish before I even thought of that), but it wouldn't have been an outrageous thought like it was now.

After what felt like an eternity, James came down to the kitchen in a turtleneck sweater that made me want to roll my eyes. He was such a loser.

James came straight for me and planted a wet one on my lips. I tensed and didn't even close my eyes. *The asshole. I told him no kissing!*

"Morning," I grumbled, trying not to sound pissed. Which was a little hard, because I was never good at faking the funk.

"What do you two lovebirds have planned for today?" Cindy asked. It was Christmas Eve, so almost everyone was down on Main Street prepping for the big festival tomorrow. I figured we'd go lend a helping hand, but it seemed James had other ideas.

"I called for a table at Angelina's for brunch. I thought Kenzie and I could have some alone time," he said, squeezing me into him.

I wanted to barf. He was laying it on thick, and if he didn't watch it, he was going to get my boot up his ass. I gave them a tight smile, but I caught Ms. Cindy watching me warily. She was already getting suspicious, and I feared she had a couple theories floating around. She wasn't stupid.

"Well, have fun. Will we be seeing you for dinner, dear?" his mom asked, and I nodded. It was tradition that I spent Christmas Eve with his folks, and he spent Christmas day with mine.

"Alright, well, you two run along, then," she said, still eyeing us carefully. "And if you see your sisters in town, remind them to be home on time to help set up!" We nodded dutifully.

Once we were out of the house and at least a block away, I used a little more force than necessary and pushed James off me. The sleaze ball. He'd been holding my hand since we left, and I suddenly felt the need for a lifetime supply of hand sanitizer.

He wasn't lying when he said he'd called ahead for a reservation. I'd assumed it was just a cover he told his mom and that we'd part ways once we got to Main Street, but sure enough, we were greeted by one of the waitresses and led to a table in the back of the restaurant.

Angelina's Restaurant and Pizzeria wasn't a super fancy place, but in my opinion, it was the best restaurant in town. And James knew it. I could eat here all day every day, and now that I didn't gain weight like I used to, the idea didn't sound so farfetched.

After ordering my meal—which could possibly feed a third world country—James cleared his throat and leaned forward. I knew that look on his face. His eyes darted, his brows furrowed, and he was biting his damn lower lip like it was a Big Mac. This was his 'I want to talk about something serious' face. I didn't know if I would like what he was about to say.

"Spit it out, Jameson. Your lip is going to be raw if you don't," I said, and he stopped mid-bite.

"Sorry," he mumbled. "I wanted to thank you for going along with this. I know it's not easy, and you probably have much better things to do." The waitress came by with a pot of coffee and poured us each a cup.

Once she left, I looked at James, who was stirring the sugar in his coffee like he was churning butter. "Dude, relax. What's going on?"

"Kenz, I miss you," he blurted out. His eyes enlarged as I sat still, holding my breath.

What did he just say?

"I know, I know; it sounds stupid and I don't deserve you, but I needed to try." He reached across the table and grabbed my hand. "Ending things with you was the biggest mistake I've ever made, and I know I'll live to regret it. I miss your smile, your laughter. The way you're so passionate about your beliefs and convictions. How strong and independent you are. Kenz, what I'm trying to say is, I love you. I always have and always will. So what do you say? Give me another chance?"

I studied him as his eyes met mine straight on. He didn't twitch or show any signs that he was lying. But ... why was his heart racing?

"James, I don't know," I muttered, because I wasn't sure how to react. I was hurt—back then and still now—about him leaving me and dating Diana, but I wasn't sure I believed what he was telling me. This was so out of the blue, and my gut was never wrong. I wanted to believe him because James was the only guy I'd ever been with. I was comfortable with him. Could we really pick up where we left off? But what was up with his pulse? There was something he wasn't telling me. Something he was withholding.

"Don't overthink it, Kenz. We're perfect together. I know everything about you, and you know everything about me. We click, and I was stupid for not realizing it sooner. I was scared, which is why I pushed you away. What we have is real, and I don't want to lose it."

His words sounded too good to be true, but he was still holding back. Something was off. No one's heart should race like horses on a track—not if they were telling the truth ... the whole truth.

"What about Diana?" I asked, and that was when I saw it— the twitch of his upper lip.

"What about her?"

"Are you still together?"

He shifted uncomfortably in his seat and adjusted the beanie on his head, covering his ears. "I plan on breaking up with her. I just felt bad doing it during the holidays," he said, his heart thumping faster. "I will as soon as we get back to the city and before the semester begins." He wet his lips nervously and I quirked an eyebrow.

No he won't.

The waitress brought our meals. I channeled all my focus on my food and avoided conversation, as well as his eyes. I was angry. Not angry enough that my wolf stirred, but rather an anger fueled by disappointment. I was hurt that he thought he could lie to me, and that he was trying to have his cake and eat it, too. I could be wrong, but it seemed like he only wanted me for winter break. Once we returned to the city, he'd change his mind and kick me to the curb again. I let it happen once, but I refused to let it happen again—no matter how comfortable I felt with him. I'd rather be alone for the rest of my life than settle with him, or with anyone who only wanted me out of convenience. I didn't want someone like that in my life for the long haul.

We finished our meal in relative silence and James paid the bill. The walk home was quieter than it was during brunch, but I preferred it. I needed to be left alone with my thoughts. I needed to figure out what I was going to say and how to keep my cool. No matter how calm I might be in the beginning, the wolf's anger always seemed to make an appearance. This was a delicate situation that I didn't want to ruin with my temper. I couldn't afford to be reckless.

James reached for my hand and I let him. We walked home hand-in-hand, and I tried to marinate in the feel of us touching each other for the last time—because this would be it. I refused to let this little charade go on any longer.

We were almost to my house when he gripped my hand and pulled me into him. With his free hand tangled in my hair, he smashed his mouth on mine. My arms were trapped against our chests and I tried to push him away without using any extra strength, but James wasn't getting the picture. I pursed my lips in a thin line, but he was still trying to force me into a kiss. With no other option and with a little extra force than strictly needed, I backed away from him.

"What the hell, man?" I yelled, wiping my mouth with the back of my hand. I had to remember to take my voice down a notch. Jonah said he'd be leaving, but I wasn't sure he actually would. Unless I misread yesterday's situation (which was totally possible), I assumed he'd still be keeping an eye on me even if someone else was assigned. Then again, I could be thinking too highly of myself.

"Geez, Kenz, what?" James said as he rubbed a sore spot on his chest where I'd pushed him.

"What? I said no kissing, asshole!" My temper flared and the speech I was prepared to make was thrown out the window. "Don't *ever* push yourself on me like that again, Jameson Theodore Carson. I swear I'll blow this whole plan of yours to Mars if you fuck with me," I growled, forcing myself to take deep breaths. My wolf was riled up, and sometimes when that happened, my canines or claws liked to make an appearance. Since it was still daylight, it didn't seem like the wisest of choices.

"Kenz, I thought we were on the same page! Don't you still love me? Even if you don't, we still have to act like everything is normal. If we don't display some affection, my family will figure it out."

"Good! They *need* to figure it out, because this morning, Nana asked me when the wedding was. I wanted to tell her *not in this lifetime*. You're nothing but scum, James! You don't love me; you just want a cheap fuck, and you think I'm desperate enough to give it to you. Well, you're *wrong*. Stop being such a little bitch and just tell them about Diana. You were never planning on breaking it off with her anyway!" I screamed.

His face turned an even deeper shade of beet red. "*This* is why!" he yelled, and I flinched. "*This* is why I cheated on your ass! Because you're too damn aggressive, and you can't hold a damn conversation with me without degrading me as a man! Always trying to tell me what to do and how to act!"

My nostrils flared as he got down in my face. This wasn't good.

"James," I gritted through my teeth, "you need to back the hell away from me."

"Or what, Mackenzie? You're gonna hit me? Go ahead, do your best!" he threatened, moving in so close, we were practically touching.

"James," I growled cautiously. I could feel the wolf bubbling to the top, and Amy wasn't around to calm me down.

"I fucked Diana because of you. I'd been doing it for months," he sneered.

That was the last straw.

With my head bent, he probably thought I just didn't want to look at him because I was ashamed, but the truth was my canines were out. I winced from the slight pain as they ripped through my gums. My body shook as I tried to grip the last bit of control, but it was no use. I backhanded him and he went flying about ten feet away from me. I growled louder this time as I hunched over on all fours on the sidewalk. I hadn't gone completely wolf—I was in that mid-stage that Sebastian flashed the night at Pete's bar. I felt the painful ripple of my bones adjusting, but the anger in me overflowed and eased the ache.

My eyesight focused and zoned in on James' limp body. He wasn't moving. I should have been concerned and rushed to help him—but I didn't. I wanted to rush over and finish him off. The lure of biting into his skin and tearing him to pieces made my mouth salivate.

A sudden snarl came from beside me and Jonah stood over me in human form. "Heel!" he barked, and my body froze in response. The wolf in me didn't think twice about defying him. "Shift!" he roared, and the wave of the Change washed over me.

My bones paused for a moment and then started to rearrange back to normal. With my adrenaline coming down from its high, I felt all the hurt and pain from the hurled truths and tears of agony—both physical and emotional—swept through me. Once it was over, I laid on the sidewalk in the fetal position, shivering in a cold sweat. My clothing had been stretched out and my jeans were ripped in certain parts. I was too tired and hurt to care or try to cover up. Jonah leaned over me, picked me off the ground, and carried me into my house. I let my head fall on his broad shoulder and closed my eyes. The fear of what I could have done took over and the guilt followed in droves.

When I first learned I was a werewolf, I was terrified of being a danger to the people around me. I considered myself a monster, but once I learned my wolf's routine and her triggers, I accepted what I'd become and learned to live my life around those restrictions. Yes, I became more aggressive and more of a loner than I usually was, but it was okay. I didn't feel bad for myself, as long as everyone I cared about was safe. But now? That monster depression I'd had many years ago flooded back and I didn't think I could survive it again. It was a dark time I'd rather not revisit.

"Shhh," Jonah cooed in my ear, and I realized I was whining like a dog.

He headed down to the basement and locked the door behind us. I hadn't spent any time down there in years. Now, it was nothing more than a storage area for us, but when we were younger it was our playroom. A futon was situated in the middle of the room with a comforter neatly folded on top of a stack of pillows. Jonah placed me on the mattress gently and started to undress me. I shook my head violently; I didn't want him to see me naked. I knew it was the last thing I should have been worrying about.

"It's okay. Don't worry, babe, I won't," he said softly, grabbing the comforter and draping it over my quivering body, and then brushing my damp hair back from my face.

I wished I could give in to him, just one time, but this—being intimate with someone else—was something I was deathly afraid of.

"James," I croaked, and Jonah's soft features darkened. His face scrunched up in disgust.

"What about that asshole?" he said tightly.

"Is he okay?" Jonah might not care, but I was the one who hit him, and the last I saw, he was lying limp on the concrete. What if I seriously injured him? I couldn't live with myself if I hurt him. I was mad at him for being a douche and cheating on me with Diana, but I'd rather wish him herpes than death.

Jonah eyed me, weighing his options, but finally realized I was more worried about his physical wounds. "I'll be back."

He was gone for about ten minutes before he returned. At least I thought it had only been ten minutes; I was dozing off when I heard the basement door open and close again.

"Hey." Jonah smiled at me as he sat on the edge of the futon and caressed my cheek.

"Is he ... ?" I couldn't finish, but he knew what I was worried about.

He shook his head. "The prick is fine. Just had a little concussion. I sneaked him into his house and dropped him in his room to sleep it off."

My eyes widened. "Jonah!" I squeaked. "If he has a concussion, he's not supposed to sleep!" I tried to convince him how important it was, but I didn't have the energy.

He chuckled. "Mackenzie, he'll be fine, don't worry. You need to rest."

I didn't know why I felt reassured by that. I shouldn't have, but if he said James would be fine, I believed him. "Jonah, what's wrong with me?"

I needed to know, because nothing like this had ever happened to me. I've been angry before and was still able to control myself, but this ... this was unbridled rage. I didn't even want to get started on what happened between us at the bed and breakfast.

"It's complicated," he said and looked away. "Let me ask you a question first ... When the full moon comes around, where do you go to shift?" He turned back to look at me, all business.

"Uh ... I have a cage," I admitted hoarsely.

He snarled, baring his canines at me in a manner that was not at all friendly. I flinched and scooted away from him. "Sorry," he said. I was still hesitant. "Do you ever run?"

I sat up slowly and leaned on my elbow. *Run?* "Yeah, when I go to the gym, sometimes I go on the treadmill," I answered, confused.

He shook his head. "No, I mean does your wolf ever run?"

Oh. I shook my head, and the look he gave me shattered me to a thousand pieces. I couldn't see his dimple anymore, and the color drained from his face. That wasn't the worst of it. The look of disappointment and pity undid me. Why did I even care?

"That isn't safe, Mackenzie. How have you been controlling the wolf for so long?"

"I don't know," I said warily. "She only comes out for the three days of the full moon. Then she sort of disappears." I shrugged.

"She disappears?" he scoffed. "No, you need to let the wolf out and be free during those days. If not, she'll come out at times like this and you could put people in serious danger." He reached for his phone and pressed some buttons.

"How am I supposed to do that in the city? If I let her roam around, she'll *really* put people in danger then. If she wants to run, she can run in the cage. It's pretty big." I knew how stupid it sounded before I said it.

"The next full moon, you're shifting with me. And we're getting rid of that cage. Is that where you were headed when I ran into you?" he asked. I'd completely forgotten about our first encounter during the last full moon.

"Is that how you found me?" I asked as I replayed that night. "How come you weren't changing and in pain?" I'd barely made it home on time, yet he was casually strolling the streets like it was nothing.

"Because I don't cage my wolf," he answered patiently, but with a hint of frustration. "The Pack isn't Moon Bound like you are. We shift on full moons in celebration, not because of obligation. That's the difference."

He was ticked I caged my wolf. It made me wonder, did he like me, or the wolf?

My mind caught on an unfamiliar phrase. "Moon Bound?"

He sighed, and after typing something on his phone, he put it away. "It's when you don't shift at all. When a full moon comes around, it calls to your wolf and forces a change on you. That's why you feel so much pain when you shift," he said.

After I processed what he was saying, it made sense. But how the heck was I supposed to let the wolf out in the city?

"So ... during full moons, you guys don't go through the Change?" I wasn't sure if he was okay with answering my questions, but this was fascinating. This was stuff I didn't know about, but that I should.

"We do, but it's not because we have to. It's like one big party for those three days."

I could hear the pride in his voice. He liked being a werewolf. I envied that.

"Where? I can't imagine you guys having a rager at the warehouse."

He shook his head and smiled. "We have an estate out in Little Falls, New York with over a hundred acres of land. We all congregate there and have barbeques and bonfires; it's a lot of fun. You'll like it."

"Jonah," I started, "I'm not going. I don't want to be part of your Pack."

He didn't look at me, but his body froze. My statement hung

in the air like a heavy weight. It might not seem like it right now, but I could survive on my own. I didn't want to be a part of their community where being a werewolf became my life. When I thought of my future, I didn't picture cleaning up after a husband and popping out little werewolf babies left and right. I wasn't born to be a housewife. It wasn't in my nature and probably never would be.

"Mackenzie ... you can't live on Pack land without belonging to a Pack," he said, his brown eyes flickering gold. "They'll kill you before they let a lone wolf roam free."

"Who?"

"The Elders. I told you about the American and European summits, remember? Well, they are comprised of Elders who are sort of like a council who governs the wolves—worldwide. Sebastian will be obligated to tell them about you. It's why an American summit was called upon ... because of you."

I didn't know what to say to that. I wouldn't want to leave New York, but if I had to—to stay alive—I would. Did I really want a bunch of wolves dictating my life? It didn't seem fair. It wasn't like I had much of a choice in being who I am.

"Where can I go?" I asked, dazed.

"Kenz," he said uneasily. I realized it was the first time he hadn't said my full name. "There's nowhere on God's green Earth that isn't claimed in some way. You have no choice, unless you want to live on the run for the rest of your life."

I soaked in what he said, taking a moment to respond. There wasn't much I could say anyway; either I belonged or I didn't, and I tended to do what I wanted either way. But that wasn't something he needed to worry about right now. It seemed that Jonah had formed an attachment to me (I swear, I wasn't being conceited), and I didn't want to stress him out. I didn't know much about this Pack stuff, but I needed to do my research before I made any decisions.

"I thought you were leaving?" I asked, changing the subject.

He cleared his throat and looked away. "I was about to when I saw you outside. What was that about, anyway? Did you know he was cheating on you?"

I could have continued to lie to him, but that would make me look stupid and weak. How would a girl as headstrong as me accept someone who cheats? Yeah, it didn't sound believable.

"We're not together," I replied, and he watched me intently. "We broke up a couple months ago because of it, but he hasn't told his family."

His eyes flickered gold and then changed back to a calming brown. I didn't know what these eye color changes were about, but they were weird.

"So, you're pretending, because … ?"

"Because he's dating a porn star and he's scared to tell Nana," I said, and his eyes widened. "Okay, she's not really a porn star, but she looks like one."

He chuckled. "Got it," he said. "You're too nice to him. He doesn't deserve your help."

"I know. At least, I know that now."

After the Change, I became difficult, not the happy-go-lucky girl I was before. Not that I was always cheerful either, but I wasn't as hot headed. To learn that James had been screwing her for months before we broke up was hurtful. I didn't think I was that bad … was I? How did I not notice?

My feelings must have been broadcasted on my face because Jonah tucked a stray strand of hair behind my ear. "Hey, don't blame yourself. It's his loss, and no matter what troubles you both went through, he had no right to cheat. That wasn't the solution."

Subconsciously, I knew Jonah was right, but it didn't erase the guilt. If I hadn't become what I was, then maybe James and I would still be together and happy. Maybe.

"Are you leaving?"

He caressed my face and I couldn't help but close my eyes. "Do you want me to?"

I shook my head without opening my eyes. It was a truth I couldn't admit aloud. Possibly only because of what happened, but either way, I didn't want him to leave my side. I snuggled in close to him and inhaled. He smelled of the woods and soap, which was peculiar, since we lived in the city. It was a good smell. I could get used to it.

He moved to lay next to me and pulled me into his chest. "Then I won't go anywhere," he whispered, running his hand up and down my back.

We stayed like that a long while.

11

Jonah and I spent the rest of the day holed up in the basement, avoiding everyone who might ask me what was wrong. Luckily, we had an old TV with a VCR and a bunch of nineties movies to watch, which we did as we cuddled on the old, rusty futon. He didn't try anything, and I was glad. We were close but he wasn't pushing me, and I appreciated it. I wasn't ready. When I finally checked my phone, I saw a ton of missed texts from my family, wondering where I was. Since it was Christmas Eve, I missed dinner with the Carsons, which earned me a load of angry texts from James. I only texted Amy before going to sleep to let her know where I was and that everything was fine. She didn't respond, but I knew she received it. Amy knew when to back off, and now was that time.

I spent the night with a werewolf, curled up with him behind me and his arm draped across my stomach. I couldn't hold back a giggle.

When I woke Christmas morning, I could smell the sausage

gravy my mom was making in the kitchen. It smelled glorious, and I planned to polish off at least a full pan of biscuits all by myself. Jonah stirred behind me and groaned when I tried to pull away.

"Where are you going?" he said. It was muffled since his face was stuffed in my back, but his grip around my waist tightened.

"I have to go upstairs and say Merry Christmas." I turned to him. "By the way, Merry Christmas, Jonah." He didn't open his eyes, but the dimple on his cheek peeked out and I smiled.

"Merry Christmas, Mackenzie." I leaned over and planted a soft kiss on top of his nose. "*Kenz*," he started, his tone turning serious.

My smile slipped. "What's wrong?"

"Nothing. I'm sorry, I just don't want to push you like I did the other day, and I'm afraid that if we get too close, I won't give you the amount of space you need. The next time we're together—when you're ready—I want it to be because *you* want me. Not your wolf."

I smiled at him. It was exactly the right thing to say. With Jonah, I didn't need to tell him what I needed—he already knew.

"Listen, my mom makes a huge breakfast, but you still better hurry up before my brother and I eat it all. If you have the same appetite I do, then you need to haul ass," I said as I headed upstairs.

When I opened the door from the basement, I had to squint and let my eyes adjust to the brightness of the room. It was mid-morning, but I'd been stuck in the dark since yesterday and hadn't seen the light in what felt like ages.

With my hand raised to cover my sensitive eyes, I dragged my tired body through the TV room into the kitchen where all the noise was coming. I walked in to see my parents, my brother, and Amy already eating. *Damn it.*

"Don't worry, Mackenzie, I made a whole batch just for you," my mother said.

I kissed her on the cheek. "You know me so well," I said, and then wished her and everyone else a Merry Christmas.

"Where were you, honey? James came looking for you yesterday," my dad asked with a mouth full of biscuits and sausage gravy.

"Dad, we broke up." All eyes were on me now. "Mom, don't burn the gravy!" I yelled at her because she wasn't paying attention to the stove. She shook her head clear and fumbled back to the pan.

"It's about damn time!" Ollie hooted and slammed his fist on the dining table.

"Oliver!" my mother scolded. He mumbled an apology, but not before he winked at me.

"That's okay, honey. Things happen for a reason," my mom said with a tight smile. I couldn't tell if she was happy or disappointed. My parents had never voiced their thoughts on my relationship with James, but they always seemed to like him well enough.

I nodded, not wanting to open a can of worms this early in the morning, and sat next to my best friend.

"Good Morning," Jonah said as he rounded the corner into the kitchen.

Ollie took the lead and made the official introductions to my parents, who hadn't formally met him yet. When Jonah hugged my mom, I was surprised to see her smile go from ear to ear at the sight of him. *Oh, good lord.* He came over and patted my brother and dad on the back. It was odd seeing Jonah here, blending in with my family like he'd known us for years. Amy was watching me, and I saw the wheels in her head spinning and connecting the dots. Once I saw her grin, I knew she'd put things together, but her version was probably dirty, while ours was no more than PG-13.

After breakfast, we moved into the living room and opened our gifts. Jonah excused himself, most likely to call Sebastian and give him an update on things. It made me wonder if wolves celebrated Christmas.

With the wrapping paper cleared away and everyone showered and dressed, we went down to Main Street for our town's small parade. While my parents volunteered during the parade, the rest of us enjoyed the festival and showed Jonah what small town living was all about.

Without knowing he was a werewolf, it was easy to tell the kind of person he was. He liked to joke around, but his body language said the complete opposite. His shoulders were always tense, and his eyes were on constant alert. He talked like he was relaxed, but it was all for show. It made me wonder what these wolves did for a living that made them so paranoid.

"Let's go on the merry-go-round!" Amy exclaimed as she latched onto Ollie and dragged him toward the ride. Watching those two was always entertaining. They sometimes acted more like siblings than Ollie and I did.

"Do they have a thing for each other?" Jonah asked as we followed a discrete distance behind them.

I almost choked on the hot chocolate I'd bought. "What? No way," I spluttered, and he looked at me with a perplexed expression. "I know it may look that way, but Ollie is almost like a brother to Amy. She's an only child, with shitty parents who barely pay her any attention. She just enjoys being part of an actual family."

Jonah's arm came around my neck and he pulled me into a hug. "You're a good friend, Kenzie," he whispered. His lips brushed my cheek, sending shivers down my spine.

"I try."

We caught up to Amy and my brother and got on one of the two-seaters on the carousel. Amy climbed onto an elephant and Ollie was on a horse, yelling "Yah!" and slapping its behind like it was real. Those two, I swear, were just plain ridiculous. Not a mature bone in their bodies.

I chuckled as I watched Amy make a trumpet sound from the elephant's trunk, and felt a rumble from Jonah beside me. I turned to look at him and noted he was fighting to keep a straight face.

"Just laugh. It'll happen sooner or later if we keep hanging out with these dummies." Once the flood gates opened. Jonah hunched over laughing, wiping tears from the corner of his eyes.

"What is *wrong* with those two?" he asked between bouts of laughter.

"We're children in grown up bodies, that's what's wrong."

"You know, that's what irritates Sebastian," Jonah said.

I looked at him. "What do you mean?"

He sighed. "It bothers him that you don't seem to take a lot of things seriously. I, for one, find it endearing," he added with a grin, and his one dimple peeped out.

I turned away toward the crowd waiting to get on the merry-go-round. The spins made me dizzy and I needed to distract myself. I wasn't sure why hearing this made me upset, but it angered me. I might not be the most mature adult, and some-times I said silly things, but ... that was just the way I was. I didn't want to live out the rest of my days in constant misery. Even when times were rough, I needed to joke about it to make myself feel better. If not, the wolf took over. Why dwell? I guess not everyone got it, and I needed to learn to be okay with that. I needed to accept the fact that Sebastian just didn't like me.

"Why are you mad?" I looked back to Jonah and saw the confusion in his eyes. He was listening to my heart beat.

"I'm not mad, just maybe a little ... miffed? I don't know, I guess I never thought I'd annoy someone as much as I do Bash."

He shook his head. "It's not that, Kenz. Sebastian has to be serious because he's the Alpha. The lives of all Pack members rely on him. He doesn't have the option to be carefree."

"Why is he Alpha?"

He cleared his throat. "Because I don't want to be."

There was a long pause as I soaked in what Jonah said. *What the heck does that mean? Is he stronger than Sebastian? Did he give him the position?* Wolf politics sucked.

"I'm going to need you to explain that one," I said, and he laughed.

"Well, my father is *The* Alpha. Sebastian only runs the Brooklyn Pack, but he reports to my father, who runs all the Northeast. It also makes him one of the Council members of the American Summit. Since I'm his son, I was offered the title of Alpha. Unfortunately for my father, it's not something I desire to be." He sighed. "I saw how hard it was for my dad, and now I see it with Bash. That's not the life I want for myself and the family I plan to have in the future."

As the ride came to a stop, it was like the world had been shut out and we were returning to reality. The noise of the festival filtered in and I had to shake my head from the daze. Jonah came from werewolf royalty. Okay, yeah, that sounded silly, but eh, it was sort of true.

We climbed off the carousel and speed-walked to catch up to Amy and Ollie, who were racing to the cotton candy machine.

"What about Jackson?"

"Jackson wants to be Alpha, but my dad is still holding out hope that I'll change my mind someday. We both can't be Alphas with my father sitting on the Council. It'd be a conflict of interest, and the wolves might think we were trying to take over. Wolves are very sensitive and territorial, so it's a slippery slope," he admitted as we reached the other half of our group.

"Omigod, I so want to take a picture with Santa!" Amy gushed as she grabbed the arm of each guy and pulled them toward the Winter Wonderland set-up where pictures were being taken.

I slowly followed just a few steps behind, thinking about what I'd learned. The wolves were a lot more organized than I thought.

After taking pictures with Santa Claus and his merry elves, Amy was coming down from her sugar high when we ran into James at the festival with his four sisters—who were glaring daggers at each of us. James was about to approach me, probably to curse me out, but Jonah came to stand by my side and James jerked to a stop. His sisters were behind him, arms crossed and shooting hate-filled glares my way. They probably egged him on, but he changed his mind once he saw Jonah. I didn't know what he told them, but I don't think I'd be welcomed at the Carson's anymore—or at least not for a very long time.

"Can we go on the Ferris Wheel?" Amy suggested, and we swerved in the opposite direction from the Carsons.

Ollie and Amy raced to get to the front of the line, almost trampling over some kids. I swore, this was the reason we never went to Dave and Busters—they had no shame.

We didn't have to wait long before Jonah and I were paired up on the two-seater. I was surprised Ollie didn't want to drive a wedge between me and the wolf. Made me wonder what was going on in his head.

"So tell me about yourself, Mackenzie," Jonah asked as the Ferris Wheel started to turn.

"There's not much to say. I'll be graduating with my Bachelor's in Criminal Justice next year. I want to be a cop, and I'm currently interning at IPP," I said as I looked over the small town of Cold Springs.

"That's pretty cool. What do you do? Buy donuts for the officers?" He chuckled and I rolled my eyes.

"Not like I haven't heard that before, but no, I actually shadow one of the detectives assigned to major cases."

"Whoa, how'd you get that?"

I laughed as I thought about my first day as an intern. "To be honest, I cheated. I used my senses on a case that was meeting a dead end, and impressed the captain. So I went from filing papers to going out in the field."

"What did you do?"

I shifted in our seat. "I sniffed out a meth lab."

"Tsk, tsk, Mackenzie. What else do you cheat on?" he joked.

I bit my lower lip to hold back a giggle. "Well, as you probably already know, I'm also a bouncer at a bar on the weekends."

Jonah hunched over the bar that strapped us in our seat. He was laughing so hard, I think he snorted.

"You are definitely special, Mackenzie," he said once he calmed down.

"Like, special, *short bus*, or special, *cute*?"

His milk chocolate eyes sparkled against the sunlight and I couldn't hold back a smile.

"Like, special *cute*."

IT WAS late in the afternoon when we got back home. My parents were still helping out with the festival, but we were wiped out from all the games and food we had. The four of us plopped down in the TV room and Amy finally addressed the elephant in the room.

"Okay, what the hell happened yesterday?"

After I went into the whole spiel on the argument with James, Jonah officially became part of the family as he shared his mutual hatred for my ex. Amy acted like she'd forgotten he compelled her, but I hoped he wasn't getting too comfortable. She forgot sometimes, but when you ticked her off, everything came back to her in boat loads and she laid it on you thick. What they hadn't questioned were my whereabouts yesterday, and I thanked my lucky stars that Amy didn't make any inferences. Even though Jonah and I didn't do anything, I didn't think my brother would be okay with us lying around in bed together all day.

"When are you heading back, Ollie?" I asked once I was no longer the center of attention.

He answered, "In two days," and I slumped against the sofa.

"What? You just got here!"

"I know, Kenz, but I can't stay long. I had to choose between Christmas and New Year's. I couldn't have both holidays."

"Well, let's not mope around, okay?" Amy said as she checked out our DVD collection. "Let's watch a movie and chill."

As she started calling out movie titles, the doorbell rang. I stiffened for a moment, thinking it might be James or someone from his family. I wasn't afraid of them—I mean seriously, what could they do to me? —but I didn't want any drama. Coming home was supposed to be relaxing, and we'd seen them not too long ago. By now, James could have changed his mind about approaching me.

"I'll get it," Ollie offered, and got up to go to the living room.

Jonah was sharing the sofa with me and leaned in to whisper, "You okay?"

I nodded and smiled, but it wasn't completely sincere. He put his arm around me and pulled me into him, kissing the side of my head. Oddly enough, I felt at home cuddled up with him. It was a pleasant feeling.

"Uh … Kenz … they're some guys asking for you," Ollie called, walking back into the room with a very tense and pissed-off Sebastian.

"Sebastian?" Jonah and I both at the same time, still snuggled close together on the sofa. The Alpha's face tightened as he took in our state.

"Kenz, who is this?" my brother asked, and in a flash, his protective side was unleashed.

"Who are *you*?" Sebastian countered. They looked like they were about to face off. *What the hell is going on?*

"Hey!" I said and got up, shaking off my state of shock. "Stop it, Bash. This is my brother." I needed to get that out there to break up the dominance competition, because while Ollie was a total Army badass, I didn't know how well he'd fare against an Alpha werewolf, and I didn't want to find out.

Sebastian relaxed a bit, but his face was still grim. His eyes traveled across the room until they landed on Jonah, who was now standing guard next to me.

"What's going on, boss?" Jonah asked, and I saw the confusion in his beautiful face.

Ugh, I sounded like a girl with a crush and I needed to get over it. I couldn't be getting all lovey-dovey with Jonah, and then having inappropriate thoughts about Sebastian. I was turning into a hussy.

I peered up at Jonah, who still looked a little perplexed. I knew he had been keeping Bash updated since we arrived, so he must not have known he was coming here. After spending the past two days together, I thought he would have told me.

"We need to talk. You, me, and Mackenzie. Now," Sebastian demanded, and stalked out of the room.

Jonah followed him without hesitation, and I wished I could say the same. I stalled for a moment, feeling the weight of Amy and Ollie's eyes on me, waiting for an explanation. Jonah stopped at the doorframe that separated the living room and TV room.

"Come on." He jerked his head to the front door and left.

"Kenzie, what's going on?" Amy asked. I wished I could tell her, but I didn't know what to say. I thought it must have something to do with the Summit. If so, I needed to figure out my next move.

"I don't know," I mumbled, and then followed the two werewolves out the door.

Outside my house was the same black SUV that had pulled

up in front of Pete's the night they kidnapped me, with two (I assumed) werewolves standing guard. Jonah and Sebastian were on the porch waiting for me.

"What's wrong?" I asked in a quiet voice. It must be bad news if he had to come all the way over to little 'ole Cold Springs to break the news.

"We have a problem," Sebastian said, keeping his back to me. I didn't know if he was talking to me, Jonah, or both of us.

"The Summit?" Jonah questioned, and Bash shook his head.

"I have news about the Summit, but that will have to take a backseat for the time being." He turned to look at us. "Jackson's been kidnapped."

I held my breath. Had I heard him correctly? Jonah's body didn't move. I was scared to look at him, so I diverted my eyes and got a glimpse of his shaking hand.

"What. Happened," he gritted out.

I peered up at Sebastian, who was watching me intently. "We don't know."

"What the hell do you mean, you don't know?" Jonah yelled, looking like he was about to pounce on Sebastian. I gripped his arm with reflexes I didn't know I had—I shouldn't have been surprised—and stopped him before he did anything stupid.

"*Jonah*," I said sternly, and he tensed.

Sebastian's jaw dropped a fraction, but he picked it up quickly, hoping I hadn't seen, but I did. He gazed at me for a while longer and then looked to his Beta. "I'm sorry, brother. I wish I had more to tell you, but this wasn't something that was appropriate for me to say over the phone. I didn't want anyone else to tell you besides me."

There was a long pause before Jonah nodded stiffly. "I understand." I released my hold on him.

"You need to come home so we can figure out what happened."

"What about Kenzie?" Jonah asked, and Sebastian's eyes narrowed. He caught the nickname.

He watched me for a moment before answering. "I was going to make her come back with us, but I think she'll be fine if she wants to stay," he said and waited for my response.

He was giving me a choice. It should be an easy one to make. I should have said I was staying, but something in my gut told me I needed to go with them. Jackson wasn't the president of my fan club, and I wasn't his biggest fan either, but I wouldn't wish this on anyone—not even Diana Stone. No matter how much of a douchebag he was, Jackson was Jonah's brother. I was stunned when I thought about how much that weighed in on my decision. What if it had been Ollie? If it was important to him, it was important to me.

I'm turning into such a chick.

"I'm going." Sebastian smirked at me like he knew what my answer would be. Jonah snapped his neck my way, his eyes flickering golden as he glared. "He's your brother. I want to help," I whispered.

He continued to glare. "No. You've done enough," Jonah growled. I jerked back like he'd slapped me across the face.

Jonah reached into the pocket of his jeans and fished out his car keys. "I'll see you back in the city," he tossed over his shoulder. He was gone before I could utter a word.

I stood there, unable to speak or move. Not even five minutes ago, we were joking and playing around. Now, I was a pariah.

"Don't take it personally, Mackenzie," Sebastian offered. "He's upset and feeling guilty."

"Guilty about what?"

"For not being there to avoid it." I heard the underlying message in that. He was too busy with me, so he wasn't around to save his brother. I was in the way.

"Do you think I should still go?" I asked. I didn't want to be where I wasn't welcome.

"Yes. I think you should," Sebastian answered, and it was settled. I was going whether Jonah liked it or not.

Sebastian followed me back into the house to find Amy and Ollie standing by the living room window that looked out onto the porch.

"Ollie, this is Sebastian. Bash, this is my brother, Sergeant Oliver Grey," I introduced, sliding in the soldier mention. This Alpha needed to learn early on that he was meeting not just my brother, but someone who understood what being an Alpha was all about. While Ollie may not be as intense as the werewolves, he was protective of the people he cared about, and when the time came, he suited up.

They shook hands, but my brother eyed him guardedly. This wasn't going to be as easy as it was with Jonah.

"What's going on, Kenz?" Amy asked.

"Jackson's been taken," I said, instantly realizing I should have kept my mouth shut. My brother's eyes snapped to me and grew an inch.

"Who's Jackson? Taken, as in kidnapped?"

What other way is there? But instead of offering a smartass comment, I merely nodded.

"You need to call the police."

He said it like it was common sense, and to the average human, well, yeah it was. But these were wolves. It wouldn't be easy to take one of these suckers down—much less a jerk like Jackson, who'd run his mouth so much, they'd change their mind about kidnapping him. Could this be supernatural? They did tell me that vampires were real, and if the myths were correct, we had beef with them.

"We can't, Ollie," I said, my gaze drifting between him and Sebastian. Could I tell my brother? Could I tell him that his baby sister was a werewolf—a monster?

"What are you involved in, Mackenzie?" he questioned in a stern voice. He said my full name, which meant he wasn't playing around anymore. He was mad.

"Nothing illegal." *At least I hoped not.* "I swear. It's just ... complicated."

"Then un-complicate it for me," he said, crossing his arms over his chest.

I blew out a breath, using the time to gather my thoughts. My hands were clammy and I rubbed them down my pants as I tried to either come up with something, or build up enough courage to blurt out the truth.

Just then, the door swung open and the hinges creaked. "Mackenzie Grey! Damnit, you better be here and talk to me!" James yelled as he stomped in, uninvited. Maybe he was good for something, the loser. "What's *he* doing here?" he snarled as he walked into the living room and pointed an accusatory finger at Sebastian.

"Jesus Christ, Jameson, what is *wrong* with you?" I said, exasperated. Seriously, the kid either needed to learn to knock, or not piss off a wolf. Because that was what he was doing for the second time this week.

"We need to talk about yesterday! You can't just assault me and then not keep your part of the deal and come to dinner!" he continued to yell as if I hadn't spoken.

"I'm not deaf, damn it! Pick that wedgie that has your undies in a twist, man. Good grief," I muttered, dropping onto the nearest sofa. So much for coming home and getting away from the crazy.

He huffed in response, but didn't say anything.

"You know him?" my brother asked James as he watched Sebastian.

I didn't blame Ollie. Bash had a menacing air to him that would make anyone question whether he'd keep you from danger, or if he *was* the danger. I still wasn't sure myself.

James puffed out his chest. Oh, please. "Yeah, I know him. He's a cop; he's protecting Kenz."

My brother's face turned tomato red and I wanted to kill James right then and there. I scowled at him and he flinched. He better be afraid. I was about to make his life hell.

"What does she need protecting from? What's going on, Mackenzie?"

I take it back. He wasn't mad, he was furious.

"It's not that serious, Ollie. I was involved in a teensy little hostage situation. No biggie." I told him our cover story and tried to brush it off like it was nothing.

"No biggie?" he exclaimed.

"Who says 'no biggie' anymore?" Amy mumbled.

"What the hell, Mackenzie! That's it – you're not going back to the city. I told dad it was a bad idea," he fumed, pacing in the small area.

"Yeah," James smirked at me, "you shouldn't go back to the city. You should probably stay here."

"Bitch, shut the fuck up," I growled. He was worried about me 'degrading him as a man'? He was about to get a hell of a lot worse.

I clenched my fists at my side and tried to calm my breathing, but I sounded like I was overweight and going up ten flights of stairs. The wolf stirred for the second time in two days, and if I kept getting my buttons pushed, I wouldn't make it to the next full moon. She wanted out, and at this rate, I might not be able to control her.

Sebastian pushed me toward the kitchen, away from the others. James and Oliver were yelling at each other, so Amy followed us out.

I was huffing now, with my hands on my knees.

"What's going on?" Amy asked, worried. I could smell the fear that was laced in her voice. I didn't hear it, I smelled it. It enticed me. I wanted her to be scared. I peered up at her and she stumbled back.

"Your eyes," she mumbled.

"Get me a bucket of ice and water, separately," Sebastian demanded quietly. He was more delicate with her than with me, and it made me snarl at them both.

Sebastian roughly pushed me onto a chair and kneeled in front of me. He grasped my face in his calloused hands and forced me to look at him. "Calm down," he ordered, but I was in full defiant mode.

No, I won't *calm down*. I growled a little louder now, even though deep down, I knew I shouldn't; the others could hear me, but the wolf didn't care. She was hungry. *Wait ... she's hungry?*

"Here," Amy said as she handed over a bowl of ice and a glass of water. "Anything else?"

"Meat. Check to see if they have any raw meat." She hesitated for a moment, but I flashed my canines at her and snapped my teeth. She turned and practically ran to the refrigerator.

"Easy there, pup. She's a friend," Sebastian chided, and I turned my hateful glare on him.

Before I realized what he was doing, he grabbed a handful of ice, pulled at my shirt, and dumped the ice down my front, using his hand to smash it against my chest.

I howled.

Everything stopped. Amy froze, and the chatter in the other room ceased as well. There were wild wolves in upstate New York that had migrated closer in the last few years, but not around Cold Springs.

Gasping for air and for the burn to stop, I reached for Sebastian and gripped the front of his shirt. His blue eyes pierced me into submission, and I felt the wolf subdue and slowly crawl back to whatever dark corner she was hiding.

"It burns," I chattered. He released his hand, making the ice cubes slide down to my belly, causing me to jump. "Ow, ow, owie!" I hopped around the melting ice as it fell to the floor.

"Do you still need the meat?" Amy whispered. She sounded nervous about getting close to me again.

"It's okay, I'm myself again," I said, and she nearly plowed me down. Her little body hugged me so tight that the chair I was in tilted back for a second.

"I was so scared! I thought you were going to eat me," she muffled in my hair.

I snorted. "Really?"

"I felt like Little Red Riding Hood," she whined.

I couldn't hold back my laugh. Sebastian snickered behind her, his mouth in a tight line, barely holding back a smile.

Sebastian walked to the counter and came back to where Amy was now on my lap, still holding me in her death grip. He handed me a plate. "Eat."

"Ew. What the hell is that?" I grimaced at the reddish-pink glob that he was trying to hand me.

"It's food, so eat. Your body went through a half-change, and your energy is depleted. You need strength."

"Dude, I don't know how to tell you this, but that's not food," I grimaced.

"Are you a vegetarian?" he exclaimed, and I thought I was going to give him a coronary.

"No! No, I eat meat, but ... I don't know what that is."

He rolled his eyes. "It's raw meat, Mackenzie. I don't have time to make it pretty for you."

"Raw meat!" Now it was my turn to shout.

"Holy hell, Mackenzie. Tell me you've had raw meat before?"

I only stared at him. The answer to that question was pretty obvious. But something was nagging me. "Where is my brother?" I didn't give two craps about James. I was hoping Ollie gave him the beat-down he so richly deserved.

"Don't worry, I'll compel them," Sebastian said, pushing the plate closer to my face. "Now, eat."

"No."

"Yes."

"No."

"Damnit, Kenz, just eat the damn thing!" Amy exclaimed.

I sighed, defeated.

This wouldn't be pleasant.

"Will I get sick from it? Like, salmonella or something like that?"

"No, you'll eat a lot worse than this at some point. What you *should* be doing is shifting and going on a hunt, but Jonah told me," he paused, "about the cage. We'll have to ease you into the hunting."

"Hunting? Like in the woods?" Okay, I admit that didn't sound like a very intelligent question.

"Yes, like in the woods, Mackenzie. Now eat."

I grumbled. "Fine, but if I puke, you're holding my hair back!" I pointed a stern finger at him and he nodded. I grabbed the plate and Amy got up to watch.

She pulled her phone from her back pocket. "I'm so recording this. YouTube stardom, here we come!"

I glared at her one last time before glancing down at the plate of what looked like raw ground beef. It was still slightly bleeding, but the smell wasn't too unpleasant. That thought scared me. I didn't want to turn into Hannibal Lector.

Taking a deep breath, I stuck my finger in the cold mound of meat and flicked a piece out. With a scrunched up face, I closed my eyes and slowly put my finger in my mouth.

I chewed on the mushiness and thought I was going to throw up, but then I swallowed and my body tingled. I opened one eye and peeked at the two people who were eagerly awaiting my analysis on my late afternoon snack. I tried a heftier scoop and stuffed my face. It wasn't too bad. Maybe with a little salt it would taste better, but it fed a hunger deep inside me—a hunger I never knew I had.

I went for another bite, but realized the plate was empty.

"Holy shit, Kenz, you demolished that junk. Must'a been good, huh?" Amy said with her phone camera still aimed at me.

"I'm still hungry," I deadpanned, looking at Sebastian. He squatted in front of me with a kitchen towel, and then gently grabbed my chin and began to clean me. I really must have stuffed my face, because he wiped at places that should have been clean. I didn't remember taking more than two bites.

His thumb that held my chin started a slow caress and I gazed into those glowing sapphire eyes. "I'll feed you," he whispered, but I wasn't sure what he was talking about anymore.

12

After two more pounds of raw ground beef and a sirloin steak, my appetite was quenched. I couldn't believe I'd eaten my fair share of raw meat without a grimace.

"How are you feeling?" Sebastian asked as he washed the dishes we'd used.

"Surprisingly satisfied. I don't know whether to be content or horrified at what I just did," I mused as I stared at the ceiling.

"Well, I'm off to go find your brother and that boy. Hurry up and pack. We leave within the hour."

"Wait. Why are you looking for them?" I jumped up from my chair and stood in the doorway, blocking his exit. What was he planning to do?

He narrowed his eyes. "What? You think I'm going to hurt them?"

I shrugged.

"Mackenzie, they heard you howl. I need to compel them to forget, or one of two things will happen: either they expose you and the rest of us, or people will think they've gone crazy and they'll end up in an asylum. What's it going to be?"

I hated how Sebastian was right all the time. No wonder he was Alpha. I sighed in defeat and stepped aside. I really didn't care about James, but Ollie was a different story.

"You better not hurt my brother," I warned as I squared my shoulders and raised my chin.

"Wouldn't dream of it."

Yeah, right.

I left the kitchen and went to find Amy to tell her what was going on and how I needed to return to the city. I told her she could stay with my family, but she didn't want to stay without me, and I couldn't make her.

Once we were all packed up—which wasn't much—we headed to the SUV that was still waiting outside. This time, only the driver was there. As we were loading our things in the trunk, Mrs. Carson came outside. I tensed at her approach because I didn't know what James had told them, and I didn't want to start pointing fingers. At the end of the day, he was their blood and right or wrong, they would take his side. I didn't blame them, I just didn't want to put them in a position where they had to choose sides and feel guilty about it.

"Mackenzie." She nodded to me and I had no choice but to acknowledge her.

"Hello, Mrs. Carson," I said, trying not to make eye contact.

"I spoke with James," she began, and paused as if rethinking what she was going to say next. "I heard what happened yester-day. I knew something was off with the two of you, but I was waiting for one of you to tell me. I don't like that you two thought you could pull a fast one on me and lie, but I'll let it go because you don't deserve it, Mackenzie." She reached for my hand and squeezed it, and her eyes watered.

Crap, I didn't see this happening. What exactly did she hear, anyway?

"Mrs. Carson, it's okay."

"No, it's not. I've already told Nana, and she's not happy with James either. What he did was wrong. No matter what troubles you had, that was the wrong way to handle them." She paused and added, "I've also told him he better not bring that home wrecker around, because then I'll *really* give him a piece of my mind."

I wanted to engulf her in a hug. I didn't realize how much her acceptance mattered to me, but it did. She chose my side.

I chuckled. "Thank you, Mrs. Carson. I'm sorry for lying."

"It's over and done with now. Just make sure you tell your folks; I won't lie to them." She looked at the SUV behind me. "Are you leaving?"

"There's an emergency back in the city that I need to tend to," I explained, and wanted to pat myself on the back. *That was very diplomatic of you, Kenz.*

"Oh. Well, I hope you're not running away because of James. I promise he won't bother you."

That was probably why he barged into my house, because he got a good talking-to from his mama.

"Don't worry, Mrs. Carson. I don't run away," I replied with a smirk.

We said our goodbyes and a few moments later, I saw my parents and Ollie down the street, walking back to the house. I waved at them and Ollie jogged the rest of the way to me.

"Hey, what's going on?" he asked as he looked at the SUV and back to me. I thought of the compulsion and figured Bash had already done it. He didn't look suspicious of anything—he looked normal.

"I have to go, Ollie."

"Is this about the kidnappers? Did they follow you here?" he growled, and I patted his arm. I guess he didn't compel everything away.

"Easy, boy. No, a friend of mine is in trouble and needs help, but I promise I'll come visit you for spring break, okay?" I said, trying to lighten the mood.

I pulled my parents inside and told them I had to leave. My father questioned me, but didn't push. That was just the kind of people they were. We weren't a close bunch, but it didn't mean we hated each other, either. We just didn't hover.

Everyone was already waiting in the car as I hopped into the passenger seat—Sebastian was driving—and my brother came up to my open window.

"Call or text me when you get there, and if you need anything, Kenz, let me know. If I have to extend my leave for an emergency, I'll do it and it won't be a problem. Okay?"

I grabbed him through the window and pulled him into an embrace. "I love you, Ollie," I whispered, and his arms tightened around me.

"Kenz, I don't know what you've gotten yourself into, but I trust that you know how to take care of yourself. Don't face the world alone if you don't have to. I'm here for you."

I placed a soft kiss on his cheek. "I know, Ollie. I'll call you when I get back to the city."

WE GOT BACK to the city in record time, only forty-five minutes, which was outrageous, but with Sebastian behind the wheel ... it was a speedy trip. He took us straight to the warehouse in Brooklyn. I wasn't sure how I felt about that, especially with Amy coming, but if we wanted to help find Jackson, I needed to suck it up.

"I can't believe Jackson's been kidnapped," Amy whispered behind me. I watched her from the car side mirror as she looked out the window. Her pierced eyebrows were scrunched in and worry lines etched her forehead.

I didn't know how much help we could be, but after spending the last few days with Jonah, I didn't want to sit around and do nothing. He might be taking his anger out on me now, but I'd like to think we were at least friends, and friends didn't back off when one of them needed help.

When we arrived at the warehouse, I realized it was packed to the hilt with men and women who I assumed were werewolves. Amy stuck close to me—smart girl—but her face was awestruck by all the very ... uh, good looking guys milling around without shirts. Jonah wasn't lying when he said they needed to wear the minimum to be able to shift at a moment's notice. The women were fully clothed, but the men barely had anything on—only jeans—and it was freezing cold out. Amy's face peeked out from the gap between her scarf and hat.

"Bash!" Jonah yelled from across the main floor and waved him over, although he froze in mild surprise when he saw me. Sebastian approached him and I started to follow, until I heard my name.

"Mackenzie!" Blu squealed and wrapped her arms around me. "I'm so glad you're okay. I was so worried when the guys went out looking for you, and then when Jonah didn't come back. How are you?" she rambled, and I noticed her eyes were bloodshot like she'd been crying.

"I'm fine, Blu. Are *you* okay?" I asked, motioning to her face. She took a tissue from her back pocket and dabbed her eyes.

"I'm sorry, it's just really hard right now with Jackson missing," she admitted. I patted her arm because I knew I had to be sympathetic. He may have been an asshole to me, but maybe he wasn't a bad guy to the rest of them.

"Do they know anything about his disappearance?"

She nodded. "He was patrolling Central Park with his team when they were attacked. Andrew was killed and Jackson was taken. Sam came back, but he's been out of it, speaking in incoherent gibberish. They think it might have been vampires," she said, her eyes wide with fear. I didn't know what to say, so I gripped her hand.

"Well, well, well ... what do we have here? An unmated Luna and a lone wolf ... pathetic," V snarked as she approached us. Amy tensed beside me and I gripped her wrist through her coat. Bash's girlfriend was our new Diana Stone, and Amy would go head-to-head with her if given the opportunity.

Blu dropped her eyes meekly and searched for something interesting on the ground. She started to worry her hands, and I put mine on top of them so she wouldn't scratch enough to draw blood.

"I'm sorry, who are you again?" I said.

The woman sneered and flicked her sleek blonde hair back. A group of three Lunas stood behind her. This was starting to look like a B-rated version of Mean Girls.

"I'm Sebastian's soon-to-be mate, and I suggest you don't

forget that. I'll soon be the Lunas' Alpha." Her pearly white teeth shone brightly as she smirked.

The thought of her being with Bash made me want to vomit, and now that I knew she would be an Alpha of some sort made me feel bad for Blu. She was obviously not part of the 'in' crowd with these chicks.

I chuckled. "Oh, yeah?" The dumb bitch nodded. "Well, I guess I'll wait to remember when you *actually* become Alpha. Until then, who are you?"

That earned me an unfriendly growl from our resident vixen. Amy giggled beside me.

"You think you're so cute, don't you—"

"Yes I do," I interrupted.

"It wasn't a question! Don't interrupt me again," she glowered.

"Mums the word," I said, and ran an invisible zipper across my lips, tossing the key behind me.

"You've never been part of a Pack, so let me school you on how it works around here. You're a Luna, which means you listen and do as I say until you're mated. Don't go around trying to change the status quo, Mackenzie Grey," V snarled. The posse behind her nodded their heads in conviction, as if this chick was the next Messiah. "Do I make myself clear?"

"Crystal," I said cheekily.

She huffed and turned around, barreling through her group of followers. Once they all dispersed, Amy and I hunched over cackling. With hands on our knees, we tried to catch our breaths between laughs.

"Kenz! You can't talk to Vivian like that! She'll ruin you," Blu chastised, red in the face.

"Ruin me? Oh, please, that girl needs a reality check."

"You don't know how things run around here. She governs all the Lunas, and she's right; once Sebastian is mated to her, she'll have complete and total control of us. She'll be *our* Alpha."

My smile faltered. "Is she really going to be mated to Bash?"

"Most likely. They've been together for years. He hasn't been with anyone else," Blu said as she pulled her phone from her pocket. She read something on the screen and then looked up to the second floor. One of the wolves was waving for her to come upstairs.

"I have to go upstairs and check on the survivor. Want to come?"

I cleared my throat. "Yeah, sure." I didn't know why I felt this irked about Sebastian and V, but it wasn't sitting well in my stomach. It wasn't like it was my business. I wasn't even part of the Pack—it shouldn't matter.

We followed Blu up the stairs and Amy sidled up next to me.

"You okay, Kenz?"

"Yeah, why?"

"Because you look constipated. What's up?"

"Nothing, just ticked off at that V chick," I lied.

We arrived at the room where they were keeping the hurt werewolf. Beside him another wolf with a mop of dirty blonde hair. It seemed as if he was once attractive, but that wasn't what caught my attention. It was the big, puckered scar that slashed across his face. It extended from just above his right eye, over his nose, catching a smidge of the left corner of his upper lip, and stretching just below his jaw line. It was intensely scary and interesting, all at the same time.

"Everything okay, Caleb?" Blu asked as we entered.

"I don't know. He started mumbling something, but I couldn't understand what he was saying," Scarface said, and then his green eyes met the three of us. "What's *she* doing here?"

Blu worried her hands and began to stutter. "Sh-she's Mackenzie. Sh-she came here with Sebastian."

I cocked an eyebrow and reassessed the man in front of me. I must have been missing something about him if he had Blu all nervous. Did she like him?

"The lone wolf?"

She nodded.

"I'm right here, you know. You could just ask me," I smarted as I approached the bed of the unconscious wolf. He looked very young—no older than nineteen. His eyes were sunken in with dark circles and slow, shallow breaths puffed out from between his purple chapped lips.

"You're not Pack. What are you doing here?"

"Man," I sighed, "you guys are so welcoming. It's a breath of fresh air, truly."

"Get out, Luna, and take the human with you," Caleb said to Blu, never taking his eyes off me.

"I have a name, tight ass. It's Amy, not *human*," Amy muttered.

"I said, *get out!*" he gritted between his teeth. My hands clenched into fists beside me.

"What crawled up his ass?" Amy mumbled as Blu dragged her out of the room.

Once it was just the two of us, his eyes roamed up and down my body. Chills racked me, but not in a hot Alpha way—in a creepy, he's-a-possible-serial-killer way.

The silence stretched over us for what felt like forever. He walked around the bed to where I was standing and stood at arm's length.

"Where do you come from, Mackenzie?" he whispered, and I got a close up at the scar on his face. We were both about the same height, and at close proximity, it was more gruesome than I thought.

"Who gave you that scar?" I countered, and he stiffened.

"I asked you a question first. Answer me."

I rolled my eyes. "Seriously? I came from my mother's womb. What's the deal with your face?"

His hand came up and grabbed my face roughly—squeezing my cheeks.

"Don't play games with me, little girl. You might have Sebastian and Jonah fooled, but not me. I'll find out your secret sooner or later."

I pulled away from his grip and scowled. "Secret? What are you smokin'? *I* don't know anything about why I am what I am. I don't appreciate you putting your hands on me, either, but I'll be nice this time. Do it again, and your balls are mine."

I turned to leave the room when I heard a grunt. It wasn't coming from Caleb, my new best friend. Times like these, I was starting to miss Jackson's brand of asshole.

The wolf on the bed tried to speak, but his mouth was too dry. I pushed past Caleb and reached over the night stand for the glass of water. Lifting the boy's head, I tipped the glass to wet his lips.

"Are you okay?"

"Get away from him!" Caleb latched onto my arm holding the glass and pulled me away—spilling the water on the bed.

"What the hell!"

"You're not a Luna, and you're definitely not Pack. Keep your filthy mutt hands off him."

"Hey, asshole! I was trying to help, since all you were doing was looking at him like he wasn't supposed to wake up," I said and stopped. I could hear the squealing of make-believe tires coming to a halt in my head. Did he hope the guy wouldn't wake up?

"H-h-hel," the patient, Sam, tried to speak, his brown eyes flashing wide and wild.

"He's asking for help; give him water—" I pleaded.

"You don't know anything. Get out!"

Caleb turned his back to me and pulled an envelope from his back pocket. I backed away to the door, but the boy's eyes were on me and I felt like they were pleading with me to stay. A tear trickled down the corner of his eye. *Oh, God ...*

I ran out of the room and to the second-floor railing. I leaned over and scanned the main floor where dozens of wolves were congregated.

"Sebastian!" I yelled over the warehouse once I spotted him in the middle of a group on the far right side of the floor. It was too loud and he couldn't hear me—no one could—it was chaos down there.

My gut told me something was wrong. I went back into the room, but came to a screeching halt just past the doorframe. Caleb was feeding the wolf some sort of hot liquid. I saw steam rising above the plastic cup.

"What is that?" I said, slightly out of breath. My heart raced as my adrenaline kicked in. Maybe I was being paranoid without reason, but there was a gnawing in my stomach that didn't trust Caleb.

"Why don't you try it?" he said with his back to me.

I scoffed, "Do I look that stupid to you? For all I know, you're poisoning him."

"Relax. It's just an herbal tea to calm him down—chamomile. You should have some; you're getting worked up over nothing."

He got up from the bed and I saw the boy was now sleeping soundly again, his chest rising slightly as he slumbered.

Caleb turned to me with the cup outstretched. I peered into it, and though it looked like tea, I still wasn't sold on the idea. Instead of messing around here, I should have gone downstairs to get help. I wanted to kick myself for being so stupid.

"Give it," I said, and grabbed the cup from him. I brought it up to my nose and inhaled. My nose scrunched up as a tangerine-like scent tickled my throat. I coughed to get the acrid taste out of my mouth, but it only built up a layer of thick mucus. Left with no other choice, I swallowed it and felt the bile rise up. That shit was nasty.

"Smells great, huh?" Caleb taunted with a smirk.

"You're an asshole."

"I can live with that. Now, I won't say it again … get the fuck out."

I walked out of the room with the taste of the tea still in my mouth, but it was diminishing. I needed to get out of there before he ticked me off and I did or said something I'd regret.

I went down the stairs and tripped on the last couple of steps. Luckily, Blu and Amy were there to steady me.

"Whoa, why do you look like you're five margaritas in?" Amy joked.

I shook my head. I wasn't dizzy, but the short trip down the stairs seemed to have zapped all my strength and I was sweating bullets.

"I don't know," I whispered and tried to get my bearings straight. I sat on the last two steps and put my head between my knees. My bones felt heavy and I didn't know how long I would be able to hold myself up.

"Did Caleb do something to you?" Blu asked, concerned.

I slowly shook my head. "Caleb?" I questioned.

Blu raised an eyebrow. "Yeah, the guy upstairs."

"Oh, Scarface, yeah. Besides being an asshole? No, I think I'm just hungry."

After a few minutes, I felt my body get control of itself again and the tight feeling in my limbs eased. I peered up and caught Blu's face. She'd been crying again.

"Don't worry, Blu, they'll find him," I reassured her. They had to find Jackson.

"Don't make promises you can't keep," Jonah snarled from behind Amy.

I turned to look at him and he leveled me with a glare. I was starting to get ticked off.

"I didn't promise anything," I replied in a neutral voice, still not feeling a hundred percent.

He snorted, "What are you doing here, anyway? Shouldn't you be back home with your cheating boyfriend?"

I clenched my fists at my side. *Okay, now I'm starting to feel like myself again.*

A thought stopped me. Maybe it was better to give him space before I couldn't control what came out of my mouth.

"Low blow, Jonah," I answered quietly. Standing on wobbly

legs, I walked away with Amy trailing behind me. What was I going to do?

Amy latched onto my arm to steady me. "Hey, what was that about? I thought you guys were, you know, *friends.*"

"I don't know *what* we are. He's pissed he wasn't around to help Jackson because he was spending time in Cold Springs, and he's taking his guilt out on me. At least that's what Sebastian said. We'll see." I approached the Alpha, who was giving orders to a team of five.

"I want Team One to take Central Park North; Team Two takes the South; Team Three West; and Team Four East. I want the tactical team near the reservoir, talking with the Fae. I need to know if they saw anyone that night. Any questions?"

He was in full-on Alpha mode, which I had to admit was kind of hot. Oh geez, there's something seriously wrong with me. While I'd been drooling over him, I didn't notice the five guys staring at me. I waved at them and got a couple smirks, prompting Sebastian to turn around.

"Mackenzie." He motioned to me and I walked over to the table. "Meet our Pack captains. Thomas, Daemon, Muhammad, Bernard, and Caleb."

I didn't recognize him in the group before, but as my gaze landed on Scarface, my smile faltered. Thomas and Daemon sent me a slight nod, and Bernard came over and gripped my hand in a firm shake. He was a burly, gruff guy who looked like a lumberjack with his outgrown reddish beard. Muhammad stood to his left. He was as tall, but more toned than Bernard. His eyes were two empty pits of black orbs, like if he killed someone, he wouldn't even bat an eyelash. I assumed he was the tactical team captain, which suited him. He appeared to be

Middle Eastern, but I could be wrong. He didn't nod or shake my hand, he just gazed at me with those dead eyes. I didn't even look at Caleb, although I could sense the cocky smirk on his face.

"Mackenzie is not Pack ... at least not *yet*," Sebastian started, and I rolled my eyes. That got a couple snickers from the captains. "Keep information limited, and make sure she doesn't leave the building."

With that last command aimed at me, my eyes bugged out.

"Hold up!" I raised a finger to him and the main floor quieted. "I didn't come here to be locked up again."

The room fell silent and I almost heard when Sebastian quirked a brow.

"What do you suppose I do with you then, Mackenzie? Send you out in the field?"

I hadn't thought that far ahead, but I was a criminal justice major. I could be useful. Unfortunately, my physical prowess was very limited. I never even took karate as a kid. Damn it.

"*Kenz*," Amy whispered in warning as she sidled closer to me, probably nervous with all these werewolves staring us down.

I ignored her.

"Are you trying to call me weak?" I heard gasps echo all around the room. My mouth might get me in trouble, but I refused to allow anyone to make me feel incompetent.

"I'm not calling you strong, if that's what you're aiming for," he countered evenly, crossing his arms over his chest.

I scoffed, "Well I am, and I can kick your ass any day of the week." Amy's grip tightened painfully and she dug her nails into my arm. I swear, sometimes my nerves made me say the stupidest things.

"Oh yeah?" Sebastian said with a hint of a smile. "Let's test this theory out."

The captains laughed with one another and started to move the cafeteria-style tables out of the middle of the floor, forming a make-shift fighting ring. Sebastian's eyes never left mine as he stripped out of his shirt and shoes, standing before me barefoot, with his jeans hanging low and exposing his V-cut that I couldn't look away from.

I gulped.

When Amy pleaded, "Kenzie, maybe we should go," I knew she was freaking out. Hell, I was too.

"Even if we wanted to, they wouldn't let us," I muttered as I carefully removed my shoes and coat, stuffing my hat and gloves in my coat pockets. I walked to the middle of the empty floor space in my jeans and sweater, where Sebastian was standing.

The wolves—and Amy—encircled us and I saw Jonah cut through the crowd. His chocolate eyes grew to the size of tennis balls. He rushed over to us and pulled me away from Sebastian, the big, bad wolf.

"What the hell, boss? What are you doing?" Jonah asked.

"She challenged me, Jonah. You know Pack rules; a challenge doesn't go unanswered."

"She's a pup, Bash! She doesn't know any of this stuff. She was not raised in a Pack," Jonah chided.

"Doesn't matter, and if you ask her, she'll tell you ... oh, how did she put it?" Sebastian looked around the crowd.

"She said she can kick your ass any day of the week, boss!" yelled Bernard.

Oh man, they're enjoying this. I'm about to get my ass handed to me. Great.

"Bash, we shouldn't waste time on a *stupid*," Jonah glared at me, "challenge instead of spending it to find Jackson."

Sebastian stiffened and his gaze traveled over to Jonah, who, even though he was irked by me, was quickly becoming my knight in shining armor. Did I want to be thought of as weak, or someone who needed protection from a male wolf? As I started to think about Pack laws and stuff, I realized that allowing Jonah to rescue me would just prove the point that female wolves were only good at being domestic Lunas and nothing else. That was not right.

"Thank you, Jonah," I started, and he turned to me with a look of relief, "but," and he tensed, "even if I challenged Bash, unknowingly, might I add, I still need to step up and follow through."

For the first time since I met him, Sebastian smiled a genuine smile and I wanted to melt right there where I stood. Which was totally lame.

"Kenz! He's an Alpha for a reason. Damn it, Kenzie, listen to common sense!" Jonah yelled, his eyes wild. He was freaking out, and rightfully so.

"Jonah, relax," I said, wishing I could take my own advice. "I'll be fine." I winked at him and he scowled. I pushed past him, and the crowd cheered as Sebastian and I bumped fists.

Let the games begin.

13

The ripples of his muscles as Sebastian moved were a welcome distraction. In the beginning, I was able to duck and swerve his punches. Which meant I was on the defense and needed to step up my A-game and try to get a lick in. I'd never had any formal training to fight, but Ollie liked to practice the wrestling moves he saw on TV as a kid, and I was his sparring partner. I'd like to think it prepared me for this precise moment. Also, I remembered a homeless man who managed to avoid a fight with someone on the subway once. He told me that if you pretended to be crazy, they left you alone. With a combination of both, I prayed to God I'd win this or at least make it out alive.

After ducking a right hook, I crawled between Sebastian's legs and popped up behind him. Wasting no time, I jumped onto his back like a spider monkey and got a good grip around his neck with my arms, wrapping my legs around his thick waist. He tried to fling me off, but I held on tight.

The cheers in the background thundered and I prayed a beat

cop wasn't walking by to hear it. I was glad it was loud enough that no one could hear me screaming—no one except Sebastian, at least. Maybe it was nerves or adrenaline, but I screamed, "I'm crazy, I'm crazy!" like a hysterical looney, yelling directly in Bash's ear.

"Mackenzie! Fight fair, damn it!"

No matter how much Bash growled, I was determined that nothing he said would get me off him. I squeezed my arms and tried to choke him—not as easy as it sounded, since he was a big guy—but it helped that his body was firm, warm, and strong, which made me want to hold on even tighter.

"Fine, have it your way," he grunted.

Charging backwards, he slammed my back onto one of the tables. I sucked in a harsh breath as it was completely expelled from my body. I tried to hold on, but with that blow, I was seeing stars and I lost my grip on him.

Sebastian stalked back into the makeshift fighting ring. Two people grabbed me on either side, and without waiting to see if I was okay, tossed me back into the fight. I slid across the floor as my eyes played catch up. I didn't see Bash approach, but felt him haul me up by the front of my sweater.

"SEBASTIAN!" I heard Jonah roar from the crowd, right before I was slammed back down on the ground. I gurgled a grunt, unable to open my eyes. I lingered a little too long on the floor, more from a fear of fighting than of the pain itself. When I finally pried open my eyes, Sebastian was crouched in half-wolf mode, coming toward me on all fours. *Shit.*

I scrambled backwards until I hit a wall, using it to stand, and then scurried out of his way. He skidded across the concrete floor and fell into a group of werewolves, giving me time to regroup. As

I edged farther from him, I saw Bernard and Caleb holding Jonah down, who was also in half-wolf mode and snapping his canines at us. Amy stood motionless beside them, but I saw the worry and fear etched on her face. I was giving that poor girl gray hairs. I needed to wrap this fight up already and quit messing around. I chuckled—as if I actually could.

Resolved to my fate, I stood up straight and grabbed the hem of my sweater, pulling it over my head and exposing everyone to my black sports bra. Whistles resonated throughout the room and Jonah ripped out a lion-like roar. He was pissed. I crouched forward and focused on Sebastian, who ran toward me at full speed. Narrowing my eyes, everything seemed to move in slow motion as I felt the wolf come out of her hiding spot. Without saying a word, I knew she was asking me if I wanted her help, and she knew the moment I said yes. My upper lip furled and I growled, showing off my canines. Just as he was half a foot away from me, I swerved to my right and jumped onto his back again, bringing him flat onto his stomach with unexpected force.

I had realized during the first half of the fight that Bash was going pretty easy on me. His moves seemed coordinated, but careful. He wasn't trying, and if I could figure that out, so could his wolves ... and then my whole purpose would be moot. Even if I did win, everyone would know it was only because he *let* me win, which was convenient and all, but not the vindication I was going for. I had to piss him off. I must have succeeded when he wolfed out, which was when our play skirmish became an actual fight.

Now that I *had* to win, I realized there was a slight problem. I must have inadvertently called out to her, or else she was always around, but I accepted the wolf's strength and agility to get me where I was now: on top of Sebastian and pinning him to the ground for my final blow. What might that final blow be, you ask? In my usual Mackenzie fashion, I couldn't go out without a bang, so I did what all crazy homeless fighters and TV wrestling impersonators do—I went for the nuts.

With Sebastian thrashing below me, I turned my body to the side and reached over between his legs for the ultimate nut snatch. *Take that, Alpha!*

The howl that ripped out of Sebastian made my ears pop and the room went silent. The cheering and friendly howls that boomed seconds ago were now mute. Everything screeched to a standstill. Jonah bounded towards me and plucked me off Bash. My feet weren't even touching the ground as he carried me across the main floor and out of sight from everyone who now sneered and growled in my direction. Amy was the only one who was running to keep up with us.

Jonah brought me into the room that I had seen Blu emerge from the day I escaped the warehouse, and I was right—it was a laundry room. Jonah set me down on one of the folding tables while he began to pace. Amy caught up and barged into the room, locking the door behind her. I couldn't tell what she was thinking or feeling; her face was unusually neutral.

"Okay, someone say something, because the silence is killing me," I said through ragged breaths. Jonah froze and stared at me mindlessly.

"Are you okay, Kenz?" Amy asked, worrying her gloved hands.

"Yeah, I totally kicked ass out there!" I said with so much excitement, I sounded like a Valley girl for a second.

Amy laughed nervously. "You so did, Kenzie," she said, and then watched Jonah warily. "See, the thing is, you've made a lot of big wolfies angry out there." Her gaze traveled back to me and she gave me her 'oopsie' face.

"I don't get it," I said, confused. "What did I do wrong?"

"It's in our nature to defend one of ours—especially from an outsider," Jonah explained as he pursed his lips. "Kenz, you just hurt our Alpha, and to make matters worse, you're a woman, a Luna, *and* a lone-wolf. The Pack is going to want your head on a platter."

I sucked in a breath. *Shit.* That was *not* supposed to happen.

"Why does being a woman matter?"

"Mackenzie, when are you going to get it through that thick head of yours? The Pack hasn't caught up to modern human times. In our world, women have a place and they are kept in line! Not doing so is considered insubordination," he yelled.

I flinched. I should have been pissed, but seeing him so angry and hearing the yells from the main floor that filtered into the room made me worry.

"Jonah?" I got off the table and went to him. "Am I dead meat?" I whispered, already feeling a panic attack rising.

He sighed. "Kenz, I don't know, but it's better if we steer clear from the Pack. They will want to issue some sort of punishment."

I shivered and he pulled me toward him, wrapping me in his warmth. I was in my jeans and a sports bra, and with my adrenaline depleted, I was cold. With my face smashed to his chest, I mumbled, "I didn't mean to."

He squeezed me even tighter. "I know, Kenz, I know."

A knock came at the door and Bernard poked his head in the room. "Can we come in?" I felt Jonah move against me and heard two pairs of feet shuffle in as someone shut the door.

"What's going on out there?" Jonah asked.

Amy came to stand next to us as she rubbed my arm. "It'll be okay, Kenz," she whispered to me.

"It's chaos," Bernard admitted. "The Lunas took Bash to the infirmary and the captains are trying to keep the Pack under control, but ... don't you feel the turmoil? She's not Pack, Jonah," Bernard said as he scratched his beard. "This won't end well. You should think about calling Charles."

Jonah shook his head. "He doesn't need to get involved. This is a Brooklyn Pack matter, not a Summit problem."

"I don't know, I have a feeling Caleb is already calling them in."

Jonah's body tensed underneath me and I pulled away. His eyes flashed a brilliant shade of gold as he snarled. Blu peeked her head in the room and entered, closing the door quietly behind her. Reaching into his pocket, Jonah pulled out his phone. He dialed a number and put it to his ear as it rang, waiting for someone to answer.

"Father," Jonah clipped out. "It's under control—no, Father ... he's a liar and a sneak. Caleb never should have jumped the chain of command and spoken with you. Yes, it is the same girl ... No, she doesn't. I will. Yes, Father. Goodbye."

Amy, Bernard, and Blu watched Jonah's conversation intently while I tried to eavesdrop on his phone call, but was unsuccessful. I didn't hear anything his father said.

Jonah sighed and ran his hands through his chestnut hair. "Well, Caleb's officially on my shit list. He told my father what happened, and now he wants us to head over to the Estate."

Bernard cursed. "This is bad timing, Jonah. We need to be out there trying to find Jackson, not dealing with this. She's a liability —no offense."

"None taken," I grumbled, crossing my arms over my chest.

"I don't think you know how much danger you're in, Kenz. We *hunt* lone-wolves." Jonah paused before continuing, "We don't usually accommodate strays like we have for you."

"Well, what do we do?" I asked.

"We *should* be heading to the Estate to talk with my father, but I think we should wait. I haven't spoken to Bash about what went on at the Summit, and I don't know my father's position on your particular situation. Until we have more info, we need to wait it out." Jonah tapped his fingers on his chin. "Bern, get me a group of your most trustworthy wolves. Then, I need you to get everyone back to work on finding Jackson. I want an update on him in two hours, no exceptions. We better have a lead."

Bernard nodded and left the room. "What about me? What can I do to help?" Blu asked.

"I need you to keep an eye on Sebastian and ask him for details on the Summit. He might not reveal them to you, but call my cell and put him on the phone. Don't let anyone in his room to see him, no matter how trusting they seem. *Especially* Vivian."

"Got it," she said and left the room as well.

"Why can't we talk to him ourselves?" Amy asked what I was wondering.

"Because we need to keep Mackenzie away from the Pack, and I won't leave her side until everyone has settled down," Jonah said.

We stood around awkwardly, as if waiting for the next shoe to drop. "So ... we're going to hole up in the laundry room?" I asked, breaking the silence.

Jonah rolled his eyes. "Of course not. We're going to look for Jackson."

LESS THAN TWENTY MINUTES LATER, Bernard came back with a group of four werewolves. Jonah directed two of them to guard the door, and the other two to infiltrate and play spies within the Pack to find out what everyone was planning. Jonah, Amy, Bernard, and I crept out through a back door that led to the small area where the Lunas hung wet clothes. Bernard handed Jonah a brown spray bottle with a label that had a picture of a deer and in bold letters said: SCENT KILLER.

"What the hell is that?" I exclaimed as he was about to spray me.

He sighed. "It's exactly what the bottle says, Kenz. It kills your scent. Hunters use it to sneak up on their prey. In this case, we need it so when the Pack eventually realizes we're gone, they'll have a harder time finding us."

After a moment, I consented and the four of us were sprayed down. It wasn't too bad, almost like mosquito repellent. When we finished, we encountered a brick wall about seven or eight feet tall that we needed to hop over. Bernard picked Amy up and sat her on the ledge, then climbed over and set her down on the other side. Jonah and I climbed over on our own, and I was surprised I was able to do so. Maybe I was still running on adrenaline from the fight or from the news of now having a bounty on my head. Who knows? I was just glad to have Jonah in my corner to back me up, because if I didn't, this would be a whole lot different.

We took the train back into the city and closed in on Times Square, stopping outside St. Paul's Cathedral. Everyone had been quiet, lost in their own thoughts on the trip over, so I didn't ask where we were going or why. With a quirked eyebrow, I watched Jonah and Bernard climb the cathedral steps while Amy and I stood back.

I wouldn't say I was devout—I mean, I believed—but I didn't go to church every Sunday, only for holiday services. I knew it would never get me into heaven, but after the Change, I didn't think I'd be allowed in. There was no way God would have created a monster like me. I was most likely the devil's work. I didn't deserve to enter holy grounds.

"You two coming?" Jonah called out.

Amy had other reasons for not going in. She didn't really look the part. With all her tattoos and piercings, they'd think she *was* the devil.

"Why are we here?" I questioned.

"We have to talk to someone who lives here," Jonah answered. Not waiting for a response, he turned back around and walked into the church.

Amy shifted uncomfortably next to me. "Are we going in?" she half asked, half groaned. I wanted to say, *hell no*—no pun intended—but I was curious about who we were meeting. It had all the fittings of a typical gothic Roman Catholic Church, including the pointy tower-looking thing in the front, but even with all the fancy architecture, it appeared a little run down. The gray paint was faded and chipped, and the little bit of lawn area around the cathedral teetered between patches of dirt with dead plants, or overgrown grass and weeds.

"I think we should go in," I finally decided. Amy sighed in resignation.

We went up the steps and entered the darkened church. The pews were crooked, and it smelled of sweet incense and extinguished candles, coupled with a hint of something old that I couldn't identify. The only light came from the altar where Jonah and Bernard stood.

"Who are we here to see?" I probed as we approached them.

"*Me*," a voice said from behind us. I whirled around to find...nothing.

"Okay, that's freaky. What the hell was that?"

"Lucian," Jonah called out with a smirk. "Stop playing games and come out. We don't have time for child's play."

"Oh, you're no fun anymore, Jonah Cadwell," said the voice again.

This time, I noticed a very delicate British accent. A figure clad in black emerged from the darkness by the entrance and walked down the aisle between the pews. He was of average height, lean, with blonde hair that was slicked back and came down just below his shoulders. He was pale, like Edward Cullen pale, which was what made my eyes bulge out of their sockets.

"No way," I gasped, causing the vampire to turn and smirk at me. His black eyes twinkled as he got closer to us and the altar lights hit him. He walked towards us—no, scratch that—he glided to us. It was so graceful and quiet, my jaw dropped and I had a hard time picking it up. He was scary—he definitely gave me the heebie-jeebies—but he was also beautiful, like a porcelain doll.

"Well, hello. And who might you be?" he asked as he approached. I couldn't resist flinching as his cold, clammy hand reached for mine and a shiver ran through me. "Wolf got your tongue?" he mocked, and I had to shake myself out of a trance.

"Mackenzie Grey," I said, allowing him to place a soft, but chilling kiss on the top of my hand.

"*Mackenzie Grey*," he repeated. "What a lovely name." His eyes lingered on me for a moment, wondering what I was, and then they traveled to Amy, who stood beside me. "And you?" he said as he raised an eyebrow to Jonah. "Did you bring me a snack?"

I snarled.

"No, Lucian. She is our friend, and resides under the protection of the Pack. Don't touch." Jonah came down from the altar to the bottom of the steps where we were.

Lucian licked his lips as if hungry, but nodded respectfully. "My apologies, young one," he said as his eyes took in Amy's small body. After much difficulty, he tore his gaze away. "To what do I owe this pleasure, then?"

Jonah didn't waste any time. "One of ours is missing. My brother Jackson."

The vampire's pale hand came up to his mouth with mild horror, but it looked exaggerated. "Oh, no, *friend,* when?"

"Yesterday. He was on patrol in Central Park with his team. One of our wolves was killed, and the other is in critical condition. Do you know what might have caused this?"

Lucian's face went neutral and he dug his hands in the pockets of his all-black dress pants that matched his black buttoned-up shirt. "Did you come here, young wolf, to know who may have caused this, or to accuse me of doing it?" he questioned. His accent was so prim and proper, I had to remind myself that what he was saying was slightly threatening.

Jonah growled. "Should I accuse you?"

"Easy, Jonah," Bernard whispered.

The vampire chuckled. "Oh, calm down, wolf. I didn't mean anything by it, but your visits are rare and short in between. I was only curious as to why *I* would be the person you went to, when the Fae seem like a more reasonable choice."

"The Fae?" I questioned. It wasn't the first time I'd heard the name mentioned, but I hadn't asked about it.

"The Fae are fairies. They're a bunch of sneaky bastards who will make you their slaves for a lifetime and then some, if you're not careful," Bernard answered, and I sensed some hostility in him.

"Were you a slave of theirs?" I asked. His disdain sounded personal.

"No. My father was," he answered grimly.

I dropped the subject. This probably wasn't the best time to rehash any of that.

"Why would we go to the Fae?" Amy asked, and I saw Lucian's two black orbs zone in on her neck. He licked his lower lip slowly and I got a glimpse of his fangs. *Oh, crap.*

The vampire winked at me once he caught me staring. "Central Park is Fae territory. If Jackson was taken from there, then I would assume the Fae would know more about this situation than I," he said, looking to Jonah for confirmation.

Ah, I see. Now I understood why the vamp might be a little defensive. I'd take offense too, if a bunch of people barged in with an assumption that I knew something. Didn't mean he was the good guy, though. He had a creep factor that made my skin crawl.

"I have a team going to see them, but I wanted to personally check in with you and see if you had ... " Jonah paused, "any information."

Lucian smirked. "I don't. As a matter of fact, you'll be surprised to know that one of mine has been taken as well."

I gasped. "Why didn't you mention it earlier?" I was a little ticked off. He was so busy being all theatrical in a freakin' church, of all places (I thought they weren't allowed in here?), and never once mentioned we were in the same boat.

"I had to make sure you weren't lying and actually holding my kind hostage," he replied, eyeing me curiously. "You seem new, young Mackenzie Grey, so I will be kind enough to explain what the wolves haven't deemed important enough to mention." He regarded Jonah and Bernard sternly and they growled in response. "Vampires and werewolves do not consider themselves close. At the moment, we walk a very fine line between associates and enemies. We have a lot of history between us that dates back to our time in Europe, from where we were seeded. So please understand, I wouldn't be surprised to find out that the wolves *did* take one of my kindred, especially since we are in the midst of territory disputes." He looked around the cathedral. "Say, where is Sebastian Steel? I would have thought the Alpha Beta would come to see me himself."

Jonah cleared his throat. "He's indisposed."

"Hm. I'm sure he is," Lucian said, baring his teeth. I stepped back from the glare of his fangs. "Now, what I want to know, if you'd be so inclined to answer, is why you've brought a Luna on what I'm assuming is a field assignment? Your kind seem so intent on keeping them hidden and safe within your own quarters, it's shocking and a rare oddity to see one here so open and in the flesh. Not to mention a Luna who doesn't seem ... how should I put it ... oh, yes, she doesn't seem *indoctrinated* yet, if you ask me."

Lucian slowly circled me. I tensed during his perusal; it wasn't hunger I saw in his eyes, but there was a gleam in them that worried me.

"We don't answer to you, *vampire*," Jonah sneered, and I felt him flush against my back. He was staking his claim. He had none, but I didn't feel the need to correct him.

I didn't think Lucian wanted me the way Jonah assumed he did. It was something else, I just didn't know what.

"Right," he said slyly and smiled. "None of my business."

He knew something. That all-knowing look he gave me was too obvious.

"Who's gone missing?" Bernard asked.

"Cassandra," he replied with a grimace, like he'd drank stale blood.

"Your consort?" Jonah asked in shock.

Consort? What were these guys into?

"Yes," Lucian said tightly. "She went out for a feeding without me and never returned. We followed her trail to Strawberry Fields, and that's where it ends."

Jonah placed his hand on my hip and gripped it tightly. "That's where Jackson's scent ends as well."

The vampire didn't look surprised. "Do you think the Fae have something to do with this?"

"I don't know," Jonah whispered, and I put my hand on top of his. He was desperate for any information on his brother. It was hard when there was nothing out there. He was grasping at straws and I wished there was something I could do—no matter how much Jackson got on my nerves.

"Have *you* sent anyone to see the fairies?" Amy asked beside me.

"No, little one, we have not. They are not fond of the undead," Lucian shrugged.

"What if they have someone missing as well?" she prodded.

"Then we need to find out. It's too much of a coincidence that both a vamp and a wolf were taken in the same place and on their territory," Bernard said.

"Are you guys beefing with them also?" I asked.

"What's up with the nineties slang, Kenz?" Amy mumbled.

"The Fae keep to themselves; they don't like to get involved in supernatural politics. That's why the only land they have in New York is Central Park, which is fine by both our kinds. In exchange, the wolves patrol their area, making sure it's safe," Lucian explained.

"If they did take one of ours, then the treaty would be void and that could bring war," Jonah said, but I think he was talking to himself. He sounded lost in thought.

"Yes it would, young wolf. It would, indeed."

14

Amy reached for my other hand and held on to me. She didn't have to say what she was thinking; I already knew. We'd gotten ourselves involved in something we needed to escape. Self-preservation at its finest. No matter how much I wanted to help, I didn't want to get involved if war was the ultimate outcome. This supernatural battle wasn't something I wanted to expose Amy to, much less myself. I'd been pulled into the danger of this Pack, but this wasn't one of my paranormal books. This was real life, and if we got involved, it meant a real death if something went wrong. I was not willing to take that risk.

My fears preoccupied my focus, so I didn't notice what was going on around me until we stepped out of the cathedral and the frigid winter air hit my face. It burned like a crack of a whip. I tried to rub my hands together, but they were still holding on to Amy. Jonah walked ahead of us with Bernard at his side.

"What's going on in that head of yours, Kenz?" Amy finally asked.

"The same thing you're thinking, that we're in over our heads."

"Yeah, I don't know about all this. I'm all for excitement and adventure, but this seems a little too scary for my taste."

The fact Amy admitted she was scared was a wake-up call. Even in the face of danger—or werewolves—she was tougher than nails.

"I think I may need to get out of town for a little while," I admitted.

Amy stopped me in the middle of the sidewalk. "Why?"

I sighed, "Jonah said I may not be able to get away from the Pack unscathed. Their laws are very strict about lone wolves, and I'd be categorized as one if I don't join."

"When have you cared about labels?"

"Amy, they'll kill me. It's Pack or death, no other options. You heard what they said: they hunt lone wolves." I waited for a witty comeback, but she examined something on my chest, avoiding eye contact. She didn't blink or move, but she was breathing, which was good news.

I hadn't planned to reveal my fears to her just yet, but I didn't have much of a choice. If I left, they wouldn't bother with Amy. She could go back to school and her life would go back to normal, but I wouldn't have the same luxury. If I stayed, there was no way Amy would be free of my mess. It would be better for everyone if I removed myself from the equation; then Jonah wouldn't be obligated to hunt me down and kill me once I refused Pack membership.

"Kenz, they can't do that," she scoffed innocently, the glimmer of unshed tears in her eyes as she stared up at me helplessly.

"Amy, please don't—"

"Don't what? Feel like I'm losing my best friend? My sister? My Mackenzie?" she gulped. "You're crazy if you think I'd let you go without me."

"Hey, keep up!" Jonah yelled over to us.

"We'll be there in a sec!" I called back and he nodded. "Listen to me, Amy. You have such a bright future ahead of you. You're a freakin' genius, for Christ sake! I mean, you'll probably graduate and work for Google. And come on, you can't *not* work for Google. They have sleeping pods for day naps and bikes to ride around! It's your dream job!"

"I don't care about any of that!" she argued. "What's the point of it all if I don't have my best friend to enjoy it with me?"

I sighed. She had a point, and if the tables were reversed, I'd be pitching the same tune to her. Amy had stuck by my side since the beginning of all this madness almost four years ago. Trust me, there had been some crazy times, but we managed. I couldn't expect her to just shrug it off and go on with her life. She was right.

"Fine, but let's talk about it later. I don't want Jonah getting suspicious."

We caught up to the two werewolves at the entrance to Central Park. I guess we weren't wasting any time. We entered from Central Park West on 72nd Street, since it was closer to Strawberry Fields. We passed the *Imagine* mosaic and headed toward one of the pavilions by the lake.

"Why are we stopping here?" Amy asked as a glacial breeze ripped through. She shivered, even as burrowed as she was in her bundled-up winter clothes.

"We have to wait for one of the Fae to reveal themselves before we can see them," Jonah explained. "They have something called glamour, where they can hide their true identities from not just us, but humans. Fairies in your culture are thought of as Tinkerbells. Unfortunately, that couldn't be farther from the truth. He paused before continuing in a guarded tone, "When they arrive, don't accept anything from them, and try to avoid saying 'thank you' or 'I'm sorry.' If you do, you'll owe them for the rest of your life."

I looked to Amy and was immediately nervous for her. Amy sometimes spoke before her brain even processed her thoughts, and it had a habit of getting her into trouble. Trouble that could cost her life. *Oy vey.*

"Uh, Aim?"

"I know, Kenz," she deadpanned. "I'll zip it, I promise. You should, too."

I rolled my eyes. At least she understood the importance of it.

"Okay, guys, look alive. It's showtime," Jonah said.

I tensed beside him as I followed his gaze across the lake where there was someone...standing on the water. I had to do a double take because I thought my eyes were playing tricks on me, but they weren't. Even more concerning, that *someone* was headed our way. Just like the vampire, it glided across the lake and barely made a ripple.

Once this person—or Fae—got closer to us, the moonlight illuminated her figure and I was able to get a good look. She wore a soft pink, spaghetti-strapped dress made of sheer fabric. Her white hair fell like a curtain down her back, flowing just past her waist. Two strands of hair were twisted and pinned back on either side, keeping her hair away from her face. And I'll be damned... the chick had elf ears. She stopped at the edge of the lake, but didn't touch land. Her eyes were a spooky, pale gray. Everything about her was just ... pale.

"Jonah Cadwell of the Brooklyn Pack, it is about time you came and paid me a visit," she said in a lilting sing-song voice. "Though I'm surprised Sebastian Steel sent his Beta wolf. I must be special," she purred.

I peered over at Jonah to see him smiling an actual, genuine smile. A low growl escaped me, but luckily no one was near enough to hear it. A possessive streak took over and I intuited that there was history between them.

"Drusilla, long time," Jonah said with a smirk.

"Long time indeed, love." She grinned as if they were in on some joke we weren't. "However, I'm glad he at least sent someone competent enough to deal with this problem," she added, exasperated.

"What problem?" I asked.

She pinned her pale grays on me, and they narrowed to slits. "Who are you?"

"Shh," Jonah shushed me. "This is Mackenzie Grey. Kenzie, this is Drusilla, the Fae Queen of Central Park."

Oh.

"Nice to meet you, uh, your highness?" I sounded completely ridiculous, which was proven by Amy's giggles behind me. *I didn't know this chick was the queen.*

She huffed, "So mundane. Did you just recruit this one, love? I feel sorry for whatever wolf she breeds. I'm afraid it won't be too intelligent."

Oh, no, she didn't. How dare she talk about the future wolf babies I'm never going to have!

I snarled. Jonah placed a warning grip on my forearm and I

snapped my attention to him. "Not now," he mouthed, forcing me to swallow my pride.

"What's the problem, Drusilla?" he asked her, completely at ease.

She eyed me for a moment longer and then turned back to Jonah, who earned her bright smile. *Bitch.*

"Branwell has been taken, and your wolves were supposed to be here to protect us. Is our treaty in jeopardy, love?"

God, if she calls him 'love' one more time, I'm going to snap.

"Drusilla, my brother was taken from here last night. We came to see if you knew anything about it, which I'm guessing you don't," Jonah admitted, running his hand roughly through his hair. He was stressed and his desperation showed.

"I warrant it's the vampires!" she exclaimed. I shook my head.

"The vampires have someone missing as well. It's not them," I inserted. From the look of Jonah, he wasn't in a position to speak. I could see the wheels spinning in his head as he tried to put the pieces together. Who was taking these people?

"Such a foolish little girl. You should never believe a breath that comes out of a night walker," she said condescendingly.

"Vampires can't breathe; they're dead."

"I think that was her point, Kenz," Amy whispered.

Oh, whatever. That was lame.

"Boss, I think we need to head back and regroup," Bernard suggested to Jonah, who nodded.

"Oh no, don't go, love. Why don't you come and spend the night?" She paused and looked to me. "You know, for old time's sake."

Okay, lady, I got the message.

I scoffed, "I don't think he's in the mood to roll around in the hay with you. Don't know if you got the memo, but his brother's been kidnapped." With that comment, I was pretty sure I made her shit list.

"Mackenzie's right, Drusilla," Jonah started. "Now is not the time, although I appreciate the offer," he said and bowed.

"Very well, love. If you need any assistance finding the missing ones, I will offer what I can. I give you my word." Without another word, she turned around to leave.

I held my breath until I couldn't see her retreating figure across the lake anymore. I hadn't realized how cold I was until a shiver came through me and my teeth chattered. Amy snuggled in closer to me.

"Is the coast clear?" Amy whispered.

"Yeah, she's gone," Bernard answered, his body sagging in relief.

I would have to remember to ask him—when the time was right, of course—what happened to his dad, and if he was still alive. I imagined it wasn't easy for him to see the Fae Queen and not want to throttle her. I know I did.

"We need to call Sebastian," Jonah said. "If it's not the vampires or the fae, then I don't know which of the million other possibilities to pursue."

"How safe is it to contact him?"

"I don't know, but we need to try. I just don't know what to do anymore," Jonah admitted.

With those words, I wanted nothing more than to take him away from all of this. *Gosh, when did I become such a softy?* I dug into Jonah's pocket, making him jump, and pulled out his phone. It wasn't locked, so I swiped it open and scanned his contacts for Sebastian's number. While I waited for someone to answer, three sets of eyes watched me. We were on a time crunch, and it seemed Sebastian was the only one who could help.

"Hello?" a gruff voice that belonged to the Alpha answered.

"Bash?"

"Mackenzie," he sighed. I couldn't tell if he was disappointed or glad to hear from me. "Where are you?"

"Safe, if that's what you're wondering." He chuckled. It sounded beautiful.

"Yes, that is exactly what I wanted to hear," he sighed in relief. "Good. Stay away from the warehouse until Jonah gets this squared away."

Yeah...I'm about to burst that bubble.

"Jonah is with me, Bash. We had to leave the warehouse." I gathered my courage before uttering those three little words. "We need you," I whispered. I could have sworn I heard a small gasp from the other end of the line, but maybe it was my imagination.

"Where are you?" Sebastian lost all the weakness from his voice and I heard the Alpha in him, loud and clear.

After I explained where we were, he told me to stay by the *Imagine* mosaic and he'd be there in twenty minutes. How he was going to pull that off was beyond me.

"What were you thinking, Kenz?" Jonah grabbed his phone from me. I shook my head and smashed my lips together. If they needed an Alpha to track Jackson down, then that's what we would get. I didn't want to mess this up worse than I already had.

The guys waited for Sebastian by the Central Park West entrance while Amy and I sat on the ground, tracing the word *IMAGINE*, which was written on the ground.

"What do you have in mind, Kenz?"

"Nothing, really. I just thought we needed his help. We have nothing but a pile of missing people."

"Yeah, well, I think Jonah's worried Bash will hurt you or turn you over to the Summit. I don't think he will, though."

My eyes snapped to hers. "He will if he has to."

Amy snorted. "Kenzie, sometimes I think you're a little slow, like special bus, handicap slow." She rolled her eyes. "Sebastian won't hurt you because he wants in your pants, dude. Just like Jonah."

I waited for her to tell me she was joking, but I got nothing. She was dead serious, and I felt the blood drain from my face.

Amy put a hand on my back to keep me up straight. "Easy there, babe. Just take some deep breaths. It's not that bad," she grinned. "Two hunks panting after you isn't the end of the world."

If she only knew ... which she didn't, and I couldn't say I was totally clear on it, either. In any event, I knew that getting involved with either of them would be disastrous. Besides having to become a Luna and therefore transform into a fifties-style housewife, the thought of being with another guy other than James sort of freaked me out.

I spent the last couple months reflecting on my past relationship, and after what happened between me and James at Angelina's during brunch, I came to a solid decision—I wanted to be alone. It took me a while to realize it, and sure, I was lonely sometimes, but it was such a momentary, inconsequential feeling. Besides, being out of commission three days out of the month with the Change didn't help my chances with anyone. It was difficult enough keeping that secret from James for almost four years. I didn't want to go through that again. Secrets could suffocate the strongest of loves.

I'd be lying if I said I wasn't attracted to both Bash and Jonah, but my self-preservation overrode it all. No matter how emotionally compromised I might be, it wouldn't change my mind. I couldn't be with either of them.

"That's not true," I said hoarsely.

"You're a horrible liar, Kenz. I know you see it, and if you didn't, you do now. I get it, you know, if you're not ready after James. That's cool. But don't pretend these guys don't care about you because they do, and it's obvious to everyone but you."

That was the worst thing she could have said—that I could become their weakness.

I shivered and shrunk into my coat, but I wasn't cold. The idea that both Sebastian and Jonah liked me caused my skin to tingle.

"Heads up," Bernard yelled over to us and we jumped to our feet. The plan was for me and Amy to blend into the night in case Sebastian was not alone.

Jonah approached warily and stood in the middle of the mosaic with Bernard. Seconds later, Sebastian came into view. He appeared sluggish from our encounter, but okay all the same.

"Don't worry, I'm alone. My pride is wounded, but I still have my sense of smell," Sebastian grumbled.

"Sorry, Boss, we're only taking precautions," Bernard apologized.

"Good. I'm glad you are. Where is she?"

"Here," I said, stepping out of the tree lines, Amy following behind me. *Damn, that spray worked well.*

In three long strides, he came to stand in front of me and grabbed my upper arms, pulling me closer to him. His glacial blue eyes pierced me in place, scanning my face and then my entire body. "Did I hurt you?" he asked softly.

For a moment I was confused by how tenderly he spoke to me. He usually hated my guts and was always pissed off.

"Uh, no, I'm fine. Are you okay?"

"Yes." His calloused hand came up to my cheek and he softly caressed it with his rough knuckles. The crinkles in the corners of his eyes appeared and he smiled at me. "Good. I was worried for a moment."

I felt like I was in an alternate universe. Why was he being— so unlike Sebastian? "Bash, are you sure you're okay? Did you hit your head?" Amy snickered behind me.

His face darkened. "Why?"

"You're never nice to me, so what gives?" After my conversation with Amy, I could see how it was possible he wanted in my pants, but to be, well, *loving* like Jonah was just plain weird.

He smirked and stepped away, leaving a gap between us that made me feel hollow. "You don't take compliments well, you know that, Mackenzie?"

"Nope, she doesn't," Amy exhaled.

We walked over to Bernard and Jonah, who looked like he'd just swallowed a whole bag of Sour Patches in one shot.

"What have you learned so far?" Sebastian asked, getting right down to business.

"Both the vamps and Fae have one of their kin missing," Bernard started, "which rules them out as suspects, unless someone within them is working of their own accord."

"What other supernaturals are out there? If one is missing from each race, then there might be more missing from others," Amy piped in.

Sebastian raised an eyebrow at her. "Very smart, and very correct. It seems like we have someone collecting different species." He scratched at his five o'clock shadow. "But for what? Is someone making a menagerie?"

"Possibly, but could it be one of us? The only thing that makes sense is if a human was collecting," Jonah said, looking pointedly at Amy.

He better not even think *about it. She would never do that.*

"A human?" Bernard scoffed. "They aren't strong enough to subdue one wolf, much less three."

"Not unless they've gotten close to us and we didn't see it coming," Jonah continued.

I shot laser beams at him. "Don't even think about it, asshole," I snarled, which got everyone's attention. Amy hadn't noticed he was insinuating it was her, but I refused to let him put any more of those ridiculous thoughts out there.

Jonah asked, "How well do you even know her, Mackenzie? Jackson was clearly attracted to her when they first met."

"Oh, wow, *now* we're on a first name basis? Got it, but if you must know, I'd stake my life on how well I know Amy. How dare you accuse her without proof! She's the only person who's been there for me since the very beginning, while the rest of you had no idea you had a lone wolf in the city who was lost and scared! If you come after her, then be ready to come after me too." I felt my body getting warm. The coat I wore itched my skin.

"I didn't kidnap anyone!" Amy shrieked. "Hello? Do you not see how tiny I am? I can't even reach the top cupboard in the kitchen!"

"Enough," Sebastian said, but it wasn't as strong as before. *Which reminds me ...*

"How's your, uh, your—" I started, looking down at his crotch not so smoothly.

"My family jewels?" He quirked an eyebrow.

"Uh, yeah..." I looked away, feeling a blush creep up my neck.

It got quiet for a few seconds and then Jonah, Bernard, and even Sebastian exploded into laughter. And I mean *really* laughing, like slap your knee, dry heaving.

I cleared my throat loudly. "Um, hello? What's so funny? This shit is serious! I could have ripped your balls off!"

Sebastian finally managed to compose himself, but still spoke between bouts of laughter. "Mackenzie, I'm fine. Nothing an ice pack can't cure."

My face fell. *Well, duh.* I crossed my arms over my chest. "Whatever. You know what I'm trying to say, so shut it."

"Kenz, you really need to learn how to fight," Jonah suggested, coming up to my other side. "You're lucky Bash didn't hurt you." He paused. "I don't think he was willing to do that."

Oh, boy, does Jonah know something? How does everyone else know but me? Better yet, this is all bullshit. He was boning V the other day in his office. They're all full of crap.

"Bash," Jonah looked to him, "I think she needs to go on a vision quest. She needs to get in touch with her wolf."

"How did we go from me needing to learn to fight, to this?"

"It'll help if you're connected to your wolf during a fight. Every Pack member does it."

"Don't worry about my wolf," I said a little too aggressively. I didn't like that they were automatically including me in Pack stuff. "She and I have an understanding." Which we did. It wasn't something we'd actually spoken about, but more like a strange feeling in the pit of my stomach. Whenever someone mentioned joining the Pack, I felt dread—and I wasn't the only one who felt it—the wolf did as well. She liked being a lone wolf, which was fine by me.

Jonah watched me and then looked to Sebastian. "What do you think, boss?"

He sighed. "If you truly had a hold on your wolf, then you wouldn't have almost shifted in front of your brother and boyfriend. A vision quest could help you with that."

"What's a vision quest?" Amy asked.

"It's a rite of passage for our kind. We spend anywhere between one to four days secluded in nature to connect with our inner wolf. Sometimes it's just guidance or understanding that we receive, and sometimes we get visions of our future. It depends," Sebastian explained.

"We'll have to wait until we go to the Estate," Jonah said.

Sebastian nodded. "In the meantime, I can prepare you for it. I won't lie to you and tell you it's easy. We usually don't take our pups out until they hit puberty and have had years of preparation. You could lose control."

"What do you mean?"

He cleared his throat. "We've had cases where the wolf overpowers their humanity. Their animalistic side takes over and they become savage—deadly. It's rare, but it still happens. Since you haven't been prepped for this all your life like most wolves have, there's a higher probability rate."

"What can we do to prevent it?" My voice sounded so small, even to myself.

"Cram as much info as we can before we go to the Estate, and in the meantime, teach you some self-defense."

"Be careful," Jonah warned, his eyes flashing gold.

"I won't hurt her, *Beta*," Sebastian snarled, emphasizing Jonah's lower position.

I rolled my eyes at the two men who pulled at my heart strings, already preparing my mind and body to get my ass handed to me. I lucked out the first time with Sebastian, but I doubt I'd get away with it again.

"Alright, let's get started," I mumbled, walking to the middle of the mosaic. I dropped down and placed a palm on top of the carving that read, IMAGINE. *I'm sorry if I mess this up, John*, I silently apologized in case we cracked the Lennon memorial.

"Hold on, Mackenzie." Sebastian approached me. "Not here."

"Where are you thinking, boss?" Bernard questioned.

"I think we should split up." He avoided looking at me, directing his command to Jonah. "You, Bernard, and Amy should find shelter for the night. Mackenzie and I will do the same."

I quirked an eyebrow. I didn't know if my imagination was running wild now that I let Amy put crazy thoughts in my head, but it was starting to feel obvious, even to someone as oblivious as me, and the look on Jonah's face wasn't helping. His nostrils flared—he was trying to keep his wolf at bay.

"Why?" he clipped out. Bernard and Amy backed away a little and I felt like copying them. I didn't want to be the reason they fought.

"Because I'm the best fighter, and the best person to teach her how to defend herself. And mainly, because I'm *Alpha*." His sapphire eyes glowed fierce.

"Whoa! Slow down there, tiger. I don't need self-defense classes. I've survived the concrete jungle for the past four years; I'll be fine." I peered over at a very quiet Jonah.

"You need to learn some basic self-defense," Jonah admitted softly. I wasn't convinced he wanted me to, but I didn't argue.

"Mackenzie, your mouth will get you into a lot of trouble in the future. This is for the best," Sebastian said.

It was hard to take offense. He was right. To think I was worried about Amy and the Fae. I should be worried about myself.

"Fine," I agreed. "But Amy needs to come with me. I don't want her out of my sight."

"If something—I'm not saying it will—but if something were to happen, I can't defend both of you. You can't afford distractions, which is why it should only be the two of us."

I looked to my best friend, who I could tell didn't like the plan any more than I did. But with a slight nod, she agreed and that was that.

"Where will you go?" Bernard asked.

"Don't worry." Sebastian finally turned to look at me. "I have the perfect place in mind."

15

As we exited Central Park through 5th Avenue, all I had a chance to do was give Amy a quick hug goodbye. I tried to talk to Jonah, but he wouldn't even look my way. I missed seeing his one dimple. He left the park with Bernard, who gave me an apologetic wave behind Jonah's back.

I wasn't convinced about the necessity of this plan because I wanted Amy as close to me as possible, but I knew Jonah wouldn't let anything happen to her. I shouldn't underestimate my tiny best friend. She was bad to the bone, and even though she'd become quiet lately, I knew she could hold her own when push came to shove.

"Where are we going?"

Sebastian looked down at me with a smirk. *That's a first.*

"You'll find out soon enough, Mackenzie."

I huffed, "Can we talk about something? I'm kind of bored just walking in silence, and my feet hurt."

I knew I sounded like the immature child that irritated him, but the suspense was killing me. I couldn't help but feel awkward around Sebastian. Aside from the intimidation factor and the fact we'd been walking in silence for miles, he was just so goddamn perfect I couldn't help but stare and drool. Okay, maybe I was exaggerating, but it was hard *not* to when the man wore shirts so tight, they looked like another layer of skin. Every defined cut of muscle was as if God himself carved them from marble.

"Fine. Why don't you tell me what's going on between you and Jonah?" he probed without looking back at me. That made me pause.

"Why don't you tell me about you and V first?" I retorted, which earned me one of his patented glares. *There's the Sebastian I know.*

"That's none of your business."

"Then Jonah and I aren't any of *your* business." Truthfully, there was nothing going on between us, but then again there was ... Did that make sense?

"Any wolf of mine is my business."

"Luckily, I'm not your wolf. If you have any questions, please refer them to Jonah." I tilted my chin up high and gave him a smug look. He wouldn't get any answers out of me—because I didn't have them. I'd get struck by lightning if I said there was nothing between me and Jonah, and the past two days we spent sequestered at my parents' house complicated our friendship further.

We stopped in front of the New York Public Library and my eyes rolled up the steps, past the two marble lions, and at the entrance to Astor Hall.

"Uh...what are we doing here?" I said with my mouth slightly agape.

The library was secretly a safe haven for me, providing access to unlimited amounts of books that ranged from classics to everyone's favorite mommy porn. A place where you could be anyone and go anywhere, transported in the pages of a book. It was magic.

"I thought this would be the perfect place to hide out. It's the last place the Pack would come look."

"I guess that makes sense," I mumbled, and followed Sebastian up the stairs. Once we made it to the door, an older gentleman opened it for us.

"Mister Steel, how nice to see you again." The older man bowed and stood to the side to let us pass. My jaw fell as we crossed the breathtaking, white marble entrance of Astor Hall.

The last time I was here, one of Amy's old socialite friends was having a birthday party and I was Amy's plus one. Standing here in the daylight was almost as amazing as it had been back then. During freshman year, I would come here to escape and beg the librarians for a free tour of the basement stacks under Bryant Park. With a student budget, I couldn't afford the costly tours. In those days, I stole toilet paper from The Brew; ate tencent Ramen noodles for breakfast, lunch, and dinner; and drank coffee from the bank. And let's get real, there were only so many times a day I could check my bank account balance—which was already a scary sight. I sighed. *The good ole' broke days.*

Sebastian cleared his throat. "Mackenzie, this is Gerard Wilson. Gerard, this is Mackenzie Grey."

I turned around and saw Gerard come my way. Without breaking eye contact, he grabbed my upper arms and held me in place. Holding me at arm's length, he sized me up and down and then grunted.

"You're a pretty young lady," he paused and quirked a bushy white eyebrow, "why do you look so manly?"

Sebastian gave out a choked sound and I knew he was holding back a laugh. The asshole.

"I don't know, sir. It's the way I'm built," I said with a tight smile.

The old man rumbled, "You need to stop lifting weights and maybe put on a dress." He turned back to Bash. "The Wachenheim Trustee's Room is available for the night. We had an event, and there are some sofas that haven't been picked up yet. Just remember, no funny business, Mister Steel." With that, Gerard pivoted to leave.

"Follow me," Sebastian demanded in his I'm-the-boss voice. I rolled my eyes, but kept my mouth shut. I was too drained and tired to argue. This plan of splitting up felt like a bunch of B.S. and I wanted to talk to Amy.

I walked behind Sebastian across Astor Hall, past a hallway, and into the first room on our left. As the door opened, I was rewarded with a breathtaking sight.

"Do you like it?"

I turned to stare at Bash, who was watching my expression closely. "Yeah," I answered cautiously, sighing as I twirled around, looking at the ceiling.

He walked to the wall and slid his hand down it. "These are walnut paneled walls, and the fireplace is made of marble. This is one of my favorite drawing rooms here at the library," he admitted, his uncharacteristically soft voice sending flutters through my stomach.

"You come here often?"

When he nodded, I was shocked. He seemed like such a

brutish werewolf.

"I didn't peg you for the bookworm type," I admitted as I settled on one of the sofas. It was a relief to my poor, abused feet. I'd put some miles on them today.

"I'm actually not. I just like the peace and quiet of a library. It's a nice escape from everyday life. I'm sure you can understand." He narrowed his eyes at me.

I looked away, uncomfortable. "Yeah, I know what you mean."

"I'll be back," he said abruptly, and disappeared back into Astor Hall.

I took advantage of my momentary solitude to lie down and pull out my phone. I missed my best friend. To be quite honest, being around Bash made me nervous. It was a feeling I wasn't particularly familiar with, and would rather not be.

I dialed her number and sighed in relief when she answered on the first ring.

"Kenz! I miss you! Where are you? I was just about to text you," she said in a loud whisper.

I smiled. "I don't know if I can say where we are, but I miss you too. Are you okay? Are they treating you good?"

"Everything is fine. We're back in Alphabet City at the apartment. I'm just bored. I didn't think werewolves could be so lame."

I chuckled. "Yeah, tell me about it. Hopefully, this will resolve itself pretty soon."

"Kenz?"

"Yeah?"

"When are we leaving?"

I expelled a heavy breath. I hadn't thought much about it, but it was as if I already knew. "After the third full moon," I whispered into the phone. Bash wasn't around, but I didn't want to take any chances with his supersonic wolf hearing. I couldn't afford to have them discover my plans.

"Okay. That gives us like, a week, right?"

I nodded as if she could see me. "Almost a week."

"Before the first night, I'll drain my trust."

My eyes widened. "No! Amy no, are you crazy? That's *your* money."

"Kenz, don't worry. I can always ask my folks for more, but when we leave, we need something to get out of here and start a new life. We need it."

Suddenly, I felt like shit. I didn't want to be indebted to her more than I already was. My debt to Amy wasn't about money, but I owed her for sticking by me when I found out about the Change. That was something I knew I could never repay. And now she wanted to throw all her money away because of me again? I couldn't let her do it.

"Amy—"

"It's a done deal, Kenzie. Drop the subject." I didn't bother arguing. "Listen, the guys are coming back, and I have to go before they start asking questions. See you tomorrow?"

"See you tomorrow," I agreed, and we said our goodnights.

I shut my eyes and covered them with my forearms to hide from the lights above. My recent conversation with Amy still resonated in my head. *Where could we go?* I couldn't imagine going too far, but I felt like that would be my only choice. The farther away I went, the safer I would be.

My body relaxed and sleep crept to take me under when Sebastian walked back into the room on soundless feet.

"Wake up!" he barked. I knew his kindness wouldn't last long. He's such an ass hat.

"What?" I snapped, not bothering to sit up.

"I said I'd teach you some self-defense."

"Can we do it tomorrow? I'm really tired." I knew I was whining, but I was tired. It had been a long day—it was still freakin' Christmas! So much happened in such a short period of time, I was surprised I was still sane.

"You can rest when you're dead. Come on, get up. I don't like repeating myself."

I grumbled as I sat up and rubbed the sleep out of my eyes. With my eyes at half mast, I dragged my feet over to an empty space by the fireplace.

"Fine. Let's get this over with," I mumbled, and saw irritation flash across his face. No matter how he made me feel, I didn't care. I was sick of all this bullshit werewolf stuff. I wanted my life back to a time when they weren't a part of it. It was easier. I guess things could never be as easy as we wanted them to be.

"Mackenzie, you may think this is a chore to you now, but one day, it may save your life. You're too young to understand now, but you will one day."

The way he spoke reminded me of my father.

"Oh, please. You make it sound as if you're so damn old. What are you, like, twenty-five?"

He snorted. "Add another ten to that."

My jaw dropped. "What? You can't be thirty-five!" *Shit.* I'd been crushing on an old guy. I know, I was exaggerating again, but compared to my sprightly twenty-two years, he was thirteen years my senior. That was a pretty big age gap.

"We age differently than humans. Our process is a lot slower," he said in a serious tone.

I plopped myself down on the ground, elbows on my knees, and rested my chin on my hands.

"Does this mean I'm going to live until I'm like, a hundred?"

He snorted, grabbing a nearby chair and sitting down. "Probably not."

My face fell. "Why not?"

"We also tend to die young. There are many dangers out there, Mackenzie, and we live off animal instinct, which means we're rash and ill-tempered. Unless we're able to communicate well with our wolf, we get killed off," he intoned, his face grave.

A knot in the pit of my stomach formed, and I wondered how long I would last on my own. Jonah said vampires hunted lone wolves. I wouldn't be running from just the Pack, but from vampires as well.

"Do you think I can survive on my own?" I spoke my thoughts out loud, shocked at how honest the question was, and how important his answer would be.

He watched me for a moment, and I shifted under his scrutiny.

"I don't know," he finally said in a gruff voice. I felt my insides tighten. "You're still a pup, Mackenzie. It's too early to tell, but you seem like a fighter. I'd bet on you."

I looked up at him, unable to hold back a small smile. I know, it's cheesy, but it meant a lot that he had some confidence in me —a confidence I wasn't sure I had in myself.

He slapped his open palms on his thighs to signal the end of the conversation, and the sound echoed in the sparse room. It made me jump. "Alright, let's start so we can at least have a couple hours of shut eye." He stood up and started stretching side to side.

I slowly got up and he came to a stop in front of me. He was close enough that I could feel the heat radiate off his skin. It gave me goosebumps.

His scent was different from Jonah's, but I caught the familiar woodsy smell. While Jonah emitted a fresh air aroma that reminded me of the outdoors, Sebastian had a rugged musk to him.

I tried to control my breathing at our close proximity. I made the mistake one time of letting Jonah catch my heart rate, but I wouldn't give Sebastian that victory. Giving him that knowledge seemed dangerous. And in typical Kenzie fashion, I babbled to distract both him and my nerves.

"How did Jonah become your Beta? Are you guys close? What about Jackson? Do you think we'll find him? What if we don't? Can—"

"Mackenzie," he cut me off, pressing his lips in a tight line. "Breathe."

I expelled a breath. *Great, so much for being discreet.*

"Jonah and I are best friends, like you and Amy. We grew up together, the three of us. But Jackson always liked to do his own thing, so it was usually just me and Jonah. That's why I made him my Beta, my second in command. I wouldn't trust anyone else."

My voice hitched, "You guys are best friends? Like besties?" I wanted to face-palm myself, but I didn't expect that. Sebastian seemed like a loner, a workaholic—I didn't think he was capable of having friends.

He nodded and I wanted to crawl into a hole. My presence here was destroying a bromance.

16

"Take a step back, rotate your right hand clockwise outward, and pull your assailant in. His grip will loosen, and then you can do the combo I showed you. Right hook, left hook, and a knee to the nose. Got it?"

"Got it."

We'd been working on fighting moves and techniques for at least two hours, and I was beyond exhausted. My legs and arms were jelly.

"Come on, Mackenzie. Your attacker won't wait for you to catch your breath."

"Yeah, well, thankfully my assailant isn't here yet and I can," I said as I rolled my eyes.

"Don't do that," he barked.

I flinched.

"Don't do what?"

"Roll your eyes," he growled, which made me do it again.

Who the hell does he think he is? Not even my parents acted that way.

"Mackenzie," he sneered.

With renewed strength, I walked over to him, looked him dead in the eyes, and started rolling them like an idiot, over and over again.

His growl grew louder, and even though I was making myself dizzy, I refused to stop. He gripped my upper arm and pulled me toward him like a defiant child. It startled me enough that a gasp escaped my lips.

"Hey!" I tried to pull away, but his hold on me was strong.

"I told you to stop," he gritted through clenched teeth.

I took a step back, rotated my left arm counterclockwise, and pulled—just as he'd taught me. Using a little extra power from my wolf, he tipped slightly forward and lost most of his grip on me. Instead of doing the combo, I pushed him off and took a couple steps back, away from him.

"I think you're getting a little abusive, so I suggest you tone that shit down," I snapped with enough anger laced in my voice so that he got the hint. I didn't know how submissive Lunas were supposed to be, but I was *not* down with that shit. If I wanted to roll my goddamn eyes, I would. I might be obnoxious, but it didn't give him the right to put me in my place. I was not part of his Pack.

His face softened just a smidge, but not enough for me to feel sorry for him. "I didn't mean to do that," he said, looking down at his hands.

"Yeah, well, I think we've done enough for tonight."

"No. We're going to continue," he argued and started towards me.

"Sebastian, I said *enough!*" I yelled. Surprised, he stopped in his tracks just two feet away from me. "I don't care if you're the goddamn President of the United States, I said I'm done." I turned around to return to the sofa where I'd tried to catch a snooze earlier, when he grabbed my upper arm again and twirled me around.

"What the fu—?"

"I'm sorry," he said, chastened. I swallowed my curse. "I didn't mean to get rough. I have to remember that even though you're a wolf, you're more human than anything. I'm not used to being disobeyed."

"I'm not part of your Pack, either. You need to chill out, Bash."

"I know," he admitted gruffly. "Just bear with me ... please?"

I narrowed my eyes so he knew I wouldn't be so easily persuaded, but deep down, I knew I'd already forgiven him. Not that I'd forget how rough he was, but I would be more careful the next time I wanted to ruffle some feathers. I wanted him to know I wouldn't put up with abusiveness, and it was best if he realized it early on.

I nodded and he released my arm. He reached around and slid his hand down my back, directing me toward the sofa. I sat down and he sat beside me, but he seemed odd sitting there. Sebastian's frame swallowed the lounger we were on, like a parent sitting in one of their children's play chairs for tea time. With his back a tight rod, he sat upright, his palms flat on his thighs.

"I need to know, Mackenzie," he said without looking at me, "is there anything between you and Jonah?"

I sat stock still, holding my ragged breaths. I didn't want to say yes or no. The only thing running through my mind was, *How the hell did I get into a situation like this?*

I'd never been a beauty queen, but I wasn't ugly, either. At least I didn't think so. My eyes were usually what attracted men; they were a rare, clear grey. While I did get hit on from time to time, I usually had a permanent resting bitch face that dissuaded anyone who was interested. But I'd never been put in the middle between two guys. Especially two guys to whom I was equally attracted.

Jonah was soft, warm, and safe, whereas Sebastian was hard, callous, and dangerous. You'd think this would be an easy decision, but it wasn't.

It wasn't fair of me to contemplate anything with Sebastian after leading Jonah on, because if I was being honest, that's what I did back in Cold Springs—unintentionally—but I did.

"Why?" I croaked, my throat going dry. I didn't want to assume he was interested in me.

"Isn't it obvious, Mackenzie?" His voice was loud in the quietness of the library.

"You act like you hate me most of the time I'm around. So no, it's not obvious."

He scoffed and dragged his blue eyes my way. "I don't hate you. You're sometimes immature, but that's because you're young."

"If I'm so immature, what's your deal?" *The same question I asked Jonah.*

He took a deep breath while I held mine, and my stomach knotted as I waited for his response.

"I want you."

My stomach lurched. This couldn't be happening to me, the

girl who never cared about having a boyfriend. Especially after James, whose shitty behavior made me swear off men. But being with Jonah and Sebastian made me forget who I was and always had been.

"That's not possible. You're with V," I stammered, confused.

He grimaced. "I'm not *with* her. She takes care of my needs, and that's the extent of our relationship," he explained with a straight face, like this was normal behavior.

"So, she's a booty call?"

"A what?"

"Never mind." I slumped back on the sofa. "Bash, things are messed up right now. Jackson's still missing, and I'm not part of your Pack. Let's prioritize."

"No."

"What?"

"I *am* prioritizing. We cannot do anything about those problems at this precise moment, so it leads me to this. I want you, and I need you to say yes."

Why couldn't I just say no? I searched the room as if the answer would be etched on the walnut walls. "You don't know me, Bash." It was true, he didn't. He couldn't want someone he knew nothing about, especially someone like me, an unknown variable from outside the Pack. They didn't even know where I came from.

"I want to get to know you, but I won't share you. I need you to be completely mine," he growled, causing the hairs on my arm to stand up.

As much of a feminist as I was, I should've been offended by his possessiveness—but I wasn't. Something inside me stirred, and I felt it all the way down to my core. I didn't understand what was happening to me.

"*Sebastian*," I hummed. As soon as the sound left my lips, he reached over and pulled me on top of him. I straddled him and felt my eyes go unfocused, a glint of silver surrounding my vision.

His mouth slid from the crevice of my shoulder and neck and brushed up until his breath tickled behind my ear. As my fingers dug into his pitch-black locks, it was like running my hands through silk. His tongue lightly traced a path down my neck and I closed my eyes.

I heard a faraway voice screaming in my head, *What are you doing?!* I ignored it.

With my chest flush against his, he bit my earlobe and growled, pushing my hips down on him. My eyes flicked wide open and I gasped.

"Say it. Say you're mine," he rasped in my ear.

"Sebastian, *please*." I tried to speak but couldn't catch my breath.

"Say it *now*," he commanded, and a shiver went down my spine.

"N-no." I pushed him away. With my hand firmly placed on his chest, he sat back against the couch. I was able to breathe once we were at arm's length, although I was still on top of him. I shook my head to clear it from the fog of sexual frustration. "Sebastian, this isn't right. I can't control her when I'm like this."

"Don't try to control her. Set her free," he argued as he tried to pull me to him again.

He was strong, but my resolve was stronger. Thankfully, Jonah had somewhat explained it to me, and I knew this was my wolf's doing. She wanted this—not that I didn't—but I was more reserved.

"No." At the firmness of my voice, he stopped moving. "I'm not like this."

I got off him with shaky legs and put a couple feet between us. My chest heaved rapidly as I held back the torrent of tears that threatened to stream down my face. I didn't want to cry in front of him. The tears weren't because I was sad; they were borne of frustration in more ways than one. I didn't know what to do. I wanted to give in and provide the wolf the release she craved, but I couldn't. My human self wouldn't let her.

God, I need to be locked up in an asylum.

"Your eyes tell me otherwise, Mackenzie. So tell me – what are you like?" He stood up from the sofa, reminding me of a panther stalking its prey as he strolled towards me. His blue eyes never left mine, and I was very aware of every part of my flushed body. I could still feel where he had touched me and where he hadn't—where I wanted him to. I shook my head.

"You're not playing fair, Bash," I stuttered.

He smirked. "I know."

"Then stop."

He came to a halt a few inches away from me. His hand trailed through my hair as the curls fell onto my chest. A shudder racked through me. I didn't know how long I would be able to keep the wolf at bay.

"I won't stop until I get what I want."

So fast I didn't even register it in time, he grabbed me.

Without thinking, I wrapped my legs around his waist and held onto his shoulders. He held me as if I barely weighed a pound.

"I don't know what it is about you, Mackenzie Grey, but I want you more than I care about being Alpha. You're different—a fighter—and that does something to me," his deep voice whispered. With one hand, he reached for the button of my jeans. "I need to mark you as mine."

The sound of my zipper echoed loudly in the room and my teeth chattered in response. I wanted it, but there was still resistance. As my humanity fought with my animalistic side, I felt like I was going crazy; too many warring, conflicting emotions and sensations ramped me into overdrive, and I felt like I would combust. His touch alone would be my undoing.

My back touched the wall, but once he started to slide my jeans over my ass, my body froze in fear.

"Stop," I croaked. "Sebastian, no, enough."

He stopped.

"I can't. It's not right. Jonah and me...I don't know what we are, but this isn't right."

My legs unwrapped from around his waist and I slid down the wall, his body still pressed against mine.

"I already asked you about Jonah," he growled, but I didn't care if he was pissed. I was having a hard time sorting through my emotions. "It's a *privilege* to be with an Alpha."

"Dude, back off! I don't give a shit what you are. I'm going through something right now, and I think I need Jonah's help. He helped me last time," I panted, out of breath. With my hands on my knees, I tried to steady myself, but I felt like the wolf would claw herself out of me.

Just breathe.

How could I want two guys at the same time? It shouldn't be possible.

Just breathe.

"What's wrong?" Sebastian barked, making me jump. His tone had gone back to being serious, and I knew it was because he was angry.

"I don't know," I stammered. "I feel like she's about to take over. She's too strong, it's suffocating."

He chastised, "You need to let her out—"

"No!" I yelled. "Do *not* take advantage of me right now," I ground out through my teeth.

He tensed.

"If you can't help me, then give me space to handle it on my own, you arrogant bastard."

His chilling blue eyes narrowed. "Get some rest. I'll wake you in the morning. Is that enough space?" Without another word, he turned around, walked to the door, and slammed it shut, leaving me alone and cold.

Just breathe.

What is going on?

My neck was stiff when I woke up the next morning. After much tossing and turning, almost to the point of calling Jonah, I was finally able to fall asleep to calm my wolf down.

Sebastian left when he clearly saw I needed help. Jonah wouldn't have left me. *Ugh.* I knew I shouldn't be comparing them, compiling a list of one's faults against the other's gifts. I should be trying to forget them. It was only fair. Once all this was said and done, I'd be gone. After the next full moon, I would leave. I didn't know where, only that it would be far away from them and one step closer to my freedom.

Just then, Sebastian barged into the room and knocked my feet off the sofa.

"Get up," he commanded. I opened one eye and stared at him incredulously.

He loomed over me and I felt a pinch of fear. I had to remember how dangerous he was, a natural predator. I couldn't let my attraction to these wolves get in the way, because sooner or later, they would get what they wanted.

"What time is it?" I answered sleepily.

"Six in the morning."

I groaned. "Seriously? I just shut my eyes!"

"The library will be opening soon. We need to go and meet the others."

I stared at him blankly. "It's the day after Christmas, and Canadian Boxing Day. I doubt the library is going to open."

"Mackenzie, let's go."

Before I could respond, he stormed out of the room. I reached for my bag and dug around for my phone. I'd powered it down last night to conserve the battery, but it didn't seem to do much good. It blinked alive at thirty-two percent.

After rinsing my mouth and splashing water on my face in the bathroom, I met Sebastian in the middle of Astor Hall. His domineering presence shrank the normally spacious room.

He didn't say anything to me when I approached; he only turned around and walked toward the entrance. I silently followed, not wanting to stir the pot this early in the morning, but this was beyond awkward.

"Where are we going?" I asked once we were walking down 5th Avenue.

"To meet the others," he clipped.

He was being short with me, but whatever, I didn't have anything left in me to argue. I was tired. If anything, *I* should be the one who was pissed off. As I replayed what went down last night, I wanted to deck him in the jaw. A *privilege*? Get real! This wasn't a VH1 reality show. I wasn't looking to fall in love with someone who thought they were important.

The walk back to Central Park was quiet, and the only people on the streets were early morning runners. We met back at Strawberry Fields, where the rest of our dysfunctional group was already waiting for us.

Amy ran up to me as if I were a prisoner of war who was being released after years of confinement.

"I missed you," she gushed, her voice muffled by the scarf tightly wrapped around her neck. I hugged her back just as fiercely.

"Me too, Aims." We probably looked like a pair of lesbians, but I didn't care. I really needed the comfort of my friend after the adventures of last night.

"Did he seduce you?" she whispered. Or at least she tried to whisper, because I heard Bernard snicker somewhere behind her.

If it wasn't so cold I might have blushed, but my cheeks were already rosy.

"No," I replied firmly, unwilling to elaborate in earshot of our audience. She caught my drift and dropped the subject.

Once we let go of each other, I nodded at Bernard and then Jonah, who looked uncomfortable. His hands were stuffed in his pockets and he was looking anywhere but my direction.

"Where to next?" I asked, looking at Sebastian. He was crouched down on the ground, touching a patch of grass.

"It's faint, but I'm catching a familiar scent," he answered with his back to us.

"Jackson's?" I saw the glimmer of hope in Jonah's eyes.

"Yes, but someone else's, too. I think it's his captor."

"You said it's familiar?" Bernard asked as he approached Sebastian.

"Yes, but I can't place it."

"I don't smell anything, boss."

Sebastian sniffed a few more times and then his face contorted in disgust.

"It's wolfsbane," he grimaced, backing away.

"No wonder," Jonah mumbled as he ran his hands up and down his very tired-looking face. It didn't seem as if he got any more sleep than I did.

"What's going on?" I didn't follow the wolfey conversation going on around me.

Sebastian ignored my question, so Bernard caught me up to speed.

"Wolfsbane is our kryptonite. It can't kill us, but it can easily subdue us. The strange part about finding wolfsbane here is that it only grows in certain parts of the world, and definitely not here in the States. Our mystery person is either a foreigner, or has really good connections."

"Have you ever been affected by wolfsbane?" I looked up at him and his face turned grave.

"Yes, and it's worse than death itself. Imagine being paralyzed with fire running through your veins. That's what it does to our kind."

His bushy red brows furrowed, and I wanted to comfort him from the bad memory he was recalling. I touched his arm and looked up at the lumberjack giant. "I'm sorry." He gave me a sad smile and patted my hand.

"There's only one person I know of with access to it," Jonah said quietly, and we all turned to him. His hands were shaking, but it wasn't from fear. When I looked at his face, I knew it was anger.

"Who?" Sebastian barked.

"Caleb," Jonah answered through clenched teeth. As he fisted his hands by his sides, I felt the waves of rage that radiated off him.

My eyes bulged out. "Caleb?" I shrieked. "As in, the werewolf that's part of the Pack, and one of its captains?"

Jonah nodded tightly.

"That's a very serious accusation," Sebastian replied cautiously.

Jonah's eyes snapped toward him. "I'm positive. I saw it with my own eyes. You know Caleb recently transferred from the European Summit."

"Are you insinuating there is a breach between the Summits?" Sebastian scoffed.

"No, I just think Caleb is a power-hungry bastard who would do anything to get in the good graces of the Summit." Jonah paused and took a deep breath. "Including kidnapping one of its own."

"I don't understand," I whispered. "How would kidnapping Jackson help him gain power?"

"If he finds him, then he's a hero," Amy supplied beside me.

"Okay, I get that, but what about the missing vampire and Fae? How do they factor into this?"

"Maybe he wants to be the one to bring an alliance between the three groups?" Jonah guessed, but I was pretty sure he was grasping at straws now.

Caleb looked scary with that slash across his face, but could he really do this? Then it hit me.

"Shit!" I expelled, causing all four sets of eyes to look my way. "He gave that injured wolf back at the warehouse some weird tangerine tea. When I smelled it, I lost my balance going down the stairs."

"I remember that!" Amy said as she covered her mouth in shock.

The three werewolves stared at me motionlessly.

"Hello? I just said that creep gave me the bane, man!" It sounded like an STD.

Bernard cleared his throat. "Mackenzie, if he did, you would have been paralyzed for at least twenty-four hours. You wouldn't be this active."

"Jonah, I don't want to accuse anyone, especially a Pack captain, without substantial proof," Sebastian replied evenly.

"How much more proof do you need? Kenzie just described it without knowing what it was!"

"It must have been something else, then, because she's fine! You know this is not how Pack law works, Jonah."

"Fuck that! The bastard took my brother!"

"How do you think it will go," Bernard started, and then trailed his eyes over to me, "if we tell the Pack that Mackenzie got a whiff of wolfsbane from Caleb? It'll be mayhem. After yesterday's events, they already want to tear into her. They won't trust her."

Jonah's face fell.

"I don't have to go back, and they don't have to know it was me. You guys can go back to the warehouse and Amy and I can hide somewhere. New York is a pretty big place. No one will find me." But the faces everyone gave me told me all I needed to know. They would never allow it. They still assumed I needed a full-time babysitter.

Well, isn't this swell?

"Do you know where Caleb lives?" Bernard asked Jonah.

"I thought everyone stayed at the warehouse?"

Bernard snorted. "Heck no. Only a few live there, like Bash and Jonah, but we can choose where to live. The only ones oblig-ated to live at the warehouse are the unmated Lunas."

My insides stirred with fury, but no one seemed to notice.

"That's bullshit!" I exploded.

The three werewolves turned to me in confusion. "What?"

"How can you force them to live there?" And how could they not understand how barbaric that was? And mainly, how could they expect me to want to join their Pack, knowing I would be stripped of my right to live wherever I chose?

"It's just Pack law, Mackenzie. It's not a big deal," Bernard said calmly, and I wanted to throttle him.

I was shaking from anger and my thoughts went to Blu. *Poor Blu...*

Amy grabbed my wrist and I peered down at her. When she mouthed, *Not now*, it took everything in me to calm down.

"He has a flat in downtown Brooklyn," Jonah finally

answered, diverting their attention from me. "It's where I saw the wolfsbane."

"What did he say when you saw it?" Sebastian asked.

"He doesn't know that I did. He'd left to pick up Chinese food downstairs, and I was looking for the bathroom. I found a room filled to the brim with that shit."

"Why didn't you say anything?"

"Honestly, I didn't think it was a big deal at the time, but now that I think about it, it just seems stupid of me. The next time I went to his place, the room was empty." He ran his hands through his hair and I saw the wheels in his head spinning. He was blaming himself. "I figured he might have been growing them for my father. I know he likes to keep some on hand."

"It's not your fault," I offered, but he didn't respond, much less look at me. "I got a weird vibe from Caleb myself, so I wouldn't be surprised if it was him."

"Bad vibes aren't proof. We need to find the wolfsbane. If he's no longer storing it at his flat, then we need to figure out where he moved it," Sebastian pointed out.

"We can check public records to see if he owns any other property," Amy suggested, causing the three wolves to stare at her, which made me chuckle.

Did these guys know anything about the outside world?

"That's, uh," Jonah started, "a good idea. Where do we check?"

Amy and I exchanged a look. Poor guys, they were so lost.

"A computer," I suggested, holding back a laugh. "The libraries are most likely closed, so we need to find an internet café or head back to our apartment."

We all stood around awkwardly, avoiding each other's eyes as we thought about where to go. My gaze traveled over to a grouping of bushes and I froze. I recognized something that was too close to be coincidental.

Jonah sighed. "I think we may need Lucian's help."

"The vampire?" Amy blurted out.

"Guys?" I mumbled as I followed my line of sight.

"Yes," Jonah answered, ignoring me. "He has connections that could be of use to us, and since one of his bloodsuckers is missing, he wouldn't think twice about helping. At least, I hope so."

"You guys might want to see this," I said again louder, but everyone continued to ignore me as they debated bringing in the vampires.

"I don't know, asking Lucian for help is literally making a deal with the devil," Bernard contemplated.

"Guys, shut up!" I yelled as I crouched in front of the bushes and carefully picked up what caught my attention, forgetting about proper evidence protocol. "She wasn't lying," I mumbled. "She wasn't crazy."

"What's wrong, Kenz?" Amy asked from behind.

I lifted the all-too-familiar piece of skin and showed it to them.

"What is it?"

"It's skin," I whispered as everything started to click into place. "We need to head down to the station, STAT. I spoke to a fairy a couple days ago, raving about how her son was kidnapped. Her son must be Branwell, although she called him John Hancock. I found skin just like this outside her apartment building. We need to talk to her!"

"Mackenzie, slow down. What are you talking about?"

I yelled in frustration. How could they not understand me?

"Remember when I told you I'm a criminal justice major, and that I intern at Major Cases over at 1PP? Well, now I'm telling you that the kidnapper is a shape shifter!"

"There's no way you could know that," Sebastian argued.

"Which is why I'm telling you we need to get down to the station. We need to talk to my superiors."

"Wait, they know you're a werewolf?" Jonah exclaimed.

"No, but they're holding Jane Hancock in a mental institute because they think she's crazy. Can you guys just trust me?"

Seconds stretched into silent minutes as we looked around at each other. I watched as they wondered if I'd lost my mind, but I knew I was right.

Jane Hancock knew what I was the moment she saw me. I brushed her off as a loony, not believing for a second that what she said was true. Even knowing I was a werewolf, I didn't believe in the impossible. We lost days because I was reckless.

"Whether you guys believe me or not doesn't matter, but I'm heading out. This is the break we've been looking for in our case. I know I'm on to something." Without checking to see if they followed, I turned around toward the exit of the park.

17

"He did *what*?" Amy exclaimed, and I hurriedly put my hand over her mouth.

We were still a couple blocks away from the station when Amy and I slowed down to talk, walking a few feet behind the wolves. The tension around us was heavy with the bomb I'd dropped just an hour ago. Sebastian was having a hard time wrapping his mind around the idea of a disloyal wolf, while Jonah only wanted revenge for the kidnapping of his twin brother.

With Amy's arm looped in mine, we dragged our feet to get some privacy. The guys were talking in hushed tones between each other, and I figured this was the best time to catch her up on last night.

"Wolves have sensitive hearing, or did you forget?"

"Sorry," she mumbled.

"It's no big deal, but Amy, I don't know what to do. This whole situation freaks me out, which is stupid, because why should I be scared about two hot guys liking me? Ugh, I'm such a loser."

She stopped walking and faced me. "No you're not, Kenz. This is already a difficult time, and those guys are just making things worse. It's not your fault, it's theirs. Do you want me to set them straight? You know I will," she declared, putting her hands on her hips.

I chuckled. "Nah, it's cool, shorty." She slapped her gloved hand on my arm.

"Hey! I told you not to call me that!" she giggled. "Okay, Kenz, but seriously, who are you diggin' more?" She wiggled her pierced eyebrows up and down.

"No way! I'm not answering that." I started walking again. "They're both...different. It doesn't matter who I like anyway, because we're leaving," I whispered.

She nodded. "I know. Now, what's the deal with this shapeshifting junk?"

Immediately forgetting my romantic troubles, I latched onto the change in subject. "Amy, it's crazy. I can't believe I didn't catch onto this sooner! Michaels and I had a case on Wednesday with a lady who was a total whack job. She actually told Garrett she was Fae. I thought she had some screws missing, but now it sounds like it was a cry for help."

"Kenz, I know how you operate. Don't blame yourself."

I nodded, but didn't say anything else.

ARRIVING AT OUR DESTINATION, we caught up to the group and congregated across the street from the fourteen story, One Police

Plaza building to hatch a plan. I stretched my sensitive hearing and sought Garrett's voice, which surprisingly enough, was easy to find.

Anderson, I want that report on my desk before I take my next breath!

The man seriously needed a Valium.

Sebastian started barking orders, which distracted me from my snooping. "Jonah and Bern, I want you to compel the guard at the gate to let us in and keep the attention of whoever is at the front desk. Keep an eye on Amy. While you're doing that, Mackenzie and I will find her supervisor and compel him to give us the report on the kidnapping."

"Why do we need to compel so many people? I have access to the building, and if I talk to Garrett, he'll tell me what I need to know," I questioned.

"We don't have time to experiment, which means we do this *my* way, Mackenzie. Instead of risking whether or not your boss gives you the information we need, we can compel him. It's foolproof."

Didn't he get it? "We can't go around invading people's thoughts and taking away their rights!"

His eyes took on a dangerous glint. "I don't care, Mackenzie Grey. Wolves don't abide by human laws. This conversation is over." Sebastian brushed past me and crossed the street with Jonah and Bernard trailing behind him.

My nostrils flared and my fists tightened as I watched their retreating figures. How could they be so nonchalant about controlling someone that way? It shouldn't matter what *special abilities* our species had. Rights were rights, and we were taking them away from innocent people.

"Kenz," Amy whispered, "it's okay. They're not doing anything wrong. There's always an exception in times of danger."

"But there shouldn't *be* an exception, Amy! Aren't you still upset about them compelling you? I know I am!"

"Of course, but in some twisted way, I understand it. You didn't object when they had to compel Ollie. Things aren't always black and white." Her flaming red hair feathered across her face in the biting wind. "This isn't our world, Kenz."

"That was different!" With narrowed eyes, I watched my best friend and realized how much being around the Pack was affecting her moral compass. She never would have said that before our lives intersected with theirs. I understood things weren't always clear-cut, but there had to be rules—boundaries —that shouldn't be crossed.

Pausing our argument for now, we crossed the street together and passed through the gate as Bernard compelled the guard. Once inside the building, Amy stood by Jonah as he talked with the female officer at the front desk, and I followed Sebastian who was waiting by the elevators.

"Where is he?" he barked.

I hesitated until a growl escaped the Alpha's throat. I was grating his nerves. "Eleventh floor."

As we rode up in silence, I felt the heat waves of impatience rolling off Sebastian, which didn't come as a surprise since I knew he didn't like to be questioned, especially by me.

"Are we going to talk about what happened?" I asked, trying to start a conversation.

"There is nothing to talk about."

"I think there is, asshole. You can't try to seduce me and then act like you do that with everyone. I mean, unless you do, then—

then you're a whore," I snapped. I scrunched my brows in consternation. *Shit, did I just call an Alpha a hoe?*

Sebastian reached for the red emergency brake on the elevator panel and we jerked to a stop.

"I'm only going to say this once, and then this conversation is over. I'm running out of patience, Mackenzie. Have you thought about why my silence bothers you? Why you can't let it go like I have? You can try and fool yourself all you want, but I know what's going on in that head of yours."

"You don't know shit, you smug son of a—"

He grabbed my shoulders and slammed me against the elevator wall.

"Unless you want to really see me angry, I suggest you don't finish that sentence," he growled, not even an inch away from me. "That mouth of yours is going to get you into some serious problems, Mackenzie. Jonah might put up with it, but I won't. You've displayed your incompetence for following orders, and it shows very clearly, but you *will* respect an Alpha. I don't care if you act more human than wolf."

My eyes were parallel to his chest, and I couldn't seem to look away as it rose up and down in ragged breaths. I trailed my gaze up to his neck to see several veins tick agitatedly on his right side. *Pop. Pop. Pop.* They flicked in rhythm to his heart, which I heard pounding against his chest. I was still trying to learn what that meant when my sight moved up and landed on his lips. They were slightly parted, his bottom lip thicker than the top. Before my brain could catch up, I stood on tiptoes and leaned in, landing my mouth on his like a feather. I reached around and ran my hands through his jet-black hair and pulled him down to me. He didn't resist.

"*Mackenzie*," he breathed, pinning me to the wall.

I wanted to blame it on my inner animal—on the wolf—but it wasn't her. This was all me. The only difference was that it wasn't an emotional attraction that I had for Sebastian. I barely knew the guy. It was purely physical—and it was a strong pull—one I'd never felt before. It made me feel dirty and wrong, but at the same time, a thrill traveled through my body like a shock of electricity. My body warmed at his touch as his hands slowly roamed up my arms until he held them above my head. Our fingers intertwined, and then he moved away.

"What are you doing to me?" he questioned, his blue eyes shining as brilliantly as if he stood under the sun. His dark features were confounded by my hot and cold personality, and I didn't blame him a bit. I didn't know what I was doing, either.

"I ... I don't know. This is out of character for me, Bash, but I just can't seem to help myself." I gazed at him under thick lashes and his face softened at my confession.

He took a loose strand of my hair and tucked it behind my ear —running his rough knuckles down my cheek in a caress. "I know, Mackenzie, which is why I'm going to stop this." He jerked away, and a cold front smacked me like a wall as he put distance between us. "You weren't entirely wrong at the library. I shouldn't have pressured you the way I did. What you may not know is that you're going through the stages of a wolf cycle at an accelerated rate, since it took so long for the Change to occur. Your mind and body are trying to play catch up, and it wasn't right of me to take advantage of your vulnerable state."

I shook my head. "No, that's not true. I wasn't like this before I met you." *And Jonah.*

"It's because you weren't around any other wolves. No matter what, Mackenzie, if you only learn one thing from me, let it be that you will always gravitate toward your own kind. It's in our nature."

I watched the emotions flicker across his face, knowing it pained him to tell me the hard truth. My face slackened and I winced as the realization of what he was saying hit me. It was entirely possible that the infatuation I had with him and Jonah might not be real.

"We should hurry up," I whispered, avoiding eye contact and working to get my emotions in check.

He nodded and released the emergency brake.

I felt like an idiot. Like an idiotic, hormonal wolf. *Great.*

As soon as we exited the elevator, I expanded my hearing and found Detective Michaels by his cubicle. It was no surprise that he was yelling at someone. The guy didn't have an inside voice.

The eleventh floor housed the Major Case Squad, filled with dozens of officers working on various cases that ranged from kidnappings to bank robberies. There was never a dull moment because there was always something to do. I loved working here and felt lucky for having such a great opportunity. It wasn't easy snagging an internship in this department.

"Grey! What the hell are you doing here?" Garrett yelled from across the squad room.

Sebastian growled beside me.

"You better control yourself, wolf. This is how we communicate in here. There is no diplomacy, so get used to it or get out," I said through gritted teeth as I smiled and waved to Garrett.

"Hey, Michaels. I got back from vacation a little early, but I had a question I wanted to ask you."

"Well, hurry up. I have a press conference in twenty, and if you're back, you might as well come in later tonight. I could use the extra hands on this case." He started walking toward one of the filing rooms.

While I struggled to catch up to Michaels, it only took Sebastian three strides to reach my supervisor and whirl him around by his arm.

"What the fuc—?"

"Listen to me carefully. I need the report you filed on the recent kidnappings. Where is it?" Bash asked as he stared into Garrett's eyes without blinking.

In a monotonous voice he answered, "In the Captain's office. Third filing cabinet, first drawer."

"Now, you will return to your work and forget that I or Mackenzie Grey were ever here."

Garrett blinked and walked out of the room, never grabbing what he came in for. I stood there motionless for a moment, unable to shake the goosebumps that dimpled my arms. Michaels would never know we were here, and it was all because Sebastian willed him to forget. It was bad enough we pumped him for information, but to mess with his memories? I still didn't feel right about it.

"Where's the Captain's office?" Sebastian demanded, snapping me out of my conflicted daze.

"Follow me," I muttered, walking two office doors down and right to the cabinet where Michaels said the report was located. Sebastian stood by the office window, making sure no one was watching us. He would probably compel anyone who did.

The drawer was locked, and we didn't have time to look for a key. With a little help from the wolf, I yanked on the handle and the filing cabinet ripped open. It would look suspicious, but I guess at this point it didn't matter. I wouldn't be working here long enough to deal with the repercussions.

I shuffled through the files and found Michael's report about half way in. I took it out and made a quick copy using the computer's scanner. Afterwards, I made sure to delete the history and tapped Sebastian on the shoulder, letting him know I was done. I tried to put everything back in place as best I could, but it would be obvious that someone had been in here. Hopefully we would make it out of the building before anyone noticed.

We took the elevator down to the ground floor and exited just as the front desk officer slid a piece of paper to Jonah with a sultry smile. His one dimple peeked out in a smirk, and I couldn't help feeling jealous of the female guard. Amy stood beside him with a bored expression on her face, but the moment she saw us, she started heading towards the exit. As we pushed open the doors, Sebastian whistled to Jonah. A few seconds later, his Beta exited behind us. We met up with Bernard about a block and a half away from NYPD headquarters and ducked into a nearby diner.

After we ordered a round of coffee, I pulled out the folded copy of Garrett's report from my coat pocket and flattened it on the table.

"Alright, so it says Jane Hancock is being held on Ward's Island at the Manhattan Psychiatric Center. That's going to be tricky to get inside. Do any of you have suggestions on how to go about that?" I asked.

"I think the easiest way in is to go through the 103rd footbridge in East Harlem. We can easily blend in," Bernard suggested. "My only question is, how are we going to get *inside* the hospital?"

"We should call Lucian. He probably has someone on the night shift there," Jonah said.

I quirked an eyebrow. "The vampire?"

"Yes. He has many connections around the city, and most of his bloodsuckers work whatever jobs they can get at night," Jonah responded.

"You're right. Call him and tell him to meet us at dusk," Sebastian agreed.

"Isn't he sleeping?" Amy innocently asked.

"They don't sleep."

18

I ate enough to feed an entire village, packing on two rare steaks with a double order of fries and a stack of pancakes. The waitress looked at me funny until the three werewolves ordered almost the same thing. Poor Amy was the odd-man out, with her tiny order of a country omelet. I was so full, I left my coat unzipped so I could rub my belly. Who was I to complain if the meal was paid for by the Brooklyn Pack? I ate as if it was my last meal, because for all I knew, it might be.

We sat around, killing time after Jonah spoke with Lucian about meeting up at the bridge. It was late afternoon when we finally decided to head out.

"There are too many of us," Sebastian proclaimed as we stepped out of the diner and into the ice box of New York City. "If we all walk into the hospital together, we won't exactly be inconspicuous."

"What do you suggest, boss?" Jonah asked.

"You and Mackenzie go. She needs to be there, because she's

the only who has met this Jane Hancock. I need to get back to the warehouse and try to get the Pack under control."

I watched as Bash and Jonah made plans for me as if I wasn't there and my opinion didn't matter. "Hello? What about Amy? She needs to come with me."

"I'll watch over Amy. No harm will come to her. She is now, and forever will be under the protection of the Pack," Sebastian responded.

Instantly, a weight was lifted off my shoulders. *Now and forever*. That was all I needed to hear.

"Bernard, I want you to meet with the Tactical team that should already be on the northeast side of Central Park, and go talk with the Fae again. Ask them what they know about someone named Jane Hancock, and then report back to Jonah."

"And to Mackenzie!" I chimed in.

"To Jonah," he said with narrowed eyes.

"Whatever," I mumbled. I swore, if I couldn't run away from the Pack and their ancient laws, then I would start a freakin' revolution.

I pulled Amy to the side as Bernard started to leave and Sebastian was busy talking logistics with Jonah.

"Are you okay with this?" I asked. I was sure she could handle herself, but to be alone with Bash was intimidating even for me.

"Yeah, Kenz, I'll be fine." She winked.

"Wait. What does that mean?"

She laughed. "Chill out, Kenzie. There's no hidden message, I'm just saying I'll be fine. Sebastian wants in your pants, not mine."

"Shhh!" I put my hand over her mouth. "Wolf hearing!"

"Yeah, yeah, as if it weren't obvious to everyone anyway. Well, good luck with psycho Fae, and come back in one piece. Preferably with a decision about your two lovers." She giggled and pulled me into a hug.

Damn Amy. She had no filter.

Once we parted ways, I walked beside Jonah down the street and to the bus stop. It was awkward. We hadn't really spoken since we left Cold Springs. So much drama happened in a short period of time, which made me feel silly stressing over it. We had all just met. Things shouldn't be as intense as they were.

"What bus are we taking?" I asked, breaking the silence.

"The Six straight down Lexington. It'll drop us off between 103rd and 104th. From there, we'll walk."

I tried to listen to his heartbeat or watch his facial expressions, but I got nothing. He was closed off from any emotion and it frustrated me. I didn't care if he was happy, mad, or whatever, I just wanted to know. It was stupid of me, but I needed to know how to approach him. Maybe I was being paranoid.

"Okay, cool...so—"

"Amy's right, you suck at beating around the bush. Just spit it out, Kenz," he said with a smirk.

Good sign.

"I'm sorry. I know things have been tense, and maybe I'm overanalyzing shit, but are we good?"

He sighed. "Listen, Kenz. I won't say I'm okay with you and Bash being together, but I won't stand in the way, either."

No wonder they're best friends.

"There's nothing between us!" I sputtered, though I didn't know why I jumped to say that. There really was nothing between *any* of us, but then again there was. Crap, this sucked.

"Are you sure? Because I don't share, Mackenzie."

Whoa.

We reached the bus stop and waited with a few other people around us.

"We kissed." Slight modification to the truth. Didn't matter, I was about to drop the real bomb. "And he said the same thing, that he wasn't willing to share me, which I'm not asking you to do!" This was turning into a disaster of an explanation. "What I'm trying to say Jonah, is that I like you both, but I don't feel comfortable having to choose. That's why I'd rather not have either of you. We just met, and we don't know each other very well. I'm a total blabbermouth with a short temper, and for all I know, you might end up hating me once you get to know me. I mean, I would suck as a Luna—I hate doing laundry, and I—"

Jonah cut me off by grabbing the lapels of my coat and closing the space between us. His lips smashed onto mine and everything I just said felt a million miles away.

What was I even talking about?

My mouth parted and his tongue swept in, melting me at his feet. With my hands trapped between our chests, he held me with such force, I knew he wouldn't let me fall—ever. I needed his stability. I was barely able to stand on my own at the mere taste of the peppermint he had put in his mouth not too long ago.

The cold air puffed out of me like smoke as he released me, and I tried to catch my breath. Don't these wolves believe in restraint?

"Uh ... " I tried to get my words in order. "Maybe, I, uh, wasn't very clear. I babble, so I probably didn't make sense, but—"

"I understood, Mackenzie," Jonah said as his dimple peeped out. No fair. "But it doesn't mean I can't kiss you—even if it's the last time—as a reminder of what you'll be missing."

"Oh," was all I could say as he let me go and I tripped over myself in my haste to take a step back. One thing was obvious, grace was *not* my middle name.

I cleared my throat and straightened up. Everyone at the bus stop snickered at me.

"Touch your nose, assholes," I growled, turning my back on them.

What did they know about my supernatural woes?

THE BUS RIDE was forty minutes long and the walk to the bridge was another ten. Luckily, he never brought up what happened between us at the bus stop and instead, spent the whole time setting up a game plan. According to Jonah, I was supposed to let him do all the talking and not get involved, much less make myself known to Lucian. Normally I would have objected, because let's be honest, there wasn't a silent bone in my body— but I was too busy replaying that damn kiss in my head, so I let him yap his gums.

It was six in the evening when we arrived at the entrance to the footpath that led to Ward's Island. Lucian was already waiting for us, dressed in his customary uniform of black slacks and a crisp, black button-up. This time he also sported an open wool trench coat—black, of course—with a pair of classic Ray-Ban sunglasses.

"Sun allergy?" I asked as we walked up to him.

"Hm, why yes, Pet. It's quite the handicap," he purred, and I couldn't hold back a laugh. This guy was unreal.

Jonah nudged me, which was his way of telling me to make myself unseen. Yeah...that would be difficult.

"Can you get us into the hospital?" Jonah got straight down to business.

The vampire snorted, which seemed out of place with his otherwise genteel demeanor. "I wouldn't have taken time out of my busy schedule to meet you all the way over here if I didn't, Wolf. Please, give me some credit."

"Stop playing games, Lucian. This is serious," Jonah barked out.

"So impatient," I mumbled, earning a glare.

"I agree with you there, Pet. He is quite *demanding*," Lucian said as he winked at me.

Jonah interrupted, "We have a lead, and she's in that mental institute. If you can't be serious and help us not only find our kin but yours as well, then you're wasting our time."

"Oh, really? Do tell." The vampire smirked and leaned against one of the bridge pillars. He crossed his arms over his chest as if trying to be casual, but it only looked robotic.

Jonah took too long to respond, so I jumped in. "Her name is Jane Hancock—I know, it's not very original—but I think she's Fae. Her son was kidnapped last week, and we think it might be Branwell, the guy the Fae Queen said was missing. Jane called the police and told them everything—literally—so they locked her up in the psych ward. We need to find out what she knows."

Lucian tsked. "Well, isn't that a mouthful?" He sighed. "If the woman is unhinged, what makes you think we can trust her?"

"I didn't say we needed to trust her; all we need to do is talk to her and see if her story adds up."

"Tomato, tomahto, it's the same thing."

"Lucian," Jonah growled, and I put a firm grip on his forearm to restrain him. "Stop with the twenty-one questions and get us into the hospital."

"My young Beta, that's not the correct way to approach someone from whom you seek help. Your kind has no manners. You're such ... animals," he chastised, flashing his fangs at us with a smile.

Jonah crouched down and snarled. This was *not* good.

With shaky legs, I went to stand between the vampire and the wolf.

"Cut it out! What's wrong with you guys? We have people missing, and you're fighting each other?"

"Oh, I like her," Lucian purred, causing the hairs on the back of my neck to stand up. He smirked at me and licked his lips. *Gross.*

"No you don't—don't even look at her." Jonah grabbed my wrist and yanked me behind him.

"Hey!" I snapped, jerking my arm back. "Everyone needs to stop trying to control me already. I'm not part of this goddamn Pack!" I yelled. With wild eyes, I scanned the other passersby on the bridge until they settled on Lucian. "You," I pointed to him, "we need your help, so let's stop bullshitting and get to the point. Can you help us?" I was irritated.

His porcelain white skin was so smooth, it reminded me of the marble fireplace from the library last night with Sebastian.

Lucian's smirk never faltered as he watched me. His beady black eyes roamed up and down my body as he stood up straighter. Employing the creepy glide from the last time we saw him, he approached me until he was only a foot away. His cold finger came up and trailed down my cheek in a caress. He felt like stone.

"*Quern tamquam ex matre*," he hummed.

"W-what?" I stuttered. I froze in place, unable to even blink for fear that he'd do something—like bite me.

"Nothing, Pet. I will help you, and *only* you."

"No, Mackenzie!" Jonah yelled, his rough hands yanking on my arm. "You can't trust a vampire!"

"Dude, get a grip. I don't have to trust him to get the information we need, and if we can't trust a vampire, then what the hell did we call him for?" I scoffed. I understood why everyone looked as if they were constipated, but if we wanted to find Jackson, we had to make certain sacrifices. I just had to protect my neck. Literally.

"Excellent point, Pet."

"Damnit, Mackenzie, why don't you ever do as you're told?" Jonah pulled at his hair. He was acting like I was deploying to Iraq. Talk about a meltdown.

I huffed, "If I ever did what I was supposed to, I wouldn't be myself. Now suck it up, buttercup. We need to chase down every lead to solve this case." I turned to Lucian, who still eyed me carefully as if he was in on some secret. "What do you need from me?"

"I want a lock of your hair," he answered without hesitation, diverting his gaze to his hands to clean his manicured fingernails. His response fell too quickly from his lips, like he was waiting for the opportunity to say it.

"Huh?"

A growl ripped from behind me and as soon as I turned around, I saw one white-hot Beta barreling towards us. Stone cold hands gripped my arm and flung me like a rag doll behind him. With his palm out, exerting no effort at all, Lucian's hand slammed into Jonah's chest, sending him flying backwards.

"What the hell, Lucian!?" I yelled as I noticed that the pedestrians crossing the bridge were now paying attention to us.

"Sorry, love, but the wolves are very sensitive toward Lunas. Thank God, I didn't bloody ask for a claw like I originally wanted."

He snickered, and I wanted to stab him in the eye. A claw?

"You guys are so damn weird," I hissed, rushing over to Jonah, who was getting up. I rubbed his back and soothed him in hopes he'd relax. "Are you calm? If you want to save Jackson, I need you to relax."

He nodded.

I eyed him for a moment before I was certain he wouldn't have an outburst again, and then turned my attention back to Lucian. "Why do you want a lock of my hair?"

Lucian diverted his gaze from me. "Don't worry, Lone Wolf, I won't do any voodoo or such. This is a personal matter, and if you want my help, you'll accept the exchange."

I bit my lip. "Fine. You got yourself a deal."

"Good," he said, clapping his hands in front of him. "Now, let's head to the looney bin before visiting hours are over."

The walk across the bridge shouldn't have taken as long as it did —maybe it was the electric tension arcing between my two companions—but I wished Amy was here with us. She would have said the perfect thing to break the ice, or at least make me laugh, like a-wolf-and-a-vampire-walk-into-a-bar joke. Man, I needed to google those when I got the chance.

Jonah was wound up like a spring and I could understand

why: I'd made a deal with a vampire without consulting him. In my defense, I shouldn't have to talk it over with anyone. I was my own woman, not part of the Pack, and if I made a sour deal with the devil himself, then I would deal with the consequences *after* we found Jackson.

"Are you two ever going to be friends? The awkwardness makes me fidgety," I said as we stopped in front of the Manhattan Psychiatric Center.

"Kenz, be serious, please," Jonah muttered.

"Oh, lighten up, Jonah Cadwell. The girl is only teasing."

We followed Lucian up the sidewalk and into the entrance. It didn't look like a psych ward. I'd imagined sterile white, padded walls, but it looked like any other hospital. We walked up to the front desk where a nurse named Betty, according to her name tag, was sitting, typing away at her computer.

"Hello, dear. We're here to see Jane Hancock," Lucian said smoothly as he perched his right elbow on the counter. He was so theatrical.

The nurse's blue scrubs swished as she stood up to address us. "I'm sorry, but visiting hours end at five. You can come back tomorrow at eight in the morning."

Shit. I turned wide eyes to Jonah, who looked as irritated as I was. We couldn't wait until tomorrow to see if this was a viable lead or not.

"My apologies, love, maybe I should have introduced myself first. My name is Lucian Young. I'm a board member of this facility, as you might recognize, and I was told it would be just as well if I came to see an old friend of mine. Could you be a dear and get us some visitors passes?"

The nurse stared at Lucian as if she wanted to bolt. She froze in place for half a beat, then scrambled to get the visitor name tags out of her drawer. I had to hand it to the vampire: he made sure his fingers were dipped in many pots. Eternity was a long time, I supposed. Might as well be set for life.

I scribbled my name on the visitor sticker and slapped it on the left side of my coat.

"Diana Stone?" Jonah read with a quirked eyebrow.

"What? We're undercover; I don't want people to know my real name," I whispered as if this were a black ops mission.

"You know these names get entered into a government system, right?"

"Trust me, I know," I said with a bright smile. *Take that, Bimbo Barbie!*

"Ready?" Lucian asked, staring questioningly at my name tag.

"Don't ask."

He smirked. "Never a dull moment with you, Pet."

WE TOOK the elevator to the sixth floor and went toward room 6-132. The floor was eerily quiet, and the nurse's station was empty when we arrived. I leaned in closer to Jonah, thinking someone was about to jump out and scare us.

"This feels like a B-rated horror movie, guys. Why is no one here?"

"What took you so long?" A woman said at the end of the hallway. We jerked to a stop and I squinted my eyes to get a better look.

"It's Jane Hancock," I mumbled as I took in her bedraggled appearance. The baggy hospital gown swallowed her thin frame.

"I expected your kind here days ago. Now get me out of here!" she croaked. She tried to walk to us, but appeared to be out of breath.

"What do you mean?" Jonah asked as we stepped closer.

"That one," she accused, raising a bony finger aimed at me, "came to see me the other day with the police. My son was taken, and you wolves haven't done a goddamn thing!"

"How was I supposed to know?" I scoffed, crossing my arms over my chest.

Jonah tsked, "We're sorry. She's new, she didn't know. Who's your son?"

"Branwell, of the Celtic Clan," she announced proudly, then nearly fell over.

"Are you okay?" Jonah reached out to catch her.

"Of course not! This place is laced with iron."

"I'll have to say that is my fault. I had the hospital remodeled with it just last year. Such a shame," Lucian sighed with fake concern.

Jonah growled at the vampire, but lifted the Fae up in a cradle and carried her over to the front desk where a wheelchair was stationed. "Don't worry, we'll get you home. We have some questions to ask about Branwell."

"I'll tell you whatever you need to know, as long as you get me the hell out of here."

Betty, the nurse, wasn't too happy with our departure—or the loan of the wheelchair—but it was easier to roll Jane out instead of carrying her off the island. By the time we left, it was nighttime as darkness encompassed the city. This had been a long, tiring day, and I couldn't wait for it to be over.

"Why did you lie to me and say Branwell's name was John Hancock?" I asked as we strolled across the bridge.

She grunted. "You were with a human. Of course I lied."

"Why don't you tell us about Branwell and the night of his disappearance?" Jonah interjected.

Her face crumpled. "I saw it. I saw him take away my boy. You have to find him! Promise me you'll find him!" she cried with wild eyes.

My heart broke for her. "We'll do everything in our power to bring him back safely," I consoled her as I stopped the wheelchair and crouched in front of its wheels. "Can you tell us what you saw?"

She wiped tears from her cheeks and cleared her throat. "I thought he was a wolf, but he smelled different. That's how I knew he was something else. He was talking to Branwell just outside our apartment building. I thought they were friends, because they spoke as if they knew each other. My son sometimes concocts herbs for the Fae Queen and other supernaturals in the city," she explained, peering over at Jonah as if she wasn't sure she should have revealed it.

"Branwell told him he'd have everything ready within a week, and the wolf got mad. He grabbed my boy by the neck and slammed him against the building. I couldn't see past that from my window, but I heard him say he couldn't wait a week. Next thing I knew, the stranger was dragging Branwell to an SUV parked across the street. That was the last time I saw my son."

I looked up at Jonah and Lucian. They were pensive as the four of us were rooted in the middle of the bridge, unmoving.

"Did you see what he looked like?" Lucian asked carefully.

She shook her head. "It was too dark, and my eyes have gotten worse as the centuries pass. But his hair was light, not dark."

"It could be Caleb, but it's still a stretch. When you say he smelled different, what do you mean?" Jonah asked.

"He smelled of the earth, like a wolf, but he also smelled like death and decay," she turned to Lucian, "like a vampire."

"Is that possible?" I asked Jonah. By the confusion on his face, he didn't know if it was.

"I've never heard of a hybrid, but in this world, it wouldn't surprise me," he admitted as he ran his hand through his hair.

"Hybrids are not possible, not biologically, at least. Trust me, I'd know," Lucian answered.

WE DROPPED JANE—WHO still wouldn't tell us her real name—off at her apartment, and Jonah called Bernard so he could update the Fae. We were at a loss about what to do next, so we ended up at St. Paul's Cathedral again. While there, Jonah called Sebastian to fill him in on our dead end. Either way this case went, if by the next full moon Jackson hadn't been found, I would still have to leave. I felt horrible for thinking like that, but I had to save myself. I couldn't wait another month for my next opportunity. If I stayed, they would either make me a Luna, or start the man hunt for my head.

"We need to talk," Lucian whispered, nodding toward an exit. I paused, noticing Jonah's back to me as he talked on the phone, then slipped away from the altar and crept in the direction of the narrow hallway the vampire had gone through. I made the only left turn and then walked through a passageway that connected to another building. I entered a room bursting with bookshelves that lined the walls and an old, dark oak desk perched in the middle of the floor, complete with chairs.

"You may come in, Mackenzie. I don't bite." Lucian grinned from where he stood near the desk.

"Very funny," I spat. "What do you want?"

"First, I want to ask you a question." I nodded. "When do you plan to leave?"

"What?"

"You heard me clearly, Pet. When do you plan to escape the Pack? I know those are your thoughts, and there's nothing wrong with it." He began to pace. "The reason I ask, is because I want to help."

Bullshit. "Why the hell would you want to help? You don't even know me." None of this made any goddamn sense. I had enough drama with the Alpha and the Beta, I didn't need a creepy vampire like Lucian in the mix as well.

"Simmer down, Wolf. I have no interest in you ... romantically."

"How did you—?"

He grinned. "Relax, I don't read minds; it's written all over your face. Come, sit." He gestured to one of the chairs facing the desk and sat in the other one.

Cautiously, I obeyed and scooted as far away from him as I could without being rude.

"How much do you know about your mother, Mackenzie Grey?"

His question took me by surprise. "What about her? She's human."

"Yes, yes, but do you know who she *really* is? Biologically."

"What? I don't know what you're trying to say. My biological mom is Joyce Grey, from Italian ancestry. She has nothing to do with werewolves."

"Joyce Grey," he whispered as he tapped two fingers on his mouth. "Is that so..."

"Yes, it is, now why do you want to know about her?"

"Nothing, simply indulging my curiosity."

He smiled, but I didn't believe him. Something was up. He crossed his right leg over his left, wrinkling his impeccably ironed black slacks. He cocked his head to the side and watched me. It made me uneasy. "Why are you so on edge, Pet? Could it be the boys?"

"Are you trying to shrink me? You're asking more than one question."

He chuckled. "I guess so. I apologize if I've intruded."

I narrowed my eyes. "Why do you want to help me?" Sneaky bastard was confusing me with all his damn questions.

"Let's just say I owe someone a favor, and if I assist you, my debt would be paid in full." He shifted in his chair. "Mackenzie, I know you have no reason to trust me. We're predators, after all. But I do hope you will take a chance this one time. You're wrong when you say I don't know you. I do, and for that purpose and many more that I cannot speak of at the moment, I wish to offer you asylum. If you accept my refuge, neither the Pack nor the vampires can touch you. You will have your freedom."

Lucian stared off in space as he spoke, providing me with an opportunity to watch him more closely. His pale, porcelain skin was unblemished, his narrow face accentuated by high cheekbones. His sleek blonde hair was tied back in a low ponytail at the nape of his neck. He sat as tall and erect as a statue—an altogether unreal visage.

The warnings from Jonah rang in my mind, but my gut told me otherwise. I didn't know what Lucian's deal was just yet, but with his curiosity about my mother, I started to think there were details I was overlooking. He implied that Joyce wasn't my biological mother, but I knew she was.

I eased my tension just a notch. "What would I have to do? Because there's no way you would offer me sanctuary for free. Not when you asked for my hair just to get us in a building. What's the catch?"

He snapped out of his daze. "No catch, Pet. You already know you cannot stay in New York City, but I don't think you want to be here long anyway. Am I right?"

Okay, he was seriously trying to shrink me. I didn't know if I wanted to stay in the city anymore; I just knew that if I stayed, I would have too much to deal with. Even if the Pack wasn't after me, I would still be running away.

I didn't answer him. "Where would I go?"

"Los Angeles."

19

My mouth fell open as I watched Lucian calmly pull out his cell phone and start typing, as if he hadn't just dropped a bomb on me. I was left speechless. Los Angeles? It was a drastic change from New York, besides the obvious benefit of being on the other side of the country. It sounded like the perfect place to go.

"How are you going to keep me safe there? Isn't the Pack everywhere?"

Lucian's eyes looked up from his phone screen. "I have a clan there that will keep you from harm."

"Wait, let me get this straight: you want me to live with a bunch of vampires?" All I would be doing was trading one danger for another.

"My people are the only ones who can keep you safe from the Pack. I wouldn't get too picky if I were you, but no, I'm not asking you to live with them, but you *will* have to interact." He paused for a moment, his chest never rising to take a breath. *Creepy.* "We are not bad people, Mackenzie Grey. If you accept my offer, you will learn that for yourself."

Without waiting for a response, he switched his attention back to his phone and ignored my outward struggle with my inner turmoil. This brought a whole new meaning to 'judging a book by its cover'. I wanted to believe he was a good person who was trying to help, but even if Lucian wasn't a vampire, I still wouldn't trust him completely. I wouldn't trust anyone who said they wanted to help. I'm a New Yorker. No one was ever just kind for no reason.

"I'll think about it," I muttered, still lost within my thoughts.

"I'm sure you will, Mackenzie Grey," he said, unfolding from his chair and standing up.

"MACKENZIE!" Jonah yelled from the hallway.

Crap, he was freaking out. He barged into the room like a bulldozer, his chocolate eyes flashing gold. When I imagined steam shooting out of his ears, the thought made me chuckle. Not just from the imagery, but from the nerves that had steadily been building in my stomach. I had a lot to think about. But first things first: we needed to solve this kidnapping case.

"Relax, I'm fine. What did Sebastian say?"

"Don't tell me to relax when I turn around and you're gone! You should have said something to me before you left!"

He was right—we were, in fact, in a secret vampire lair—but he was also wrong. "If I would have said something, you'd have stopped me!"

"You're damn right I would. You can't trust him, Kenz."

Lucian stood idly by, not saying a word as Jonah berated him. Call me a softy, or maybe I didn't know the whole truth about their relationship, but I felt bad for Lucian. Since I met him, he hadn't done or said a thing against the wolves, yet all they did was talk shit to him at the same time they asked him for help.

"Don't fret, Mackenzie Grey. It all just rolls off my shoulders." Lucian winked, and I turned my silent anger toward Jonah.

"What did Sebastian say?" I asked through gritted teeth. I was mad at Jonah, but I wouldn't bitch him out with an audience. I would have to learn to restrain myself.

"He told us to get back to the warehouse so we can regroup. He's issued a warning for the Pack to stay away from you, so you should be safe." His face was stone cold—no dimple in sight. "Now let's go. This place makes my skin crawl."

At that moment, I wanted to lose all control and punch Jonah in the face for trying to commandeer me, but the lightbulb in my head picked that moment to go off.

I gasped as I raced to Lucian's bookcase and started reading the spines. "Do you have any books on species?" I asked as I scanned the books in a rush.

"Why, yes, of course. They're over here." Lucian pulled a thick textbook from the shelf behind his desk.

"Mackenzie, what the hell are you doing?" Jonah growled and tried to pull me away. "For once, just listen to me!"

"Skin, Jonah! We found skin!"

"What?"

"Oh my God, Jonah! For one minute just stop thinking about me not listening, and think about what Jane Hancock said and the skin we found at her apartment *and* the park. Don't laugh, but I saw this on a TV show once. Could this kidnapper be someone who sheds skin? Like a snake?" I felt the answer at the tip of my tongue, but couldn't piece it all together.

"Jonah," Lucian stared, mouth agape. "She may be onto something. We could have a Skin Walker on our hands." The vampire hurriedly flipped through the pages of the book he'd shown me until it landed on what he was looking for—a section that detailed the Skin Walker.

"Shit," Jonah muttered, running his hands through his hair, which I'd realized he only did when he was anxious. "They're almost impossible to find."

"It makes sense. Branwell was probably making an herb to mask his smell," Lucian said.

"But who is it?" I asked as I read the short definition of a Skin Walker.

SKIN WALKER—LEGEND *says that this creature, with the skin*
    of its prey, can take its form and walk and talk as they desire.

"IF HE HAS Branwell to mask his odor, there's no way we'll find him."

"We have a suspect, Jonah. Caleb," I whispered. It made sense. What better way to infiltrate the Pack than through one of its captains? The only question now was why.

A CAB RIDE was the quickest form of transportation to the warehouse. Even better, Lucian offered to foot the bill. He wouldn't take no for an answer when he said he'd be coming with us, which Jonah tried to persuade him against. We didn't know how the Pack would react. It could start an uproar, and of course, my favorite excuse, the vampire's presence would just give them another thing for which to blame me. I definitely felt the love.

We arrived in record time and my nerves surfaced again at the thought of what we were about to do. We were going to accuse someone of something, yet we didn't have any proof of wrong doing. It was exactly what Sebastian didn't want us to do, but Caleb was the most suspicious of all the supernaturals I'd met thus far.

As the double doors of the warehouse swung open and we walked into the cafeteria-style room, all eyes fell on us and the floor quieted. Sebastian was standing with the captains—including Caleb—by a white dry erase board in the middle of the room. He turned around when Bernard nudged him in our direction.

Sebastian's cold blues landed on Lucian first, and his nostrils flared out of control.

"What's going on, Jonah?" he barked, his voice reverberating across the main floor.

While the Alpha and Beta were at a stand-off, I scanned the room for Amy and found her on the second-floor landing with Blu. She waved and I smiled—glad that she was okay.

"I would expect this from *her*," Bash pointed at me, "but not from you!"

I was about to say something in my defense when Lucian caught my attention. He shook his head, which I interpreted as him telling me to keep my fool mouth shut.

"I didn't have a choice; he was going to show up either way, so I'd rather it was with me," Jonah said, standing firm on his decision.

Sebastian walked across the room toward us with the captains trailing right behind him. They stopped about five feet away.

"What is the meaning of your visit, Lucian?"

"Oh, it's quite simple, Alpha—you have a traitor in your midst," Lucian declared as he leaned forward and cupped his mouth, pretending to whisper, but knowing the whole warehouse could hear.

The gasps traveled like wildfire, which only angered Sebastian more.

"Quiet!" he roared, and it was like hitting the mute button on your TV. Not a sound. "Explain."

"You can't trust them, Sebastian! That lone wolf brainwashed Jonah and brought a bloodsucker into our home. This is unholy!" someone yelled from within the crowd of werewolves.

"Unholy?" I laughed, no longer able to contain myself. I needed to be defended, and if no one else was willing to do it, I sure as hell was. "What the fuck do any of you know about what's sacred? Not a damn thing. This vampire might know more than you," I said as I jerked my thumb toward Lucian. I mean, he lived in a damn church. There was probably a Bible lying around there somewhere.

"Mackenzie," Jonah warned, but I ignored him.

"What's *unholy* is the fact that you have a wolf in your Pack who's growing wolfsbane without permission; that he tried to feed me some, and force-fed it to Sam, who's lying in bed, barely holding on; and … " I paused for extra effect. Lucian wasn't the only one who could be theatrical. "… he's a Skin Walker."

Cue the gasps.

I didn't tear my gaze away from Scarface and I'm glad I didn't.

While the room erupted into chaos, I narrowed my eyes and caught the slightest twitch of his upper lip. *Gotcha, bitch.*

Not waiting for permission, I ran towards him and tackled him to the ground. The only ones who noticed were the wolves in our immediate vicinity. Everyone else was busy arguing about my accusations.

I swung at him—right, left—then he flipped me over and wrapped his hands around my neck. I clawed at his face, my inner wolf awakening. My canines emerged and snapped at him —trying to inhale some oxygen.

"You stupid bitch," he whispered in my ear as someone finally pulled him off me.

It took me less than a second to jump up and crouch down on all fours. My throat hurt and my eyes watered, but it didn't stop my wolf from belting out a roar that could put a lion to shame. The room froze as all eyes flashed to me. I watched as my nails extended and scraped the concrete floor, the hairs on my arms thickened, and my face scrunched up like a prune. I'd halfway shifted. My tongue glided across my canines and I felt hunger rear its ugly head.

"She attacked me! Do something about it!" Caleb yelled, his eyes wild.

"Stand down, Caleb! We will figure—"

"No, Sebastian! I've had enough of your sympathy for this outsider. It's obvious you're making exceptions for her. Letting your feelings cloud your judgment is *not* a sign of an Alpha who puts the needs of the Pack before his own," Caleb sneered.

A growl ripped from my throat, followed by a deeper, deadlier voice I didn't recognize as my own. "Are you trying to challenge him?" I questioned, the pieces starting to fall into place. This was his plan all along—he wanted Sebastian's position. "Who the hell are you?" I growled as Lucian came to stand beside me. He must have come to the same conclusion.

"Don't question me, little girl. I don't have to explain myself to a disgusting lone wolf such as yourself!"

"Answer her, Caleb. Who are you?" Jonah asked, coming to stand on my other side. I was worried he would side against me, but I was glad he didn't.

Caleb scoffed and turned to address the crowd that had formed. "You see this? Who's the traitor now? Taking the side of a mutt instead of his own kin!"

"Caleb!" Sebastian barked. "If you have nothing to fear, brother, then you should have no problem answering the question."

Scarface looked around at the wolves waiting expectantly for his reaction. It was one thing to be indignant because you were wrongfully accused, but to respond as defensively as he did sparked some curiosity.

I tried to remember what the book had said about Skin Walkers—it said the skin was sewn just under the chin. I looked at Lucian and nodded. I didn't know how he was always one step ahead of me, but now wasn't the time to ask. I lunged for Caleb.

"This is ridiculous!" he snarled just as I climbed onto his back like a spider monkey.

My claws reached around and under his chin. I felt the ridge in his skin, dug my nails into it, and pulled.

The fear of being wrong gnawed at my gut, because if I was, I'd have the whole Pack to deal with. I knew that wouldn't be something Jonah or Sebastian could get me out of. They would kill me with or without the permission of their Alpha if I hurt one of their own. Luckily, I hadn't.

I pulled the flesh of the Caleb lookalike face over his head to expose him for what he really was—a Skin Walker. His face was raw meat and sinewed muscle, but there was no mistaking the fact that he wasn't Caleb. The structure of his face was all wrong.

Lucian hissed and howls erupted through the warehouse. I was still holding onto Caleb's face—a werewolf I had never met.

Mohammad and Bernard held the imposter, who was thrashing wildly against their grips. Jonah's face burned with so much rage, I even feared him for a moment.

"Where is he?!" he yelled. "Where is my goddamn brother?!"

The Skin Walker laughed. "You'll have to kill me, because I'll never tell you."

Jonah swung at him, but it only made the Skin Walker laugh more. My mind scrambled as I tried to think of something, anything to use as leverage over this creature, but there was nothing. We hadn't learned enough about his species. Learning his identity was just a lucky break.

I moved between him and Jonah, who jerked to a stop from his out-of-control anger. My eyes narrowed at the Skin Walker and I whispered, "Tell me where they are, and I'll let you live. I will risk my life to save you from the Pack. I have no allegiance to them; you know this to be true." I didn't know if he would believe me, but I had to try.

"And if you're lying?" he questioned in a voice I didn't recognize.

Without hesitation, I grabbed Jonah and wrapped my hand around his throat as I stood beside him. Claws piercing his skin, he froze beside me as did everyone else in the room.

"Let him go!" I yelled to Mohammad and Bernard. "If you don't let us walk out of here, I'll rip his throat out."

"What are you doing, Kenz?" Jonah croaked, his heart thumping wildly against his chest.

"Mackenzie, don't do this," Sebastian said, trying to negotiate with me.

If my gamble worked, the Skin Walker would be set free and the Pack would slaughter me. I deemed it a worthy sacrifice for Jackson and the rest of the taken.

"I said let him go! Don't make me repeat myself."

The two captains slowly released the Skin Walker. He stood in place for a moment, waiting to see if it was a trick. When he concluded that he was really about to be let go, I started to back away with Jonah at my side. I looked up and saw Amy flying down the stairs towards me.

"No one comes near us. If you do, I'll kill him."

Sebastian grabbed Amy just as she was about to approach me. Even Lucian watched me with concern. For once, I did something he didn't expect.

The three of us backed away, and as soon as we got to the double doors, the Skin Walker whispered in my ear, "The basement of Caleb's apartment."

I had one shot and one shot only. Everything depended on me getting this right. I pushed Jonah as hard as I could toward the crowd of wolves that were on the brink of losing control, then I turned around and dug my claws through the Skin Walker's back. With my other hand, I grabbed hold of his neck for stability and forced my hand further until I had a firm grip on his heart.

I didn't know what was going on behind me, whether the Pack was going to attack me or not, but I fervently hoped that someone had heard the Skin Walker whisper the location where Jackson was being held.

Placing my mouth to his ear, I growled, "I have allegiance to no one."

Then I ripped out his heart.

20

Interning at IPP taught me many things, but I was most grateful for the wisdom of Detective Garrett Michaels. He always told me that being a good officer wasn't the most important aspect of the job; it was about making the tough decisions, the ones that could leave you scarred for life, that made you great in this field. Even if people didn't like you for it, someone had to do it—and sometimes you had to break the rules.

I didn't know how I would feel after killing the Skin Walker. I didn't set out to do it; it was a last-minute decision, but I knew it was one I had to make for the good of everyone else. Jonah would have killed him before ever finding out where his brother was or if he was even alive. I prayed he was. I may not be religious, but if there was a God looking down on me, I hoped he was listening. As I went against one of his commandments, I prayed he'd forgive me—because I wasn't sure if I could forgive myself.

The murmurs outside the door made me keep my eyes closed. If I opened them, then I'd have to admit to the things I'd done. No one uttered a word when I stood at the entrance of the warehouse with a crumpled Skin Walker at my feet and a bloody, un-beating heart in my hand. The commotion behind me dulled to white noise as someone dragged me away, my hand dripping a trail of crimson in my wake.

I didn't remember much afterward, but I knew it had been six days, thirteen hours, and twenty-three minutes since the killing. Every time someone came in to either check on me or bring me food, I closed my eyes and pretended to be asleep. I wasn't ready to face anyone. Not yet.

For all the smack I talked, I wasn't prepared to feel this devoid of emotion, to feel stripped of my humanity, and overall, to feel this dirty. I didn't understand the myriad of emotions. He was the bad guy! I should feel elated because I did something good, right? So why did I feel this way?

The door creaked open and I smelled who it was—Amy. She'd been visiting me every day as I laid in bed, unmoving.

"Hey, Kenz." She sat on the bed and gripped my hand. "Tomorrow's the full moon and everyone is heading to the Estate. I know I'm not allowed to go because it could be danger-ous, but I need to speak to you before you go. Sebastian said he's taking you whether you wake up or not. Please, Mackenzie. If not for me, at least for Ollie. He's been calling your phone nonstop and he's worried. Please, just wake up already. Everything is alright now. Jackson's back. I've been helping Blu take care of him." She paused. "Okay, well, I'll check on you again this after-noon. I love you, Kenz." She planted a kiss on my forehead and left the room.

I waited a few minutes before gazing at the ceiling again. I needed to get my bearings together before the full moon.

I heard someone turn the door knob and I shut my eyes quickly. Maybe I wasn't ready to interact just yet.

"Mackenzie Grey, you need to wake up. I'm tired of everyone crying over you and your nonresponsive ass. Just because I'm not at a hundred percent and need some bed rest, doesn't mean I'm the next Doctor Phil. So either you pop those gray eyes open, or I flip this mattress. You have thirty seconds to decide."

I knew I hadn't missed Jackson that much. What a douchebag.

"If you lay a finger on this bed, I'll cut you," I said—or at least tried to say. I hadn't spoken a word in days, and my throat was as dry as the Sahara desert.

"Ah, there she is. Welcome back to the world of the living."

I opened my eyes as he handed me a glass of water. I sipped it as I lifted my sore body into a sitting position. All I'd done was lay in bed and occasionally use the restroom, but my muscles ached.

"Who's been crying over me?"

He leaned on the bed on one elbow. "Oh, you know, the usual suspects: Amy, Blu, Sebastian, Jonah, hell, you even got big ol' Bernard concerned. Man, even the vamp has been visiting the warehouse on a daily basis. When'd you become best friends with *that* leech?"

"Since he helped me save your sorry ass. When am I going to get a thank you for that, anyways?"

He snorted. "Not in this lifetime, doll."

Figures.

I bit my lower lip and deliberated with my next question. "How bad is it?"

Jackson cocked his head to the side. "Is that why you've been in a self-induced coma for almost a week? You think you're in trouble?" I couldn't respond so I nodded. "Man, I wish I could say that was the case, but no, you're a damn hero to these idiots. Get out of your feelings and go say hi to your admirers. Even my father is excited about meeting you."

I waited to see if he was joking, but he wasn't. I thought that would make me feel better, but it only made me anxious—and not in a good way.

"On a serious note, Mackenzie, get out of this room and go face your fear. It's the only way."

"I know," I muttered as I worried my hands.

"Then get up. Amy's concerned about you. Don't do that to your friend."

It was my turn to cock a brow. "Amy, huh?" I smirked.

He pushed my shoulder. "Zip it. She's cool."

"Mhm...sure."

He shook his head and stood up to leave.

"Jackson?" He turned around. "I'm glad you're okay."

For a moment I thought he would actually say something nice, but I shouldn't have had such high expectations.

"Don't get soft on me, Mackenzie. Now hurry up, they're waiting."

I SHOWERED, brushed my teeth and hair, and meticulously cleaned every tainted part of my body. I put on a pair of clean jeans and a long-sleeved shirt that were folded on top of the night stand, and slipped my feet into a pair of slippers beside the bed. Cracking the door open, I stepped onto the second-floor landing and peered down to the main floor. The cafeteria-style room had a few occupants, but it wasn't overflowing like it usually was. I scanned the group to ensure that the people I needed to see were there.

They were seated at one of the tables eating lunch. I didn't move from my spot as I spied on them. They laughed at something and Blu tipped her head back, spotting me from where I stood.

"Mackenzie!" she exclaimed, everyone at the table immediately following her line of sight.

I hadn't looked at myself in the mirror, so I didn't know if I looked like shit or not, but I could only hope I was at least half way decent. The anxious stares and awkward silence made me uncomfortable and I shifted my feet, trying to find the courage to move.

Jackson nodded, and I wanted to slap myself that he was the reason I found the nerve to get out of bed. But it did the trick. I headed down the stairs slowly, my muscles adapting to moving again, and met Amy at the foot of the stairs. She wrapped her arms around me in a soft embrace, when I had expected and was preparing for a hug that would knock me off my feet.

"I missed you, Kenz," she whispered, and I felt my eyes water. I swallowed my tears and hugged her back.

"I missed you too, Aims."

She released me and walked with me over to the table. I was grateful that no one else got up to greet me. I couldn't take it, not now. I got a nod from Sebastian and Jonah, and a smile from Blu. Other than that, everyone went back to their lunchtime chit chat. *Thank God.*

Once lunch was over, Sebastian pulled me to the side and told me to meet him in his office in ten minutes. Those were the longest ten minutes of my life.

Amy and Blu had been keeping me company—talking about anything that wasn't recent—when I excused myself and went down to the basement. I stood outside of Bash's office for a minute, feeling the heat crawl up my neck and rubbing my clammy palms on my jeans. I was nervous because I knew what we had to talk about, and I didn't want to have this conversation just yet.

I knocked on the door twice before he gave me the okay to enter. He sat behind his desk and Jonah sat in one of the seats across from him with his back toward me.

"Hey, uh, you wanted to see me?" I mumbled.

Sebastian raised his head from the stack of papers on his desk. "Yeah, come have a seat and shut the door behind you."

I took two deep breaths and steadied my heartbeat. Shaking out the nerves, I relaxed and did as I was told—for once. I looked straight ahead at the bookshelf behind Sebastian and tried to read their titles—anything to distract me from looking at him or Jonah.

"We didn't want to bother you so soon, but with the full moon tomorrow, we need to talk about some things," Jonah started. "We didn't have a chance to talk about it in detail before, but as you know, the Pack heads upstate during this time of the month. Instead of forcing you to go, we wanted to give you the option."

My gaze snapped to Jonah. They were giving me an out.

"This isn't a trick, Mackenzie," Sebastian intuited. "You've been through enough. We don't want to push you."

I wanted to cry and break down, I felt so broken inside. Maybe I was being dramatic, but one thing was for sure, I didn't want them to see me that way. I didn't want to be handled with kid gloves, or be treated as if I were made of porcelain. That was how they treated their Lunas, and I definitely wasn't one of them. My pride wouldn't let me.

"I'll be fine to go."

"Kenz, you don't have to make a decision now. Think it over —" Jonah started, but I cut him off.

"I said I'll go. My decision is final."

"Okay, that's settled. Don't push, Jonah. Now we need to talk about what happened."

"What about it?" I said in a flat tone. I wasn't ready for this...

"Mackenzie, when we head to the Estate, questions will be raised regarding the Skin Walker. Mainly, how you knew for a fact that Caleb wasn't who he said he was."

"I didn't." I could have lied, but this was what had been eating me up alive: the fear that I could have been wrong and possibly killed an innocent person in cold blood.

"You can't say that to my father."

"Well I won't lie!" I exclaimed. "I didn't know for sure. I took a chance and lucked out. End of story."

"Mackenzie, he's not telling you to lie, but you *do* have to be careful with what you tell Charles. All we're trying to do is keep you alive. We don't want anything to go wrong," Sebastian added calmly.

"I appreciate the sentiment guys, but I'm screwed either way. No matter how you paint the picture, I'll never be one of your Lunas." I stood from my chair and left the office. Neither one tried to stop me.

I ambled stiffly back to the main floor where Amy was on her phone, probably checking Facebook. I slid onto the bench across from her and she perked up.

"Oh my gosh, you should see the pictures Diana Stone just posted on Instagram. Nana Carson would freak if she saw them. I'm tempted to screen-shot them and mail it to her with the note, *This is your future daughter-in-law* written on the back. What do you think?"

I chuckled. "I think you're insane. Let me see." She passed me her phone and sure enough, there were some scandalous pictures of Diana Stone dancing on top of a bar wearing next to nothing. "These would give Nana a heart attack."

"Oh, but the revenge would be ever so sweet. That stupid bimbo," Amy mumbled as I heard the click of her taking a screen-shot on her phone.

"Aims, we're busting out of this joint. At least for a couple hours," I joked. "I'm heading to the Estate with the rest of the Pack tomorrow for the full moon, but tonight, let's hang out. I owe you for being such a shitty friend this past week."

"Heck yeah, you owe me! No one else would have put up with your fake sleeping."

I rolled my eyes. "Yeah, yeah. Well, where do you want to go?"

"Honestly?" I nodded. "I kind of want to go home and have a Netflix day. Maybe order some Thai?"

"Amy, that sounds like pure bliss."

21

"Pass me the Pad Thai," Amy asked. I handed over the to-go container.

"Anymore sticky rice?" I asked.

"Yeah," she said, passing me the container. We proceeded to dig into a cold, second helping of Thai food. We'd been sitting on the living room floor watching re-runs of *House of Cards* and trying to eat with chop sticks. "I swear, I'd totally do Frank Underwood. I love his side notes."

"Ugh, gross, Amy."

"Oh, whatever, like you don't salivate over Mark Harmon from NCIS."

I scowled. "He's freakin' hot for an old guy!"

"So is Kevin Spacey!"

We watched until episode thirteen of the first season, interrupted with a few interjections from Amy trying to prove why Frank was doable. My phone was plugged into the charger when I heard it ding, notifying me of a text.

Jonah: When are you coming back?

Me: Tomorrow, why?

Jonah: Curious. Be safe.

I didn't respond, and I didn't think he expected one. I appreciated his concern, but I needed to detach myself from the infatuation I had with him and Sebastian, especially if I was still planning to leave after the third day of the full moon. Regardless of what happened, the plan was still the same—I was *not* joining the Pack.

While Amy made hot chocolate, I went into my room and called Ollie. From what Amy told me, he had been calling every day and knew something wasn't right. He answered before the first ring ended and I heard the sigh of relief when he heard my voice. I made up some bullshit excuse about coming down with a cold and how I didn't want to worry him. I knew he didn't buy my cover story, but he didn't press me. It was how our family functioned.

"You know I'm here for you, Kenzie, with anything you need, no matter what," he said.

It made me smile.

"I know, Ollie."

We said our goodbyes and I mulled over our conversation. I hoped I made the right decision again—for everyone involved.

I went back to the living room where Amy was looking up something else to watch on our Netflix queue. She'd cleaned up our cartons of take-out and replaced them with two steaming mugs of hot chocolate with floating mini marshmallows.

That was how we spent the rest of our time before the full moon. Remembering that we were still human.

"Okay, so on the last night, you're going to rent a car and head back to the city?" Amy asked as she helped me pack my duffle bag.

"Yes, Amy, no worries. We've gone over this. I'll rent a car from wherever it is we'll be at, then I'm scooping you up to hit the road to freedom. So have only your basic necessities packed, not your whole closet," I warned as I narrowed my eyes at the little deviant. If I didn't restrain her, I'd be tugging along a U-Haul filled with just her clothes.

"I know, I know!" she exclaimed as she jumped up and down. For some reason, the entire idea of our escape excited her. I wished I felt the same way. The nerves in me made me want to take a Xanax. Just before I left, I pulled her into a death grip hug.

"I love you, Amy. Thank you for being an amazing best friend. I couldn't have done any of this without you," I mumbled into her red flaming hair as her tattooed arms hugged me back. I thought back to when we first met and how even though she was human, she knew exactly what to do when I went through my first Change. Unknowingly, she had protected me all these years from the normal *and* the paranormal. I owed her more than I could ever repay. I just hoped I was doing her justice by my choices.

I took a bus and a train to get to Dumbo, Brooklyn, where the Pack headquarters was located. I spent the whole ride trying to relax with some of the greatest hits from the Beatles on my iPod. Unfortunately, Paul and John weren't doing it for me today.

With my duffle bag slung over my shoulder, I pushed on the double doors into the warehouse and was met by a busy crowd of wolves packing for their three-day trip. I roamed through the crowd trying to find a familiar face, while many waved and smiled at me. Some patted me on the back. For the first time, the Pack accepted me as one of them. No more glares or weird looks. They now looked upon me with admiration, as family, which made my leaving that much harder. I couldn't say I was attached to them—I mean, I barely knew them, but it was nice knowing there was a group of people just like me, who understood the troubles I went through and wouldn't judge.

I couldn't find anyone I knew on the main floor and didn't see anyone on the second and third landing. I headed toward the basement to Sebastian's office. The door was open, and I saw that everyone except Blu was inside.

I knocked and all eyes turned to me. "Can I come in?" Sebastian waved me in and Bernard offered me his seat. "Uh, no thanks, I just came by to find out if there's anything I need to do. A lot is going on out there," I said, shifting on my feet awkwardly.

"If you're packed, then you're all set. We're leaving in about an hour," Jonah said. "You can ride with us up to Little Falls. Blu is coming as well." I nodded and took comfort in the fact that Blu would be in the car with us. I would be uncomfortable if it was just the boys.

"Can you all excuse us?" Sebastian motioned to the captains that were in the room. One by one, they trickled out. On his way out, Jonah paused a moment by my side and pulled me into an embrace.

"Everything's going to be okay, Kenz."

He left and I was alone with the Alpha. He leaned back in his chair and motioned for me to sit down. I didn't argue.

"Listen. I know what happened with the Skin Walker was hard on you, but you need to get over it. This isn't you, Mackenzie. You're stronger than this and you need to start showing it," Sebastian demanded. "So you killed the bastard. So what? What you don't know, is that he was collecting different skins from all over the city. He was trying to infiltrate the Pack and take over to start a war with the Vampires. He killed one of my best captains and made us doubt that Caleb was a good wolf. He was a *bad guy*, Mackenzie, and you did the world a favor. Instead of moping around, why don't you give yourself a pat on the back and walk around here with some pride? You didn't just prove yourself to the Pack—you're changing the status quo with the Lunas. This is groundbreaking. Be proud of that."

I nodded but didn't say anything. I wanted to and I knew he was expecting it, but if I opened my mouth I would start laughing. This was the worst and best pep talk ever.

"Whatever." He rolled his eyes. "Before you go, this package came in for you." He handed me a FedEx envelope. "This isn't your personal post office, so unless you're joining the Pack, don't use this address again."

"Yes sir," I saluted him and grabbed my mystery mail from his desk. I turned around to leave, assuming I was dismissed.

"And Mackenzie?" I looked back to catch a smirk on his face as his blue eyes glinted with something I immediately knew was dangerous. "This only makes me want you more."

If I could swoon into a puddle of nothing, I would—but I couldn't. I wouldn't give any of them the satisfaction of seeing how much they affected me.

Halfway down the hallway, I started to open the envelope Sebastian had given me, unable to stop the smile that crept across my face when I saw its contents. It couldn't have come at a better time. I stuffed it in my duffle bag and went to look for Blu.

THREE HOURS AND FORTY-FIVE MINUTES. That was how long it took us to get from Brooklyn to Little Falls, New York. The scenery was beautiful, but *Ninety-nine bottles of beer on the wall* was grating my last nerves. Did they have to sing every road trip song known to man?

As we drove through Main Street, it reminded me of my home in Cold Springs. I supposed a lot of these little upstate towns were similar. The only difference was that Little Falls was surrounded by so much nature, I felt compelled to roll my window down to suck in the fresh air. The small town was less than ten miles away from the Estate, which means I couldn't miss it even if I were lost. The tall, wrought iron gate with concrete pillars on either side welcomed you to Cadwell Estate: one hundred and fifty-seven acres of pristine land that housed the werewolves of the Northeast once a month. The three-mile drive through the estate was just as picturesque, and my face was glued to the car window as I stared wide eyed, and mouth agape.

"Welcome to the Estate, Mackenzie Grey," Blu whispered beside me and I smiled. This was unreal. I snapped pictures just as we pulled into the driveway of a three-story home, quickly texting them to Amy.

The trail of cars that followed us pulled in and began to unload their cars. I got out and went to the trunk of our SUV to help Bernard, but he waved me off.

"Go check out the grounds. You have the same glow in your eyes that I had when I first came here. Go on, have fun," Bern cajoled.

Blu giggled and pulled me along to show me around. "Oh my

gosh, Kenzie, we're going to have so much fun! I can smell burning wood already, which means the bonfire has started!" she squealed. I had to double-time it to keep up with her.

"Not so fast there, girls." Jonah stopped us in our tracks. "I need to borrow Kenz before you start showing her how to misbehave." He winked at Blu and she nodded.

"Fine. I'll look for you later, Kenz," she giggled and ran off toward the bonfire.

"Am I already in trouble?" I cocked an eyebrow toward Jonah.

His dimple peeked out. "No, Kenz." He shook his head. "My father just wants to meet you."

Oh, shit.

I followed him back around the house and to the front door. He pushed it open and we walked into a massive foyer decorated with an array of tasteful art. The only furniture was a solitary table with a vase of flowers in the center, situated right beside a winding staircase.

"You grew up here?" I was having difficulty keeping my mouth from hanging open.

Jonah chuckled. "Yeah. A lot of us did. Come on, his office is this way," he said as he motioned me to his left. We passed through two enormous living rooms and a dining room until we came to a stop in front of a set of closed doors. "Don't forget what we talked about," he whispered as he pushed the doors open.

The smell of wood, rain, and cigars hit me the moment I walked in. The office was the size of my whole apartment, filled to the brim with books and art. The massive oak desk situated in the middle of the room was bigger than my dining room table. Behind it stood a man about the same height as Jonah, with the same brown hair that was slicked back and tossed into perfect waves. The anticipation was killing me as I waited for him to turn around. He wore khaki slacks with a tucked in, plaid long sleeve shirt. He held a tumbler of dark liquid in his right hand, with his left resting on his lower back.

"The prodigal son returns, and with none other than the infamous Mackenzie Grey. What a delight," Jonah's father said. As he turned around, I was met with identical milk chocolate eyes that twinkled against the wood burning in the fireplace.

"Mackenzie, this is my father, Charles Cadwell," Jonah introduced.

I nervously rubbed my sweaty palm on my jeans before reaching out to shake his hand.

Charles looked down at my open palm as if I were passing him a piece of turd.

"I guess the rumors are true; you don't act like a Luna," he said as he finally shook my hand.

"Father," Jonah hissed, but I waved off his concern.

"Don't worry." I smiled. "But yes, Mr. Cadwell, I'm not your typical Luna."

He narrowed his eyes and then nodded. "Hm. I see that. Have a seat, Ms. Grey, we have much to discuss." I did as I was told and sat across from Charles. He offered me bourbon, but I declined. I needed to be sober for this conversation. "Jonah, son, we won't be needing you just yet. Why don't you go seek Sebastian and help him situate everything for Ms. Grey tonight?"

Jonah was hesitant at first, but I smiled at him reassuringly and he put his hand on my shoulder before leaving.

"He has gotten quite fond of you, hasn't he?" Charles asked shrewdly.

"We've become good friends," I answered, trying to be diplomatic and keep my heart from racing.

"Right. Of course. Then again, it seems you have everyone in a frenzy at the moment," he hinted as he swished his drink around. "Killing a rogue Skin Walker and saving my son. That's not something you see every day, much less from a Luna, which begs the question ... where did you come from?"

"I told—"

"I know, I know, that was a rhetorical question. You see, I think I have an idea who you are, and if I'm correct, you will soon be a hot commodity within the Lycan world, Ms. Grey."

I sat motionless as I tried to absorb what Charles was telling me, working hard to keep my face and body neutral, all while my insides were about to explode. I knew who I was: Mackenzie Grey from Cold Springs, New York, daughter of Thomas and Joyce Grey, sister to Oliver Grey, a twenty-two-year old, aspiring detective with the NYPD, and a werewolf. I didn't need anyone coming along and trying to tell me otherwise. But I couldn't say I wasn't curious, because I was.

"What are you trying to say, Mr. Cadwell?"

He eyed me and smirked. Instead of one, he had a dimple in each cheek, which reminded me of Jonah. The similarity between them was uncanny.

"What I'm getting at, Ms. Grey, is that the people who you *think* are your parents, are not. You're adopted."

I busted out laughing, the hysterical kind, which in result made Jonah burst into the room like it was on fire.

"What the hell is going on?" he ordered, but I couldn't answer, much less see his expression.

I was laughing so hard my eyes were squinted into slits and

filled with tears, blurring my vision. There was a tightness in my chest and I thought I was going to have an asthma attack.

Me? Adopted?

I must be getting punk'd, because there was no way. Ollie and I looked a lot alike, like the siblings we were.

"I told her the truth about herself. She's adopted," Charles explained calmly, which only made me laugh harder.

"How do you know that?" Sebastian asked.

In my fit of hysteria, I hadn't even heard him enter the room. Either way, I wasn't in the right frame of mind. Was everyone eavesdropping on my conversation with Charles?

"From the blood samples you provided me two weeks ago. They don't match that of her family, and if I put them up against who I think are her parents, I bet we'll get a match."

That sobered me up.

"*What* blood samples?" I jerked to a stop, looking around at the three men in the room, but landing on the two I had started to trust.

"While you were sedated, we took some of your blood to run tests. We needed to know who you were," Sebastian answered with a straight face, as if he hadn't invaded my privacy.

"And you didn't think to ask me, much less *tell* me what you did?" I yelled, wide eyed.

"Ms. Grey, what's done is done. No sense crying over spilled milk," Charles answered.

"I don't give a *damn* what you think," I gritted through my teeth. "My parents are Thomas and Joyce Grey, and that's final. Are we done here?"

Charles nodded.

"Good. Now, if you'll excuse me, I'll be with Blu." I hauled ass from the room, not even glancing at the two people who had betrayed me.

I jumped off the porch and inhaled some much needed fresh air. I stood in front of the house with no idea where to start looking for Blu. She could be anywhere on the massive grounds . Closing my eyes, I listened for voices and headed in the nearest direction. It would have been great if I could ask someone for directions, but unfortunately the first person I ran into was V— my werewolf arch nemesis.

"I'm not in the mood, Vivian," I sighed as I tried to go around her. No luck. Her minions stood in my way.

"Where are you off to in such a hurry? Why don't you shift with us tonight?" She giggled to her cohorts, keeping me out of whatever joke she'd just made.

"Oh, I would love to, but I'll be shifting with Sebastian and Jonah tonight, and the next two nights, for that matter. I can't wait," I said with just enough sarcasm to make her squirm. I pushed past her gaggle of friends, but stopped when I heard her speak.

"You might think you've won them over, but you haven't. Don't get too cocky, Mackenzie Grey. You're a nobody, and soon, everyone will realize it."

"Yeah, yeah, I'm heartbroken," I chucked over my shoulder and pushed deeper into the woods. I wasn't going to lose sleep over the werewolf version of Diana Stone. She was the least of my problems.

It took me a while to find Blu in the sea of wolves milling around the grounds. The estate was huge and there were tons of people—way more than at the warehouse—celebrating the full moon. Some of them barely spared me a look, while others recognized me and nodded my way. The animosity I once felt from the Brooklyn Pack was gone. I had been accepted.

Once I found Blu, I shelved Charles' claims into the back of my mind and tried to forget. Obviously, his theory was pure nonsense.

Blu was standing with a group of Lunas and a couple of male wolves. They were huddled around a campfire with a few tents scattered behind them. She introduced me to the group, but I completely forgot their names within seconds. What I had hoped to forget, I couldn't. I barely paid attention to the conversation. I smiled when I needed to and laughed on cue, but nothing felt natural.

Why would Charles say I was adopted? What an asshole.

I contemplated texting or calling Amy to tell her what happened, but there was no cell service on the grounds, this far from the house. Being disconnected to the outside world should have freaked me out, (they could be planning on sacrificing me or some crap!) but I had too much on my mind.

"Kenz?"

I turned around to find Jonah in a pair of khaki shorts and barefoot. I tried to look anywhere but his bare chest, disappointed that I couldn't.

"Yeah?" I said breathlessly. There were tons of male wolves walking around here shirtless, but since they weren't Jonah, I hadn't spared them a glance.

"Let's go for a walk."

I hesitated for a moment, but realized I couldn't ignore him forever. Eventually I would have to meet up with him and Sebastian tonight for my first full Change outside of a cage. That was another thing I was nervous about. I got up from the log and followed Jonah deep into the woods, away from the milling throngs of people.

"I want to apologize for my father. He doesn't always have tact. I guess that's where Jackson gets it from. He shouldn't have ambushed you that way, and on a full moon. It was wrong."

"Whatever."

He came to an abrupt stop and turned me toward him. "Don't do that, Mackenzie. Don't shut me out."

I chuckled. "Jesus, Jonah, don't shut you out? It's not as if we were best friends or some shit. Relax."

"You're right. We weren't best friends, and I'm not Amy. I'm more than that, whether you want to admit it or not. We might have only known each other for a couple weeks, but that's all the time I need to know how I feel about you. That's enough for me. If you're not ready, that's fine, I'll wait. But we are destined to be together, I know it."

His brown eyes drilled into me and for a moment, I felt bare and vulnerable—but just for a moment. I didn't know what I felt. I never even imagined life without James. So much had happened after our break-up, that I never really thought about life after him.

"Jonah," I started, but he shook his head.

"Don't answer me. I don't want a response right now, not until you've had enough time to think about it."

I nodded and he started to walk again as if nothing had happened. I stumbled over myself trying to keep up.

"Where are we going?" I asked as I hopped over a pile of broken branches.

"To our campsite for the next three nights."

"What? Why? I thought we were going to shift near the rest of the Pack?" Thoughts of being butchered and killed in the middle of the woods ran through my mind.

"Are you crazy, Kenz? You've never shifted around other wolves! You'll go berserk. We need an isolated area, and Bash and I can handle you just as well." We came out to an opening where a tent and some firewood were already stacked.

"Where's Bash?"

"He'll be here soon. He's still doing some damage control with my father. He wasn't too—uh—happy about the way things went down earlier," Jonah said. "Help me set the tent up."

I grabbed the poles and started attaching and passing them to Jonah so he could slide the tarp in. Once we finished, we walked around the area and collected more wood to start a campfire, keeping the conversation light and discussing mundane things. It was nice. We worked well together. Jonah was a jokester, so each time he gave me a friendly shove or tug at my hair, I'd kick his tush. Even with his declaration, things weren't awkward. Maybe he was right. Maybe we *were* meant to be together.

We'd just sat down when we heard footsteps half a mile away. My ears perked up.

"Don't just use your hearing; smell who's nearby," Jonah suggested.

I closed my eyes and took a big whiff. I could smell the woods, the residue of rain on the soil and leaves, but I also got a hint of burnt wood and musk oil.

"It's Sebastian."

"Correct," he said, and we waited for Bash to make it to our clearing.

In a pair of low hanging, worn-out Levi's, a barefoot Sebastian came into view. I licked my dry lips and my jaw was at the brink of dropping.

What was wrong with these werewolves and their insatiable need to always be shirtless?

"You might not be Pack, Mackenzie, but common courtesy is universal," Sebastian announced.

I quirked an eyebrow. "Excuse me?" There was only so much I would put up with before I exploded. Plus, since it was a full moon, my patience was already short.

"With Charles, Mackenzie. Don't act as if ... Never mind, it's getting dark."

Oh, hell no. "As if what? As if he didn't drop a major bomb on me? You're damn right I acted without common courtesy. He wasn't very gentlemanly, either!"

"All you needed to do was hear him out, Mackenzie. It was about your life."

"Are you serious? Look at my face! I got a goddamn planet growing on my forehead, and it's from all the stress of this damn Pack. Look at this monstrosity!" I said as I pointed at the pimple that had started to take over my face.

"Kenz, relax."

"No, I'm *not* going to relax! Listen, I don't know what made me get involved with the kidnappings and the werewolf politics, but the stress from it all is really doing a number on me, and *now* you want me to go further down the rabbit hole with this whole adoption theory? No, fuck that."

"Decisions don't need to be made right away. We can talk more rationally about this after the third night, okay?" Jonah tried to mediate, but I was burning holes into Sebastian's perfectly sculpted chest.

"You people are giving me an ulcer," I mumbled as I stomped into one of the tents we'd set up.

I hid in my tent for as long as I could, but eventually, Jonah had to come in and knock some sense into me. It was almost time for the full moon, and I could feel my wolf getting restless. She stirred in anticipation, and I knew she couldn't wait to get out and run free for the first time.

"It's time, Kenz. I know my father and Sebastian can be intense at times, but they mean well. Just give this situation some time, okay?"

I sighed. "Can I ask you a question, Jonah?"

"What's up?"

"How do you stay calm all the time? Shouldn't the wolf be out of control around this time of the month?"

He chuckled. "Kenz, there's a lot you need to learn about what we are. It'll all come with time. You're still very new at it, and you still need to go on a Vision Quest. Once you do that, many of your questions will be answered."

I nodded and followed him out into the dark woods. It was later than I thought, and the night was quiet and still, except for the sound of rustling trees and paws hitting the damp earth. Two sets of glowing eyes stared at me and I felt my insides tighten up like a rope. I gulped loudly and fidgeted with my hands.

Shit.

22

"Take off your clothes," Sebastian commanded.

My head popped up like a groundhog. I should have expected this sooner. I completely forgot about the technicalities of the Change, but unless I wanted to shred my clothing, I had no other choice.

"C-can you guys turn around?" I stuttered, immediately wanting to slap myself.

"We don't have all day. Get on with it."

Sebastian and Jonah crossed their arms over their chests, and I expelled a breath in defeat. If I was going to shift with the Pack for the next three full moons, I might as well get used to being naked in front of others.

I gripped the hem of my sweater firmly and slowly pulled it over my head, dropping it on the ground without a thought of possibly dirtying it. In a plain black bra, I stood there with nerves that ate my insides like Thanksgiving dinner. Even though I wasn't cold, a shiver traveled through me and I gulped it down.

My fingers traced the button on my jeans, and it felt like every sound was audible from a mile away. I could hear the pop and zip so loudly, it consumed the sound of my racing heart. I shimmied out of them and when I stood back up, the boys weren't paying me much attention anymore. They'd started to undo their own jeans and I felt flushed. This was normal for them, but not for me. In my black bra and panties, I'd never felt as vulnerable as I did now.

"Mackenzie," it was Jonah, "don't overthink it. It's no big deal."

Without meeting his warm chocolate eyes, I finished taking off my undergarments—waiting for further instruction.

"She'll be coming out soon. Don't fight her. Don't fight the pain."

I nodded, anticipating the first pinch of pain as if I were getting a flu shot. My sweaty palms rubbed against my skin and I gripped my thighs as soon as I felt the first snap of my shoulders, doubling me over—a scream ripping out of my mouth.

"It will hurt, Mackenzie. Welcome the pain; don't give in to it."

Blue eyes penetrated my own and I steadied my breathing. *I can do this.*

I shut my eyes, breathing in through my nose, out through my mouth, and closed myself off from the outside world.

Let's do this together.

It was like having an out-of-body experience. I could see her. See *me*. We were beautiful. A coat of silky black, with silver eyes that leaned toward white. I kneeled in front of her and hesitantly reached out a hand. She didn't move or flinch.

I've never seen you before, I said breathlessly as I ran my hand behind her ear and stroked. She didn't move.

It's a full moon and our first night out of the cage. Can we work together?

I didn't know why I was asking her. It wasn't as if she could answer me. I sort of knew the answers to my own questions. I knew what she wanted. She didn't want to join the Pack, she wanted to stay free.

I can keep us free. I can keep us safe.

When she leaned into my hand and gave me permission, it was a done deal. I shut my eyes and howled up to the moon. The instant I opened my eyes, everything was different. I was no longer with the wolf. I *was* the wolf. I sat in front of two very human, naked men, Sebastian and Jonah. They watched me with calculation and awe—just as I'd seen myself.

Jonah was the first to kneel before me. "You're an amazing creature, Mackenzie Grey. You're stunning."

For once, I was glad I couldn't respond. I didn't know what to say, mainly because of the unabashed adoration he lavished upon me—a look of love. He stood and backed away, giving Sebastian the opportunity to come forward. He didn't kneel, he just stood before me, forcing me to look up to him. He didn't say a thing, he just watched me. His chest rose up and down at a faster than normal rate. His blue eyes glowed and his hands clenched into fists at his side.

He turned back to Jonah without saying a word and they nodded to each other at an unspoken question. Then I witnessed the most amazing thing in the world—they shifted.

Sebastian and Jonah fell on all fours and I watched as their bones broke and reshaped in unnatural ways, yet they didn't utter a sound. They didn't scream or cry for help. They looked peaceful. The only thing that never changed was their eyes—sapphire and gold.

Sebastian's fur was like slate, almost grey but darker, while Jonah was a golden, honey brown with highlights of amber. Bash came up to me in all his Alpha glory and nudged me behind the ear —almost like a caress. My coat bristled from the sensation. When Jonah walked over to my other side, it was the perfect definition of how I felt: caught between the Alpha and Beta, between Sebastian and Jonah—and I couldn't choose—not even now. I howled once more and they both took a step back and ran toward the wood line.

This was it. This was the moment I'd been anticipating since I met the Brooklyn Pack. The moment to finally run free—for the first and last time.

FOR THE PAST three nights on the estate, I'd felt things I'd never dreamed of since finding out what I was four years ago. I not only connected with my inner wolf, but I connected with the earth and world around me. And my wolf—well, she felt like home. I finally understood her. If there was one thing I was grateful to the Brooklyn Pack for, it was the chance to experience these three full moons. It was breathtaking.

I laid on the ground, on top of damp soil, rocks, and broken twigs, with leaves in my hair, sporting my birthday suit, as I stretched and inhaled the clean, crisp air. It was the third morning I'd woken up like this and I was going to miss it. I now understood the negative side of caging the animal.

I looked on either side of me and found Jonah on my right

and Sebastian on my left. They were both sprawled out naked and passed out asleep, disheveled and dirty just like me. Being uncaged over the course of three days didn't cure me of my modesty, but I *did* feel more connected to them and I was glad they'd befriended me. However, it was time for me to go.

I got up, shook out my sore bones, and looked down at the two men who had captured my heart in such a short period of time. I felt the heat creep its way up my neck as I took in Sebastian and Jonah. They were perfect—not a flaw in sight. Unfortunately, I couldn't stay and marvel them. Good things didn't last forever.

I tracked our paw prints, sniffed out where our campsite was, and entered our tent. Grabbing my duffle bag, I quickly put on the extra set of clothes I'd brought. Slipping on my worn-out pair of black and white Converses, I started my trek back to the Estate.

The grounds were quiet, since everyone was resting after the three days we'd just had. I should have been too—I was exhausted—but I had a plan to follow through. The driveway from the entrance of the estate to the mansion was a three-mile walk. As stealthily as I'd entered the mansion, when the door slammed shut behind me, I jumped.

"Smooth, Mackenzie," I mumbled to myself.

"Not really. I think you woke the neighbors," Jackson said from the top of the staircase.

Shit.

"What are you doing up?" I asked, trying to keep my nerves at bay.

"I'm not strong enough yet to shift, so I've been resting. However, I should be asking *you* the same question."

"I need a, uh...shower. I reek."

"While I don't disagree with you there, I don't believe you, either. So why don't we just skip all the excuses and dancing around the subject, and you tell me the truth—you're leaving." He finally came down the stairs and stood a few feet away from me.

"How did you know?"

He chuckled. "Mackenzie, you're so predictable, I'm surprised no one else figured it out. You're not cut out for the Pack—"

"Hey!"

"... and I don't mean that as an insult." He leaned against the rail. "I'll deny it if anyone asks, but you're not meant to be a Luna, you're meant for greater things. Regrettably, the Lycan world hasn't caught up with modern times. Hopefully, someday we will, but it's not now. You need freedom, so you should seek it."

I watched Jackson with wide eyes and a dry mouth. I looked around the foyer, waiting for Pack members to jump out, yell "Sike!", and then capture me, but nothing.

"What have you done with Jackson Cadwell?"

He laughed. "Listen, kid, do you have a plan of action, or are you just winging it?"

"I have a plan."

"Good. Then you should head out before everyone starts to wake up."

"Okay." I started to turn toward the doors, but stopped. "Jackson?"

"I'll look after Amy, don't worry. I won't let anything happen to her."

I smiled. Things were going to be okay.

LITTLE FALLS, New York might look like a small speck on a map, but boy, was it a hike to the bus station. It was ten in the morning and I had ditched my phone before my bus transfer in Philadelphia. I opened the manila envelope I received in the mail and took out the rest of its contents. New passport, a Los Angeles driver's license, a burner phone, a key, and a letter—from Lucian.

My dear Mackenzie Grey,

I hope this letter finds you well and that you've accepted my help. Inside you will find the documents needed to travel, including a new identity and your bus tickets. Once you arrive in Los Angeles, they can no longer lay a finger on you. But for this to happen, you will need to dispose of your cell phone so you are not tracked. I have arranged everything at your school so you can finish your last semester online. As for your internship, I have some connections in the LAPD if this is something you'd like to pursue. I also spoke with Pete at Pete's Bar (not a very pleasant fellow, I might add) and submitted your letter of resignation due to personal problems. I will have someone at the bus station waiting for you—you will know who he is when you see him—and he will be your tour guide once you arrive in the great city of Los Angeles. Please remember that you cannot have any communication with anyone from home for a very long time—including your human best friend, your family, and the Pack. You will now be public enemy number one; do not trust them, even when you think you can.

I wish you the best of luck and we will talk soon. Take care, Pet.
-Lucian

. . .

I READ the letter three more times before tucking it away in my bag again. I felt crummy for leaving Amy the way I did, especially when she was excited to come with me, but I just couldn't do that to her. I couldn't risk her life, not knowing what these vampires were capable of. She was safer with Jackson looking after her.

Things were going to change—*I* was going to change. I was being given a chance at a new life—a new me, and it was time I took advantage of it. The enemy of my enemy was my friend. That was my current mindset, and I needed to adapt fast.

It was time for a *shift*.

Continue with CAGED (Mackenzie Grey: Origins #2)!
Click here to start reading!

READ ON FOR A SNEAK PEEK AT

CAGED (Mackenzie Grey #2)

ABOUT THE AUTHOR

For teasers and giveaways on the next book, join my Facebook group, **Karina's Kick-Ass Reads!**

Reviews are very important to authors and help readers discover our books. Please take a moment to leave a review on Amazon. Thank you!

ALSO BY KARINA ESPINOSA

Mackenzie Grey: Origins Series (Completed)

SHIFT

CAGED

ALPHA

OMEGA

Mackenzie Grey: Trials Series (Completed)

From the Grave

Curse Breaker

Bound by Magic

Stolen Relics

Bloodlust

The Last Valkyrie Trilogy (Completed)

The Last Valkyrie

The Sword of Souls

The Rise of the Valkyries

From the Ashes Trilogy (Completed)

Phoenix Burn

Phoenix Rise

Dark Phoenix

CAGED

No. Way.

No FREAKIN' way!

This had to be some cosmic joke from the universe—not that I should've been surprised—Lucian had a way of making you do uncomfortable things, still. I crossed my arms over my chest and tapped my foot in annoyance. My duffle bag was slung over my shoulder and I oozed bad attitude. I was cranky and hungry. The bus ride to Los Angeles didn't make enough pit stops for a girl with a wolf inside her. Where was the justice in that?

"Are you just going to stand there or are you going to get in?" said the vampire that was my tour guide once arriving in LA. He wore head to toe black, with messy dirty blond hair, and hazel puppy dog eyes. Lord Jesus, help me. I focused on his paleness to divert my lingering eyes and reminded myself that the individual before me was a FREAKIN' VAMPIRE.

"I am not getting in that death trap you call a vehicle. I enjoy being *alive*," I smirked.

"As if I hadn't heard that one," he chuckled. "But in all seriousness, are you going to get in the bloody Jeep, or am I going to have to carry you in myself? I'm not opposed to either option," he grinned.

I scoffed. "Touch me and you die—again."

The vampire put his hands at his hips and sighed. "Two to zero, you're a real Ace there."

I shrugged. "I try."

"Well try some more inside the car. We're late."

"Late for what?"

"It's a secret," he grinned. His pearly whites shone in the city night and I caught a glimpse at his fangs. Gross.

"I don't like surprises," I growled.

"Someone's cranky," he laughed and took a step toward me. "Easy way or the hard way, Ace, your choice."

I scanned the busy parking lot of the Greyhound station in downtown Los Angeles. It was unusually crowded for this time of night. Lights were flashing, people were yelling, and it would be impossible for me to make a run for it.

"Don't even think about it," he said and I rolled my eyes.

"Fine," I relented. "At least tell me your name," I said as I bypassed the vampire, tossed my duffle into the back of his Jeep and climbed in.

"Roman," he said as he dug in his pockets for his car keys. It was an old Jeep Wrangler, its paint peeled and rusted. It squeaked when he sat in the driver seat.

I snorted. "Are you serious? Talk about a cliché."

"Excuse me?" he gave me a sideways glance as he turned the ignition and pulled out of the parking lot.

"Dude, you have such a vampire name. Did your folks know you'd turn into a blood sucker?"

"Ha-ha. Very funny," he deadpanned. "So what's your name? I was only told to look out for the wolf with bright gray eyes."

I dug into my back pocket and pulled out my new driver's license, curtesy of Lucian Young—the Head Vampire of New York. "Well according to my new ID, my name's Hillary Clinton," I wrinkled my nose. "Any way I can get this changed?"

Roman laughed. "Yeah, I know a guy."

I nodded. "So are you going to be my tour guide? What are your tour rates like—a pint of blood a day?" I smirked.

"Ouch," he crossed his hand over his heart. "Who leaked my rates to you?"

"Probably the one who dressed you," I muttered and looked out the unzipped window. His laugh was background noise as I took in the quiet streets of 3AM. I was used to the city that never slept, and felt out of place in this strange new world. My human best friend, Amy, wouldn't have liked it out here—she needed 24-hour pizza joints and Gray's Papaya.

"Penny for your thoughts?" Roman asked.

I sighed. "I would tell you to mind your own business, but I'm curious about where we're going."

"Has anyone ever told you how...*demanding* you can be?"

"All the time, but you still haven't answered my question."

"That's because I can't. Not until we're closer to our destination." He turned on the radio and U2 played against the harsh gusts of wind passing through the vehicle. "Just sit back, relax, and welcome to Los Angeles," he winked and I nearly blew a gasket.

The worst part about this two and a half hour car ride: how easy it was for my thoughts to wander. I thought about everything—where we were going, where would I be sleeping—was I safe? All of these questions raced across my mind and then it went back to a few days ago during the last full moon. The time spent with Sebastian and Jonah was something I would never forget. Leaving them was hard, but if given the option again, I wouldn't change a thing. I needed to free myself from the Pack—I couldn't live under the thumb of men who didn't believe I had the brains to think for myself. This wasn't the fifties, and I wouldn't be giving up my freedom—ever.

I squinted as the wind picked up and sand blew in my face. I checked the dashboard and saw it was pushing five in the morning. The sun peaked over the horizon, giving it that mesmerizing orange-pink glow.

"Hey, check that sign over there. We're here," Roman said as he pointed.

I looked over to my right and saw the sign that said, **Mojave National Preserve.** As if that answered any of my questions.

"What the hell are we doing here?"

He sighed. "Damn. Lucian told me you were a pup, but I didn't think you were clueless. We've entered the Mojave Desert, home of the Desert Wolves. Their lineage goes further back than the almighty European Summit you wolves love to worship. Grab a paper and pen, and start taking notes, Ace."

"My name is Mackenzie, not Ace, and I don't worship anything but coffee and possibly bacon," I said, feeling good about my declaration. That's right, no one had a hold on me, much less the Pack. I was a lone-wolf.

"Yeah, okay," Roman snickered. "Listen, once the quest is over, I'll make sure to get you back to your Pack safe and sound. You don't have to act tough around me. Vampires and Wolves are peaceful here in SoCal."

"Quest as in a Vision Quest?" I didn't care that he thought I was Pack. I couldn't believe Lucian arranged a Vision Quest. I didn't know the exact details but from what Bash said, I needed a lot of training before I could go through a quest or the consequences could be fatal. The wolf could consume me and I would lose my humanity. If I completed it unharmed, then it would be the most freeing experience of my life. I wouldn't be angry or have this emptiness in my chest anymore. I'd be whole.

I wasn't ready.

"What other quest is there? Relax, you pups prep for this your whole youth. Although you're kind of old to be doing it now. Either way, it's like one in a million who fail. I haven't met a bugger that's failed yet. Don't be the first, Ace," he winked and I felt as if I were going to throw up.

I just might be the first.

"What is up with your eye? Do you have Tourette's or some shit? Stop with the winking."

He laughed. "You're a funny girl, but relax. You'll pass the quest."

I shifted in my seat. "So...let's say for argument sake that I don't pass...what will happen...to me?" I debated about whether to jump out of the car in mid-ride and make a run for it. How could Lucian set me up like this? Could I find my way back to the city from the desert? Shit, I didn't drink enough water as it was, I was going to dehydrate. Oh my gosh, I was stupid to trust a damn vampire.

"You're looking a little pale over there, what's going on?" he said as he pulled onto the shoulder of the road. He cut the engine off and got out of the Jeep. "Listen, it's no big deal. You go out there, be one with your wolf, get a vision, and you're done. It's gravy."

Shit, shit, shit. "Uh, where are you going?" I stumbled out of the car and followed Roman to wherever it was he was headed.

"We have to walk from here. The Desert Wolves aren't too far off the main road. Come on, no worries, Ace."

The early morning was windy and I squinted to avoid getting sand in my eyes. My hands itched from the dry air and I began to miss the East Coast humidity.

We stepped over dry plant life and small cactuses, but what worried me was the idea of running into a snake or scorpion. As a city girl, rats and cockroaches were the vermin I was used to. I tip-toed behind Roman in my now dusty black-and-white converses. In only a black V-neck and ripped jeans, I was not prepared for a hike.

"We're almost there. See the fire up ahead?"

"Yeah," I responded as I watched about a quarter of a mile ahead, there was what looked like a bonfire. "I don't see anyone. Where are they?"

As paranoid as I was, the first thing running through my mind was that this blood sucker had brought me out to the middle of nowhere to slaughter me into tiny wolfey bites and add me to his salad for dinner. Morbid, I know.

After a few minutes, we made it to our destination and the vampire sat on one of the logs that encircled the fire.

"Where—"

Before I could ask, a small figure emerged from around the flames. A woman, around her eighties—shuffled toward us. She wore salt and pepper hair in two braids on either side that reached all the way down her hips. Colorful beaded necklaces and bracelets adorned her, clanking against each other as she walked. Her skin was the color of rotted oranges and as rough as leather—but it was her eyes that froze me in place—they were yellow.

"Hillary Clinton, I'd like you to meet the Alpha of the Desert Wolves—La Loba," Roman introduced us and from the little bit of Spanish I knew, her name was the She-Wolf. My jaw dropped as I realized what Roman had said—she was an Alpha. How? I guessed things really were different on the West Coast.

I extended my right hand to her and like most wolves I'd met, she stared at it as if I were offering Ebola.

The vampire snickered. "Uh, what are you doing, Ace?"

"Ignore him, Mackenzie Grey—Lone Wolf. I am familiar with your customs and admire you for them," she said, her voice of a three pack-a-day smoker. I was taken aback that she knew my name...and status. I thought Lucian was going to keep it a secret.

"Wait—lone-wolf?" Roman choked out but I ignored him.

La Loba shook my hand and she was warm like a freshly brewed cup of coffee on a winter morning. She felt like home—but she wasn't—I knew that, she was just familiar. I could sense her wolf. Sebastian told me that I'd always be attracted to my own kind.

"You seek a Vision Quest. Is this true, Mackenzie Grey?"

My eyes fell to my sweating hands. I wasn't one hundred percent sure this was what I wanted to do. I hadn't prepared for this experience, and mainly out of fear—the fear of the unknown was worse than anything. What if I didn't make it? I used to be very angry with this life I'd been dealt, but now I would never want to give it up. Not in a million years.

"I'm sure," I said as I stared La Loba straight in the eyes. I didn't flinch or waver. She needed to know I was certain and there was no doubt in my mind, because I could not go into this Vision Quest fearing a negative outcome. If I wanted to succeed, I had to do what I knew best—survive.

"Then follow me, Mackenzie Grey," she said and turned back around in the direction she came from.

"Hold on a second, Mackenzie, what Pack did you belong to before?" The vampire asked as his cold hand latched on to my upper arm.

"I've never belonged to a Pack. Didn't Lucian tell you? He's hiding me."

"Wait, what? Shit, wait—that bastard—hold on, Ace. Don't go through with the Quest. You'll fail," he said, his brows scrunched up in concern. "Forget everything I said before and don't go through with this. This is hella dangerous, you need proper training."

"I thought you said this was gravy?"

He shook his head. "Not for you. Definitely not for you."

"I'll be okay, *Ace*, relax," I mimicked him.

"You don't know that!"

"Why do you even care?" I arched a brow.

"I don't. But it doesn't mean I can't warn you of the potential dangers. This is ludicrous, you're unprepared and you won't make it out."

I shook my head, and chuckled. "I won't fail, Roman. It's not in my nature."

It was my turn to wink at him, leaving him frozen in my wake as I followed La Loba out into the cold and unforgiving desert.

ABOUT THE AUTHOR

Karina Espinosa is the Urban Fantasy Author of the Mackenzie Grey novels and The Last Valkyrie series. An avid reader throughout her life, the world of Urban Fantasy easily became an obsession that turned into a passion for writing strong leading characters with authentic story arcs. When she isn't writing badass heroines, you can find this self-proclaimed nomad in her South Florida home binge watching the latest series on Netflix or traveling far and wide for the latest inspiration for her books.

For more information:
www.karinaespinosa.com

ACKNOWLEDGMENTS

First and foremost, I have to thank my family (and I mean everyone) far and wide, you have all been so supportive of me and my writing career. Especially my mother who pushes me when I feel like giving up—thank you.

My editor extraordinaire—Daniella Brooks—I wouldn't trade you for the world! Like I've told you many times before, you're stuck with me so you can't quit—ever. Ha! Thank you for being not just my editor, but such an amazing friend!

To my awesome cover designer, Laura Hidalgo—thanks for putting up with my diva antics. Only God knows how fickle I can be and you took it with grace and a dash of tough love.

Last, but not least—thank you to all the great author friends I've made in this past year and to all my amazing readers. Your support is mind blowing and I couldn't have finished SHIFT without you.

Printed in Great Britain
by Amazon